Comeuppance at Kicking Horse Casino

and Other Stories

Comeuppance at Kicking Horse Casino

and Other Stories

by

Charles Brashear

American Indian Studies Center
University of California, Los Angeles
3220 Campbell Hall, Box 951548
Los Angeles, California 90095-1548

NATIVE AMERICAN SERIES NO. 10

Books in this series are published for the purpose of encouraging American Indian authorship in expressive literature.

Publications Editor: Duane Champagne
Publications Manager: Pamela Grieman
Cover design and layout: Lisa Winger

ACKNOWLEDGMENTS

Several of these stories have appeared in magazines, to which grateful acknowledgement is made:

"Betjegen," *Four Quarters* 28:1 (1978): 13–19.
"It's What We Want," *Appalachian Heritage* 16:1 (Winter 1988): 41–49.
"Chanco," *SAIL* (*Studies in American Indian Literatures*), Ser. 2, 2:2 (Summer 1990): 34–42.
"Rough Creek, Texas—1888," *Four Quarters*, 2nd ser. 4:2 (Fall 1990): 47–54.
"When the Fry-Bread Molders," *Fiction International* 20 (Fall 1991): 84–91. Reprinted in *Looking Glass*, ed. Cliff Trafzer, Publications in American Indian Studies, San Diego State University (1991), 84–91.
"How Beans Make Decisions," *SAIL* (*Studies in American Indian Literatures*), Ser. 2, 4:4 (Winter 1992): 18–27.
"Cookies and Milk for Jackie," *New Frontiers*, The Magazine of New Mexico 3:1 (Spring 1996): 25–28.
"Chitty Harjo," *American Indian Culture and Research Journal* 21:2 (1997): 255–264.
"Ghost-Face Charlie," *Cimarron Review* (Native American issue) #121 (October 1997): 12–21.

Library of Congress Catalog Card No. 00-101309
ISBN 0-935626-51-4 (paperback)
Printed by McNaughton & Gunn, Inc.

Copyright ©2000, by American Indian Studies Center, University of California. All right reserved. No part of this book may be reproduced in any manner whatsover without permission.

Contents

Author's Introduction	1
When the Fry-Bread Molders	5
Chanco	10
It's What We Want	19
Tell Them We Have Started the War	33
Hiss-Til-Toyoo	43
Rough Creek, Texas—1888	53
A Hunting Story	63
Maria Has-Red-Shoes	71
Tommy Turtle-Back	82
How Beans Make Decisions	92
Ghost-Face Charlie	102
Dillie's Den	113
Betjegen	119
Cookies and Milk for Jackie	128
Chitty Harjo	137
Tour of Ácoma	147
Return to Zuni	155
Cowboy	163
Comeuppance at Kicking Horse Casino	173

Author's Introduction

This collection of stories is a mix of historical and contemporary fictions about Native Americans. The historical stories provide a background for the contemporary stories, so that the entire collection becomes a loose chronicle of the Native American experience since the European settlement of North America. A wide range of tribes is represented—Blackfoot, Powhatan, Cherokee, Creek, Comanche, Lakota, Navajo, Ute, Keres, Ácoma, Zuni, and an unnamed southern California tribe. Each story highlights some individual's quandary—and often alienation—in negotiating and adapting to a face-to-face encounter with the whites.

Until very recently (until approximately the triumph of Indian gaming), the dominant impact of the encounter has been a limited destruction of the Indian—not always as extreme as the suicide in "When the Fry-Bread Molders," but common enough to make that story a kind of keynote to this collection, at least until the comeuppance at the end. From the beginning, Native Americans have been invited and/or forced to join white culture and have see-sawed back and forth—as "Chanco" wavers—between a passionate attempt to embrace white culture and an equally passionate alienation from it. Some tribes and some individuals have undergone a transformation of the myth by which they live into something more harmonious with white culture, as in the Cherokee transformation of myth in "It's What We Want," a fiction based closely upon historical fact. This evolution of consciousness has allowed some tribes and individuals to assimilate more successfully than others. Other tribes have preserved or reinvented their cultural integrity, as in "Tell Them We Have Started the War," where Indian traditions remain triumphantly opposed to and unreconciled with white culture.

And yet, assimilation (a recurring theme in this book) has been the effect, the subtext, of our history, and the school has been its primary instrument. Almost half of these stories involve the effect of school upon Native American children—some from Indian boarding schools, some from church schools, some from public schools, all destructive in some ways, enabling in others. The boarding school rape of both mind and body is, to me, the shrewdest metaphor for what the white man has done to the Indian. Some children—Jimmy

Lame Crow, Maria Has-Red-Shoes, Tommy Turtleback—are destroyed by school experiences in different ways. Others—Eddie NightWalker, Dillie Ci-yáh-n-ree, Betjegen, Billy Duc-Doc—learn to make profitable use of their school experiences, even if the blessing is mixed.

Several of these stories involve mixed bloods, products of Indian-white marriages, a situation which nearly always generates divided loyalties and identity crises. In "A Hunting Story," the old man is still trying to deal with a youthful violation of his cultural loyalty to an Indian grandmother. In "Rough Creek, Texas," a young girl is thrown into an identity crisis by the discovery that she had such an Indian grandmother. In "Return to Zuni," the tribe is the problem, rejecting Zima's identity until the old grandmother comes forward to endorse his loyalty and identity. Even the coach in "When the Fry-Bread Molders" finds it sometimes difficult to deal with his divided loyalties.

Another facet of family is the continuity of generations. "Betjegen" and "Return to Zuni" illustrate reintegration of an individual into family after some time of assimilation. "Ghost-Face Charlie" illustrates the destructive aspect of that reintegration, while "Chitty Harjo" shows beneficial results of a cross-cultural integration. One segment of "Comeuppance at Kicking Horse Casino" touches on the older generation's perception of continuity and change.

Two of the stories involve pyschological projection. Jackie Bullbreath fills her anomie, not with cookies and milk, but with her vicarious projection of her consciousness into the lives of other people. It is not her fault that she fails to assimilate; the fault lies with the shortcomings of the white culture she is exposed to. Jake Backturn, driven by his insecurities and guilt, is slowly becoming Chitty Harjo, the fallen hero. He is progressively taking Chitty's place in the family, on the stomp ground, even with Chitty's girl-friend. His projection of himself into the personality of Chitty Harjo is a sort of reverse assimilation.

The characters in "Dillie's Den," "Betjegen," and "Cowboy" have worked their way through assimilation and have rediscovered at least some of their native heritage, partly through a limited rejection of white culture.

The overall result of this American/Indian interface has been a limited assimilation of the Indian into white culture, which is probably the Native American's ultimate doom and ultimate survival. Perhaps the most America can hope for is not a "melting pot," but a society modeled on a "salad bowl," in which differences are recognized, yet widely accepted as irrelevant. These differences must be perceived as posing no threat to either culture, which happens when they become economically profitable, as when some Anglo discovers that he can make a buck on the Saint Patrick's Day Parade or the October Fest. Then cultural differences become quaint and picturesque, rather than threatening. I already see signs that the powwow is on its way to assuming such a valence.

One recent development that whites see as threatening (probably because they aren't the ones making the bucks) is Indian gaming casinos. In my home county, San Diego, three bands of Kumeyaay are makings piles of money on gambling. They are spending it on housing projects for Native people, a satellite campus of D-Q University, contributions to the local symphony orchestra and the local Public Broadcasting Service, a pan-Indian regional hospital, and health center. One of the bands is talking of buying and operating a bank. Another is putting in a discount shopping mall that may well out-compete those in the suburbs. In Northern California, where I went to high school, the tribe is buying back the good farmland that was taken from them more than a hundred years ago. These Indians are not acting like Indians at all; they are acting like bankers, entrepreneurs, businessmen. Money has made it possible for them to take charge of their own assimilation, whether the multicultural departments are ready for it or not.

Cultures are not static or fixed, but ever-changing. The arrival of the horse transformed almost all of the cultures between the Appalachians and the Rocky Mountains. Within barely more than a generation, the people could hardly imagine a culture without the horse. The gun worked a similar transformation. The domestication of the dog and the turkey in the Southwest must have been similar transforming events. The arrival of the copper pot and the steel butcher knife, the adoption of weaving, and the introduction of needles and buttons, looking glasses, scissors, matches, and dozens of other items each worked their miracles of change.

Nor is cultural change limited to material culture; it happens also at the social level and even can happen in myth and religious life. Several matrilineal cultures were changed to patrilineal cultures, by force it is true, but changed nevertheless. Courtship and marriage customs evolve; even the cult of the warrior has developed through patriotic service during World War I, World War II, and America's other wars. I am told that one of the reasons that so many Indians are on forest-firefighting crews and do so well is that it appeals to their concept of themselves as warriors: they are pitted against a difficult and dangerous enemy and they are defending and preserving environments.

Reservation gaming and the comeuppance it makes possible are already transforming Native American cultures. It is also galvanizing white attitudes about the otherness of the American Indian. I don't have a good solution to the problem of changing white America, but I can see Native America evolving rapidly. It will be much more beneficial to all parties concerned if both the dominant culture and the new Native American can develop an attitude of sameness of human beings, which means the rediscovery of a tolerance that the Indian has not had nor enjoyed for perhaps two hundred years. I hope my stories contribute to that tolerance.

Charles Brashear, San Diego, January 2000

When the Fry-Bread Molders

Mr. White, the principal, came into the noon faculty meeting a little slower than usual. He held a sheaf of papers in his hands, but he wasn't reading when he announced: "Jimmy Lame Crow has committed suicide."

The whole faculty of Benjamin Franklin High School could never have been quieter. Mrs. White, who taught sewing and cooking, even lay down her embroidery, brushed the back of her hand lightly across her mouth, and turned to stare out the window. We were in the Home-Ec room on the second floor, so we had a pretty good view of Blackfoot, but I couldn't tell where the Fort Hall Reservation started. I'm not even sure you could see it from here. Miss Pietsch, our English teacher, glanced at Mr. Daniels, the shop teacher, then bent forward, cupping her face and eyes in both hands. We all knew Jimmy had been her pet.

Mr. White picked up his papers again after that long pause, then lay them back down. "Coach," he said, and all eyes turned toward me. I'm the only mixed-blood on the staff, so they always expect something from me. "Coach, I'd like to ask you to—"

I nodded and looked at my fingernails. I figured he wanted me to drive out to the reservation and take the news to Jimmy's family. I'd been out there a few times, to pick Jimmy up when we had a game away from home. An image of his grandmother came into my mind and wouldn't go away: the image was as real as a dream—a little old wrinkled woman so shrunken with age and twisted with arthritis that she was hardly four feet tall. She couldn't speak much English, just a string of heavily accented syllables with a recognizable word now and then. "Shame" was the word she was using in my vision, but it sounded a lot like "same."

"Same! Same!" she had screamed when I took Jimmy home after his baseball accident. A really hot, low line drive had taken a bad hop at second and hit Jimmy in the face. It broke his nose and cheek-bone, so I had to take him out of the game. His whole face swelled shut and got black. After the game, I took him to the Indian Health Service clinic and the nurse pulled the bones out to where they're supposed to be, as best she could, then taped him up. I had to hold him down, the pain was so bad. He came out of it with a crooked nose and his cheek bones uneven. It made him look mean, but he was the mildest thing around. When I took him to his grandmother, his whole head was a huge white mask, with just holes for eyes, nose, and mouth. She kept crying, "Same! Same!"

"Coach, he's still—" the principal began, but Miss Pietsch cut him off.

"Why?" she moaned, lifting her face and fidgeting around in her seat. "Why?" she cried, "Why, when he has so much—"

"*Had* so much," corrected Mrs. Christopher, the American history teacher. "But you're right," she went on. "He was my best student."

"Mine, too," said Mr. Cox, the math-science utility man.

Even Mr. Daniels and Mrs. White nodded their agreement, and Jimmy Lame Crow hadn't taken shop or home-ec.

"I had him figured for Stanford next year," said Mrs. Christopher. "I hadn't told anyone, but I got word that his essay on Manifest Destiny had made it to the finals in that contest he didn't even know he'd entered. I'm sure he was about to win a scholarship."

"I know that essay," said Miss Pietsch. "I helped him with his grammar on it. He brought me a piece of fry-bread afterwards. It was awful. So greasy and rancid. I thanked him, of course, but I put it in my desk drawer. 'I'll save this for later,' I told him. But I couldn't eat it. It turned all moldy, but I just couldn't throw it away. I guess it's still in my desk. I'm so ashamed. I should have been able to be a better person. So ashamed." Her voice trailed off, but she couldn't seem to stop. "He gave me a copy of *The Pre-Columbian Cook Book* at the same time. Said he had made the fry-bread himself. From a recipe in it."

So that's how Stanford heard about Fort Hall. Jimmy was our best hitter, no question of that, and he could play ball with just about any college you want. But I couldn't understand how the Stanford scout had heard about us, so isolated as we are way up here. But there the guy was at a couple of our games. He was prohibited from talking with Jimmy, of course, but he cornered me twice. He wanted to see the batting averages for last year and the year before. He kept making bad jokes: "We want to take the chief down to Palo Alto and make him into an Indian." That sort of thing.

"Why?" repeated Miss Pietsch.

"I suppose we'll never know," said Mrs. Christopher. "It might even be that we don't *want* to know. Some skeletons are better left in their closets."

Mr. Daniels started coming out of the shock. "How?" he asked, pausing, as if to search for words. "How did he do it?"

Mr. White shuffled his papers again, then muttered: "With a piece of nylon rope. The sort you use on a boat. Hung himself from the pipe in the Boys' Room."

"Do you have to give us the details, Henry?" asked Mrs. White.

"Well, no, I guess ... Someone asked." He looked at me again. "Coach, uh—uh—I was wondering if you—"

"When?" This time it was Mrs. Christopher who interrupted him.

Mr. White cleared his throat, glanced at Mrs. White and his papers. "Uh—Ah—We aren't certain. Mr. Arter—" He stopped again, looked at the women, shuffled his papers. "The custodian," he said, as if he needed to identify Mr. Arter for us. "Uh— Charlie found him in the Boys' Room when he came to work. He must have done it last night."

"Stop!" cried Mrs. White and Mrs. Christopher in unison.

"Well, uh— That's just it. I can't stop. We've got to do something about— Uh—Coach, I've been trying to get a word in edgeways. Could you go take him down?"

"What?" cried Mr. Daniels, Miss Pietsch, Mrs. Christopher, and Mrs. White all at once. I think I even asked "What?"

"Yeah. Well, you see— Ah—You know how Charlie has that gimpy leg he got in Vietnam? Well, Charlie couldn't lift him. He's still hanging in the Boys' Room on the first floor. Could you—Ah— Could you go take him down?"

I stood up so quick, I knocked my chair over with a big crash, and started for the door. That meant that Jimmy had been hanging down there for several hours.

Mr. White shuffled his papers and looked out the window. Then he added, just about the time I got to the door, "I thought you could— You know— Since you've met his family. I thought you could take him out to—"

"Henry! Stop! I won't hear another word."

I heard Daniels' heavy boots right behind me, and then the clacking of several women's heels on the stairway. It sounded kind of like the whole meeting was adjourning.

I burst through the Boys' Room door. Several teenagers were standing around: Billy Daitschee, Oscar White Owl, Tommy Red Knife, Taitee Maunee, and some others. They were standing back away from the swinging body, acting guilty, as if I'd just caught them playing with themselves at the urinal.

Jimmy Lame Crow had made a hangman's noose in the nylon rope, climbed up on the toilet back, and hung himself from the plumbing for the upstairs restroom. The drop hadn't been enough to break his neck, so it looked like he had choked. His eyes were bugged out like a frog's, and his mouth was open wide. His lips and tongue were black and swollen. There were several scuff marks on the wall, as if he'd changed his mind too late, and died trying to climb the wall.

"Sheeee-zussss," said Daniels, behind me.

"I'm not going in there," said Mrs. Christopher from the door. Mr. White was holding the door open with his forearm.

"Did you call the sheriff?" I asked Mr. White.

"He—Ah—He said go ahead and take care of it. He'll come around later and check it out."

I stopped Jimmy from swinging. His body was stiff with rigor mortis. His bladder had let go and wet his pants, but the urine had dried into a stiff stain.

"You boys," said Daniels. "You get on out of here."

"Let them stay," I said. "They're his friends."

Several of them started for the door. "Billy, Taitee," I said. "Hold his legs. Lift him up." I took out my pocket knife, climbed up on the toilet, and cut him loose. The nylon was hard to hack through with a small blade. I could hear Billy and Taitee grunting. When Jimmy dropped into their arms, I heard the whole crowd sigh. Billy and Taitee laid him down with extreme gentleness, as if they were afraid of hurting him.

I climbed down from the toilet back and tried to take the noose from his neck. As slippery as the nylon is, it had gotten tighter and tighter with each bit of struggling, but the knot wouldn't let the rope loosen. I'd need something more than my pocket knife to get it off.

I heard Miss Pietsch running for her room, which was about halfway down the hall. Then I noticed there was something in Jimmy's hands. It was a big wad of moldy fry-bread. His right hand was a tight fist that I couldn't get open, and I could see he held another fragment of the same bread in the other hand. There was also a bulge of it in his pants pocket.

I motioned for Billy and Taitee to carry his legs as I lifted his shoulders. I guided them toward the parking lot, where my pick-up was. He was no more trouble to carry than a log would have been.

I'd been out in the country gathering firewood, so there were several sticks and limbs in my pick-up. We lay Jimmy among them. I didn't even have a blanket to cover the body with. I worked at the nylon rope with a pair of pliers and finally got it off.

"He say anything to you guys lately?" I asked Billy and Taitee.

They glanced at each other and at me. I knew if I weren't a mixed-blood they wouldn't say anything. "He's been getting quieter, ever since we took world history," said Billy.

"It got worse, with that Manifest Destiny stuff," added Taitee.

They both scuffed the ground with their toes and glanced at me again. I nodded to indicate I understood what they were getting at. "Is that why he did it?" I asked.

"He didn't want to buy into that stuff," said Taitee, pointing with his chin to the cornice of the school building.

I looked up and read the name: Benjamin Franklin High School. "Sheeze," I said, "that's been around a while. He had gotten used to that a long time ago. There has to be something else."

They looked at each other again. "That Stanford guy," said Billy, "that Stanford guy finally talked to him."

"That's against the rules," I said.

"They wanted to take him to California and make him into a white man," said Taitee.

I paused, to let an interval pass. "Well," I said, "I expect I'd better get him out of here, before someone comes along and wants to bury him like a white man. You guys want to come along?"

They both shook their heads and turned to stroll back to the school building.

I hesitated before getting in my pick-up. I felt like I wanted to kick the door in, or something. It occurred to me that I could take some of that fry-bread and go stuff it down Miss Pietsch's throat, but I realized it wasn't her—at least not just her.

Finally, I got in the pick-up and drove out toward the reservation. I could already hear his grandmother crying "Same! Same!"

Chanco

Chanco sensed his brother's presence before he saw him, for he knew he waited there in the shadows of the short palisade. "You are to kill them tomorrow morning," his brother said in their own language, the language of Powhatan. "You are to kill him. And her and the baby too. When the sun shines through the first branches of the trees. Ope-tsan-kano has ordered all the villages to attack, all up and down the river. We will strike everywhere at once."

The dog, a big slobbering mastiff, growled then at his brother, and Chanco had to calm him, thankful that it covered his confusion. *Me? Why me?* he thought. *I'm only fourteen; that's a man's job.*

"You can do it, can't you?" his brother asked.

Chanco hesitated, glad to be in the darkness, glad that his brother could not see the quivering in his lip, the protest in his eye. "I— I— How? With a knife?"

"Take his musket. Use his own musket on them. He has taught you to use it, hasn't he? Or has he made your heart blue?"

The words struck Chanco like a fist. His brother had stepped close, so that his breath beat Chanco on the side of the head, hard but without anger. "You're getting to be a man," said his brother. "You've got to do a man's duties. We've got to get rid of them. Before they destroy us and our way. We will burn Jamestown, burn their farms, kill all these thieving English, and push their ships back into the sea. That is Ope-tsan-kano's plan. You must go along with it, like a brave warrior, or you will have no one to go along with you."

Chanco held the mastiff's collar and said nothing. If he had said it was treachery, his brother would have hit him. If he had said they only want us to be civilized too, his brother would have hit him again.

"Answer me," said his brother. "He has taught you to use the musket?"

"Yes," said Chanco.

His brother turned on his toe and faded away toward the west outbuilding where Chanco slept.

Four years before, Chanco had been captured when the English raided his village for slaves. At first, he had hated the English—and Richard Pace, his captor, in particular. He had tried several times to escape. Each time he was recaptured, Pace had not punished him, but had treated him with kindness, and, slowly, Chanco had come to be content with Pace and the English. The Reverend Alexander Whitaker, who had taught Pocahontas to be a Christian, had taught Chanco how they were all really brothers in soul, and how the Indians were really one of the lost tribes, who were now found, and would live hereafter in peace and prosperity. Then Chanco had become a Christian, too, and tried to live, not as Richard and Isabella Pace's servant, but as their son, as an older brother to little George. He no longer had a desire to escape.

But now, old Wahun-Senock-qu-a, the Powhatan, was dead. And Ope-tsan-kano, Powhatan's half-brother who had fought the English from the beginning, had sent Chanco orders to kill his benefactor. Chanco did not know where to turn, so he stood in the shadow of the short palisade, holding the mastiff's collar and trying to pray to Jesus, until Isabella Pace called him to supper.

At the supper table, Chanco kept glancing at Richard Pace. *He wants me to tell*, thought Chanco. *He would want me to tell, but I won't do it.*

When Pace asked about his brother, Chanco pretended to have food in his mouth.

"That *was* your brother you were talking to, wasn't it?" asked Isabella.

At last, Chanco mumbled, "Went west," pleased that he had told the truth about where his brother had gone, but had not revealed anything. He knew his brother would be waiting in the shed. Chanco had already slipped a wild turkey leg into the belly of his shirt.

"Any news of Opechancanough?" asked Pace.

Chanco tried to hold his outward expression absolutely still, as he had been taught when a very young child. He gazed at Pace to see if there was any knowledge in his eyes. At last, he shrugged.

"I just thought maybe your brother—"

At that moment, Chanco hated his benefactor more than he had ever hated anyone. And hated him even more, because Richard Pace was so insensitive, he could not even see that he was hated. Pace's contempt for all things Indian was supreme. *I'll kill him*, thought Chanco. *Because he is our enemy, mine, all the Real People's. Even though he has been more father to me than anyone, I'll kill him.* With pleasure, Chanco thought of a way to mislead without lying. "Ope-tsan-kano, no change," said Chanco. "No change since last year."

"That's good to hear," said Pace, sipping his wine with satisfaction. He leaned back in his chair and became more voluble. "George Thorpe said he had a message from Opechancanough only a week ago. Some had heard ugly rumors, about which Thorpe sent to inquire."

Chanco just gazed at Pace, pretending ignorance.

"Well, you know of the peace we concluded last year and ratified and stamped in brass, as Opechancanough wanted, and then nailed to the witness tree?" Chanco nodded in the English fashion.

"Well, the messenger came back, saying that Opechancanough held that peace so firm, that the sky should sooner fall than it dissolve." Pace sipped more of his wine and straightened his vest.

"I tell you, Chanco, it's good to know that we are secure in our houses and the civilization of the savages is progressing well. I reckon now that there was no substance to the rumor that Opechancanough had tried to bribe some of the coastal tribes to poison all of us. I tell you, Chanco, this New England is fair on its course to be a paradise for us."

As Pace talked on and on, Chanco realized that it was not Pace's insensitivity that allowed him to say these things to a person who had been dispossessed and made a slave, but that Pace was talking to Chanco the way he would talk to another English man, or to a son. And Chanco was pleased. Perhaps they were brothers of the soul, after all. Perhaps there could exist a world in which Indians and English lived as equals. Hadn't the Reverend Mr. Whitaker died in the river while trying to give help to an Indian woman? Hadn't he gone to her aid as soon as he would have gone to the aid of an Englishwoman?

Pace's voice broke through Chanco's thoughts again. "I tell you, Chanco, this is the first day of spring, and a new world is a-borning. Look at me: I've patented my plantation almost four miles from Jamestown, with nothing around me but a short palisade. And all up and down the river, men are living harmoniously with the natives, as we are living here at Pace's Paines."

Chanco looked down. It was true. He was living more comfortably now than he had before, more comfortably than he had his whole life. He was warm and well-fed, and, more importantly, Richard and Isabella Pace seemed to care for him genuinely, and little George crawled on Chanco's knee as if Chanco were no different from his parents. They were Chanco's parents, too, now. How could he raise a weapon to kill them?

Pace was still talking: "Perhaps Mr. Whitaker and George Thorpe were right; maybe we could castrate the mastiffs to make them tamer, even though some maintain it unwise to drop security so far. Let us pray." Pace and Isabella drifted into the prayer with closed eyes, "Let us thank the Almighty with all our hearts for the success He has seen fit that we enjoy as we so nobly pursue and advance our projects of buildings, plantings, and in effecting the savages' conversion by peaceable and fair means—"

As Pace talked, Chanco gazed at his plate and at the candle on the table, unable to pray. He sank lower in the chair the white man had made of tree limbs. *Maybe he won't see me*, he thought. *Maybe I'll look up in a while and both he and my brother will be gone. Maybe the task will vanish. He would want me to tell*, thought Chanco. *If I were really his son, I would be bound by duty to tell.*

Chanco slipped the wild turkey leg from beneath his shirt and returned it to the platter. Then, he waited those minutes he had been taught were polite and said good night. He went out without calling Pace 'father.'

Even before his eyes had adjusted to the darkness, Chanco heard the mastiff sniffing at his leg like a friend. He knew Chanco. *Ope-tsan-kano will send assassins to the plantations where the dogs know them*, he thought. *Then they can get in without waking their victims.*

The big dog followed Chanco as he moved away from the main house. That made Chanco feel secure, for the dog would keep away the spirits of dead people that lived in the woods and frequently tried to do mischief to the living. He heard one in the woods down by the river, squawking like a turkey that had just been caught by a fox. Even though he was uncomfortable in the dark, he dallied, looking back at Pace's house, knowing, dreading, that he would have to face his brother again in the shed.

All of Chanco's life, the tribe had tried to deal with this same dilemma. When the English had been here only a year, John Smith had gone to Nansemond village and demanded corn: "You know our want, and we know your plenty. Somehow, by peace or by force, your plenty is going to serve our want." To which, Wahun-Senock-qu-a, the Powhatan, had replied, "Why should you take by force that which you can have by love?" But Smith stuck to his line and extorted corn from the Indians as a condition of peace.

Even Powhatan was then ready to let Ope-tsan-kano execute Smith, but Pocahontas begged him to change his mind.

"You can't trust these English," said Ope-tsan-kano.

Not long after Pocahontas had saved Smith, they kidnapped her and held her as a hostage to ensure peace. Chanco, too, had been kidnapped and held hostage in the same kind of extortion that just happened to produce slaves. *Yes*, he thought, *Ope-tsan-kano is right. They will never accept us.*

"Do you think we will find a place in their God's sight?" Ope-tsan-kano had once asked in council. "Don't you know they say we are infidels, servants of their devil in our dark and howling woods, not even so good as scum or sweat, until we consent to take their God by the arm? But do you think they would let us live among them? Would they let us work at our trades? Or theirs? Would any of them follow an Indian commander, or let an Indian be governor of Virginia, even if he were as wise as Powhatan? They tell us that they are the chosen people; but who chose them? They themselves. They have no room in their hearts for brotherhood; they have no room for anything but their greedy admiration of themselves."

The tribe had always offered good faith, and the English had responded with extortion. Ope-tsan-kano was right. They would have to be exterminated—to the last man, woman, and child. And Chanco would help. He would be glad to help. He hurried toward the shed.

His brother growled at him from the dark of the room. "What kept you so long? Didn't you know I was waiting?"

"I got away as soon as I could," said Chanco.

"Haugh!" said his brother in disgust and disbelief.

Chanco let it pass. "Here," he said, "I've brought you some food." He handed his brother a small loaf of corn bread and a turnip.

"What *is* this?" scowled his brother. "Squaw food! Do you think I want to eat that kind of truck and become stiff like the roots? No! I want to be able to spring lightly and swiftly through the forest. Couldn't you get me any deer meat? Or at least some turkey?"

Chanco hesitated, then decided to make no excuses. His brother fell to eating the food.

Chanco opened the shutter and stood listening to the night. He had grown up in the Powhatan's village, where his first memories were of men arguing to kill the whites, countered by Powhatan's world-weary answers: "We have not achieved our ends by force, nor will we. Is it not better to lie secure in our lodges with our women and children near, than to strike these men, after which we must lie on the forest floor, eat what grubs and roots we can find, and forever be on the secret watch to attack again, lest we be attacked? Who of us can deny that their weapons are superior to ours? As friends, we will have like weapons. Who of us can deny that their copper pans are better than our clay pots? We, too, will have copper pans. And what man among us does not already carry one of their knives at his waist?"

Chanco hardly knew what to think. Pocahontas adopted them as family, and look how comfortable she became. Even the Powhatan had come to accept and approve of her choice. *What man among us could not adopt a family of them as his own?* thought Chanco.

Most of the tribe had said Powhatan was a great man, but Chanco's uncles and brothers had followed Ope-tsan-kano.

"Have you seen our uncles lately?" he asked his brother.

"Yes, of course. Everyone is a part of the attack. All the villages, all the sub-tribes, all of the peoples that Ope-tsan-kano leads. Your uncles will strike at George Thorpe's place. The black servant there may know of the plan, but he will run away to save himself. We will bash in Thorpe's skull, then cut his body into small pieces, to be lost in the dark woods, so that his soul will find no rest."

"So much?" cried Chanco. "Does he deserve so much?"

"He deserves more. But we cannot cut his spirit in pieces."

"But he has been so good—such a good friend—"

"Friend? Ha! Is it being a good friend to humiliate even Ope-tsan-kano by dogging him to say that Thorpe's God is a loving God? Better than the Great Spirit? Or force us to say we love Thorpe and his mastiffs? For he rips out our souls, even as he has trained his dogs to rip out our guts."

His brother was right, of course. Thorpe had done those things. The thought of Thorpe's guts being scattered in the forest thrilled Chanco. It would serve him right, serve all the English right to be ripped to pieces so ruthlessly, as they had trained their mastiffs to kill Indians. *Yes,* he thought, *rip them to pieces and feed them to their own dogs!* His brother was eating the last of the food.

I hope some of the assassins stop to have breakfast with the English, thought Chanco, *before they kill them with their own tools.*

His brother was still talking, though more quietly. Whitaker had been a fool and a meddler, who might have been a good man, had he been born an Indian. Thorpe and Pace and those other English were not friends, but thieves; they professed their undying love, but Indian corn and wild game still found their way to English tables, which left the Indians to eat grubs and roots in the forests.

Yet, any Indian who wished to could live with them, thought Chanco, *and be well-fed, secure in their souls, warm against the winter,* even as Chanco had lived these last years. He felt paralyzed. What could be done? There was no solution for both these men.

I could run away, he thought, gazing at the dark woods. *I could go into the forest and walk toward the hills under the sunset and never come back. Then I wouldn't have to answer to either of them.* But, in anguish, frustration, outrage, he knew, *I will have to do it. My brother is here to make sure I do it.* Hopelessness burned in him like the fires of damnation themselves. He leaned against the sash, sinking in his despair.

Then Chanco discovered with a start that he had dozed on the window sill, for his brother was shaking him awake. By the night sounds, Chanco could tell it was not long before first light.

"I have to go now," said his brother. "You too must awake and do your duty."

"Go?" asked Chanco. "You are going?"

"Yes, of course." His brother's voice had turned bitter and sarcastic. "My job is to bash in 'Mister' Perry's skull. I'll teach him what his slaves think of him and his slobbering dogs."

Then Chanco's brother was gone. Chanco sat long, listening to the quiet place in the woods where his brother had passed.

Their ancestors were out there. The ghost of Powhatan was there, too, in the woods. Were those great men still arguing after death? Did their souls carry on the problems they had struggled with in life? They had come to no conclusions in life, but was there something, some idea, some information that the immortal soul knew that the mortal did not? Could they tell a mortal? Could they give a sign?

Chanco got up and walked out the gate, leaving the mastiff behind. His skin shriveled in goose bumps, though he was not cold. He could hear his heart thumping as he entered the woods. Everything was absolutely quiet.

Was that the sign they gave? Their absolute silence?

He walked a short way on a path he knew, then stopped. He tried to speak, but no sound came. Then he whispered, "Wahun-Senock-qu-a." He waited a moment for an answer. "Wahun-Senock-qu-a, great father, elder uncle. Are you there? Give me a sign."

He waited. Nothing. He felt a chill in his backbone, and his hands shook. Was that the sign? Were they telling him to look into himself?

"But why me?" he whispered. "I'm only a boy. I'm only fourteen. How can I know a man's thoughts? Oh, Sweet Jesus, help me in my misery. Deliver me from my weakness, lead me from my confusions into righteousness. Purify me that I may see."

He paused to listen. There was not a sound in the forest, not a speck of light.

It would soon be dawn on March 22, 1622—Good Friday. It was the day the Lord Jesus had been tormented and crucified. Chanco felt profoundly sorry for Jesus, because Pace had impressed upon him what a holy man Jesus was—how infallible, how forgiving and loving, how unselfish, how divine. This Jesus had promised to carry even Chanco's worries, if Chanco would only give freely of his love. How could Chanco not love such a brave warrior, who invented his own weapons and led his tribe in his own ways?

The Israelites were the chosen people of God. Yet they were constantly at war with the people that tried to push them out of their Holy Land, constantly in danger of suffering genocide, driven on all sides by angry enemies, as a desert wind drives the sand, as the English had pressed the Powhatan people. What they saw as justice, others saw as greed. What the English saw as honor, the Powhatan people saw as thievery. What the English called plantation was invasion and war. And God had said, let there be a stop to this. Yes, God had said, gird up your loins and slay them with their own swords; let there be a stop to their evil.

Chanco returned to the house, picked up the axe he chopped Pace's wood with, and headed for his adopted father's bedroom.

He could not see Pace in the darkness, but once in his presence, he had no doubt. He shook Pace awake, saying, "Forgive me, father. Your life is in danger."

Pace was confused. "What? Who? Is that you, Chanco?"

"Yes, it is Chanco. Your life is in danger, master. Oh, please forgive me that I could raise your axe against you. I cannot—"

"Axe?" cried Isabella Pace. "What do you mean?"

Then Chanco told them of Ope-tsan-kano's plan, letting it tumble out, disorganized and apologetic.

"Quick! My shirt!" shouted Pace, throwing off his nightshirt. "We've got to give the alarm."

"No!" cried Chanco. "My uncles. They will be killed."

But Pace had already gone out, dragging his pants onto one foot, leaving Isabella Pace to hold a quilt to her breast. In the yard, Pace was shouting, "To arms! To arms!"

Chanco stood, stilled by shock. He had meant to warn only Pace. It meant less to him if all the other English were smashed. But not Pace. And yet, Pace was only a part of the whole English tide. If it were right that he live—

Pace broke through the door again, shouting, "Come on, Chanco! This is an emergency!" And he dragged Chanco out by the arm.

Pace had put his boat in the slough and lay the oars across the thwart. "Get in!" said Pace. "We've got to get over to Jamestown, quick!"

"No!" cried Chanco in his native language, as he ducked, turned, dashed toward his shed.

Pace grabbed at him as he passed, catching only his sleeve. The seam gave way at the shoulder, and Chanco slid free. But it had slowed him enough that Pace got his other hand on the shirt.

Chanco spun, running backward, twisting to allow the shirt to slip over his head.

Then he was free, free soon of the homespun trousers also, running west in first light, in his own red-clay skin, springing lightly like a deer or turkey over the fallen logs in the woods, running, gaining a second wind.

When he came to Perry's place, he leapt over the mastiff with the crushed skull and knew that Perry was dead. By the river, he found Perry's skiff and rowed across to George Thorpe's place. They had cut Thorpe into pieces, as they had planned.

In all, 347 of the 1100 English were to die that morning, according to the records of the Virginia Company of London, but Chanco could not know that. He did know that Pace had rowed the three miles to Jamestown and warned the Governor, for he heard the cannon booming and the muskets cracking.

"My uncles!" he thought. "They are killing my uncles." Chanco found other bodies near Thorpe's burned house. It was a pleasure to kick them. For a moment, Chanco wanted to run after his uncles, catch up with them and his brother, join in the slaying. But they would soon know that Chanco was the traitor who had informed and allowed the English to prepare their defense at Jamestown. "If it weren't for you," they would say, "we could have killed them at their breakfast tables. We could have killed them all. Every last one."

Nor could Chanco ever go back to Pace, now that he had said "No!" in his own language, now that he had his own red-clay skin back. To Pace, Chanco would now be just an Indian, to be whipped, to be enslaved, to be guarded by a slobbering mastiff.

So Chanco ran west. Toward the hills where he could hide. Toward the hills where he could lift up his arms and ask the falling sky to forgive him, where he could beg the cold earth to receive him, where (he knew) none of the powers of the six directions would nurture him. For he was lost in the universe, with no place to turn. Neither the Great Spirit of All nor God the Father would have him now, for he was a traitor to both his fathers.

It's What We Want

When settlers from North Carolina and Virginia moved across the line you couldn't even see in the woods and into Cherokee hunting grounds and went so far as to build several of their cabins, even on the banks of the Watauga River, John Stuart, King George's Indian agent at Charles Town, and Alexander Cameron, his assistant, sent them strong talking papers and threatened to bring their red-coat army to force the greedy Americans back. We Cherokees were shocked by the idea. How could anyone think of raising the war hatchet against people of the same tribe, who spoke the same language and followed the same customs? Stuart and Scotchie sent us a talking paper, saying we should stay in our houses and not take up the war-axe ourselves. Scotchie reminded us that Stuart was the voice of King George himself and that he would make the Virginians move. But the whites were still on our land. They were interfering in our lives. We didn't like it but didn't quite know what to do about it.

Our Head Man, Oconostota, the Great Warrior, sat in his white seat, the Peace Seat, in the town council house, put a big hand on each knee, and told Ellis Harlan, a trader at Chota, what to write in a talking paper, which he sent to Stuart, saying "we think the Virginia People don't hear your talks, nor mind; nor do they seem to care for King George's. . . . We would that they would move off our lands and leave us alone; it's what we want."

"My voice is for war!" Dragging Canoe said in council, not waiting his turn to speak. He threw back his blanket, so all could see the muscles in his silver armbands, a signal that he was ready to do what he was calling on others to do. "Forty strong warriors of Mialaquo-town are ready to take up the bloody war-axe with me and strike the black pole. We are ready to drive them off Cherokee lands." He made chopping motions to emphasize his words and turned to each clan's area as he referred to them. "There are fifty warriors in Tuskegee, a hundred in Toqua, a hundred in To-ma-tli, not to mention over two hundred here in Chota. I say we are not weak. We are fourteen towns here in the Over-the-Hills district alone. And there are the Valley Towns, our brothers; and the Middle

Towns; and the Chickamauga Towns. We do not have to quail against the wall and wait for them to come even to our door. Scotchie said we should burn their cabins and send them back to Virginia, if they came into our land. They have crossed the line in the woods, which they agreed to stay behind; let us go and kill them."

But Oconostota did not give permission for a raid. He listened quietly until Dragging Canoe was finished, as is the Cherokee way, then pointed out that, since the trade with the Carolinas has been so meager, we have little powder and lead, and, when that is gone, the white men's guns will be far superior to our war-axes. Then there would be another of those disasters that Dragging Canoe is a little too young to understand. Or too hardheaded. The tribe listened to the old man, for he has no battle scars on his back. He has always faced his enemies.

Of course, Dragging Canoe's father, Atta-kulla-kulla, whom the whites call the Little Carpenter, and his niece, Na'nye-hi, our Beloved War Woman, are for conciliation. They have relatives among the whites, and they both speak the language. They will say renegotiate. Live peacefully with them as brothers. Marry with them. Come to know them as we know each other.

From his seat as Second Man of the Cherokees, Atta-kulla-kulla stood up and turned so we could all see once again, at his neck, the gold medal that King George gave him personally when he went to England as a young man. He walked clear around the sacred fire, then spoke in the town council house. "We are fortunate that the white men love us as brothers. For I, who have been across the big water, Ostenaco, who has been across the big water, others of you who have been across the big water, know how powerful they are. They want the sun to shine in our land, and the waters to flow in our rivers, just as they want that in their land. They have much to teach us. Then we will be as strong and powerful as they. I say, perhaps there has been some mistake. I say, we should go and ask them if there has been some mistake."

Taska-ya, the Conjuror of Chota, has cast his divining stones, but the red stones and black stones and white stones are all mixed together every time he casts them. There wasn't much there to read.

And we, the Cherokees, we hardly know what to do. We have to know that the power and knowledge of our ancestors, who still live here, whose bones are buried here, are in and with the Cherokee spirit. We have to have the Thunder, the power of the Spirits, if we are to influence the whites to lay down their enmity and pick up the good will of a friend.

If that's what we want.

We have asked the spirits in all the directions to be with us, just as you must when you are re-making ceremonial tobacco.

If you've ever done that, you know how good it is.

You start with ordinary brown tobacco from the earth. In the slit of time between the top and bottom rim of the sun coming up, you hold up the tobacco and say the four charms.

From the East, which is Red and which contains the powers of creativity, success, life-giving, you ask that your beginnings may be bright.

From the North, which is Blue and which contains the powers of suspicion, defeat, trouble, you ask that your decisions may be made with caution and a just pessimism.

From the West, which is Black and which contains the powers of death, the transfiguration from this inner world to the outer one, you ask that you may know the long-range effects of questions.

From the South, which is White and which contains the powers of peace, prosperity, and happiness, you ask that you may know the wise use and continued sustenance of conditions.

Four times, you lift the tobacco and pray.

Softly, sensations of knowledge run through your body, as you repeat the charm.

Then, as the sun breaks loose from the earth's rim, you feel the Thunders of the directions balancing on your tobacco, and your arms shake because it is almost impossible to hold it still while the powers are entering the tobacco.

When you bring it down, it is no longer ordinary brown tobacco, but Red Tobacco, far too strong for any mere man to smoke.

When we burn it in the ceremonial fireplace, which is the pipe bowl of the Galun-kwiti-yu, the smoke rising is their breath. When we walk through the smoke, it is their breath blowing on us and their power entering us.

We Cherokees know these spirits are always with us. When we go into the forests of Kaintuckee to hunt, when we go to the swamp lands of the south to fight a war, when we go traveling to the Mississippi to trade, and beyond, just to see what is there, these Guardian Spirits go with us. They tell us how to act; they tell us how to be; they fix our place and responsibility in earth and the seven layers of heaven. What a great comfort it is, to know these Powers will take care of us.

Even the half-bloods among us know this. And I don't mean just those like Red-headed Will and Sequoyah, who can't even speak English, but also those like The Bench who speaks English as well as his father who was once a red-coat soldier, or Bushyhead, John Stuart's own Cherokee son, who has been to school in Charles Town and can even read and write the English tongue. In fact, he's taught a lot of us to understand English, but he's a Cherokee first. Even some of the traders who have lived among us for many years follow Cherokee laws, and they know it, too.

The flesh and bones of our ancestors may have long since decayed, but their spirits are living here still; their spirits watch over the living and are responsible for all good things—for the fertile earth, the weather, the Green Corn that is the sustenance of life.

That's what we feel.

That's what we know.

The Virginians don't seem to know or care about these things. They leave the graves of their ancestors and go wandering off into the forest to molest anybody they can find. And they don't seem to mind. They're awfully hard to understand.

Atta-kulla-kulla and six of his warriors went for a walk to Virginia and held talks with the invaders. The people on our land recognized that The Little Carpenter was their good friend, so they said, "We are sorry, we made a mistake about where the line was."

"When a Cherokee discovers a mistake," observed Atta-kulla-kulla, "he corrects it."

"Oh, we will. We will," they said. "But you see our crops in the ground. The corn is up to a man's thigh. We cannot go back to Virginia now. There is not enough time to plant new crops. Then, when the winter comes, our women and children will have nothing to eat. Surely, you do not want our women and children to starve."

"No," he agreed, "No one wants your women and children to starve. But none of us want you on our land. It is our land. The Great Kana-ti gave it to us and the Great Buzzard shaped it in ways that we love. It is ours. It has been ours for a thousand years. Go back," said Atta-kulla-kulla, "and return when your crops are ripe. Then you can pick your corn, and go feed your women and children."

At every cabin door, we heard the same song.

Then, after a few days, their leader, John Carter came seeking us out. "Our people are peaceful, hardworking people," he said. "They have worked hard to build their cabins and clear the farms where they had hoped to feed their families. We have discussed this in our councils, and we have an idea to present to you.

"Our people do not want to leave the cabins they have built or the farms they have cleared, so we suggest that we pay the Cherokees for the use of them for a while."

They offered $6,000 in trade goods—blankets, knives, shirts, trousers, axes, things like that—mostly things they could make themselves. And they would give us all that pile of goods if we would just let them stay there eight years.

We have to admit that those Virginians are very clever at making things. Why, they have a big wheel where they build a fire and heat up metal, like they were one of the demons of the fiery place itself. One of them will reach in with a big pair of tongs and take that metal out, spit their power onto it, and lay it on a big block of metal; then another one will hit it with a hammer, here and there. They sweat and curse and grunt, just like they were praying, and they look frightful with all the smoke and soot on them and their eyes and arms gleaming in the red light of the fire, and after a while they have something in the tongs that looks like an axe. Of course, it's not very good for splitting a skull, but it works okay for a lot of other things. And then they prove they've got real power with the spirits, because they heat that axe-head up, and do all the right charms, and then put it in a pot of water where it shrieks and smokes and talks back to them, like it was angry, and it comes out hard enough to last more than a day or two. And they don't even have to say their charms aloud.

Some of the Cherokees think they are the Thunder priests of the destroyer devils; some say, "No, it's not devils in them, it's the creative power of the Ancient Red in the sunrise"; others say, "There's nothing special to it at all, and even a Cherokee can learn to do it if he wants."

Their women are clever, too; true handmaidens of the Spider power. They'll take a regular trade blanket, cut it to pieces, and then sew it all back together, so that you get a coat that buttons up the front and even covers your knees. They made Atta-kulla-kulla one where the red stripes all matched. He was really proud of that coat, almost as proud as he is of his medal. If he hadn't been such a high officer—he's Second Man among all the Cherokees, you know—we'd all have wanted one of those coats. They're real good in winter, too. Keep you warm without letting in a lot of air.

Atta-kulla-kulla held out for a while, he said, and told them how like a child without a father we are, now that King George has been unable to bring us any presents. He once gave us a medal and a coat, which we wore faithfully, but it has grown thin. Atta-kulla-kulla asked the Virginians if they could make us a new coat and maybe give us something for our women, too. He asked them for more of their copper pots. They're so much better to cook in than our clay pots and they last a lot longer, too. The Virginians said they didn't have any to spare, but that in future years they could get some from their cousins on the shore of the ocean. They offered us some of their flat pans. There is a man among them who can make a pan from a sheet of metal and glue it together with another metal, just like you'd put bark together with pine pitch. They're good pans, too. They won't stand much heat, but if you're careful, they'll serve you pretty well.

Ostenaco, who is Head Man of To-ma-tli and who crossed the ocean with his son-in-law, Henry Timberlake, just eleven years ago and stood at the throne of the new King George himself and talked with him like a man and received a big medal that he wears around his neck, even in battle. Of course, it's not as nice a medal as Atta-kulla-kulla's, which he got from the first King George forty-two years ago, because Atta-kulla-kulla's medal is real gold and says that we are King George's children and if we're cooperative, he will take care of us forever. Anyway, Ostenaco pretty much agreed with the idea of a lease to the Virginians on the Watauga River. He was right when he said, "They've pretty well ruined the place for hunting, because you can hardly find a deer, much less a buffalo or a wild turkey, between the Long Island of the Holston and the line Colonel Donelson drew in Virginia, which they were supposed to stay behind."

They really mess a place up, first with their hunters and then with their plows.

That's what led Ostenaco to tell John Stuart while Atta-kulla-kulla was at Watauga that we had little use of the land the Virginians want to borrow. In council, Ostenaco gave a short speech that ended: "If we let the Virginians live there, it will be in their power to supply us with goods, which would be very fine, as we have no trade at present, except with the South Carolinians, and that road is long and their trade houses often empty."

Atta-kulla-kulla gave a nice speech in council, too, saying that it was but a little piece of land, compared with what we have, and that he pitied the white people because they were getting so thick over by the ocean, and that these close by could be of great service to us, especially if they would agree to send us a man who could start a school among us.

"Look around you," he said, "and pick out the men who can read and write, and those who can't. Notice which one is dependent, which one is the father, which the child. Look around you: you see Cherokee children who must be leaders when we oldsters have passed on, as must we all. They will be leaders in a new time when our times have passed, as surely they will. As loving fathers, we should want all Cherokee children, and Cherokee children yet unborn, to be strong and not have to depend on others. Those who must lead in the new time will need to know how to make talking papers and how to decipher them, if they are to be good fathers and take care of their children. If the Virginians would establish a school among us, we should be very happy about it."

That part went over really well with us Cherokees—the part when Atta-kulla-kulla proposed that we ask the Virginians to help us start a school as a part of their payment to us. That's something a lot of us want.

So we talked for three days about the plan. The Cherokee way is that everyone has his say in council and gets to answer everyone else until we all agree on what to do. That way we get to hear the blue thoughts and red thoughts and the white thoughts and think out the uses and the black effects of a proposal. Finally, we agreed to let the white people borrow the land on the Watauga River, and about three hundred of us walked up there to take part in the talks and watch our Head Men put their marks on the papers the white people are so fond of making up.

They took good care of us, too. Gave us a lot of small presents, in addition to what they were going to pay us. Mostly little things, like a piece of rope for this man, a knife blade for that one, a ribbon or two for the women. Not many mirrors or much war paint or anything very valuable, but still it was nice of them to think of us and give us gifts. They gave us food, too—some of their cooked pig and cow and some gummy yellow stuff they said was made from cow milk. It tasted pretty good, too; it stuck to your teeth for a while, but it was creamy and smooth as it slid down your throat.

Then they suggested we make a nice day of it and have some games and races and contests. Of course, they couldn't play Cherokee ball, but they watched while some of our people played. Then we had some wrestling matches, and foot races, and horse races. They even let the black people with wooly heads out of the little houses they keep them locked in and let them race and wrestle with us. We were all having as good a day as you'd want to have anywhere.

Then a vicious man from Wolf Hills shot and killed The Raven of Chota's clan-son.

Raven's clan-son had just won a race, and this big ugly man with teeth missing called Raven's son over toward the edge of the clearing and just put his rifle in his face and shot him. Raven's son didn't live but just a minute.

Of course, The Raven and Dragging Canoe started to attack them, with just their belt knives. But even brave warriors know knives are no match for flintlocks, so they had to back off. We all ran and got what weapons we had with us, but the man and his six or eight friends had managed to hide. Some of our warriors wanted to turn on all the whites right there, but we hadn't decided to go to war and hadn't done any of the necessary ceremonies, so we just faded as quickly as we could into the surrounding countryside and headed back to Chota. Because we all knew this meant war, as soon as we could get prepared for it.

The Raven of Chota was Oconostota's sister's son, so The Raven's son was like a son to Oconostota, and since Oconostota was Head Man, there was no question that we'd have to go to war. It took us no time at all to agree to that in council. At a time like that, the Peace Chief has to step aside and let the War Chief take over. But since Oconostota was both Peace Chief and War Chief at that time, all he had to do was move from the white seat to the red seat and change his advice.

Even Atta-kulla-kulla and Na'nye-hi admitted we'd have to go to war. Na'nye-hi was The Ghigau, Beloved War Woman, so it was her duty to make the black drink to cleanse the warriors who were about to go to war. We had danced and prayed all night and gone to the water at dawn, and the leaders had put blood-paint on a war-axe and had struck the black pole, and The Raven had been chosen to lead one war party, and Dragging Canoe, Atta-kulla-kulla's son, had been chosen to lead another, and we were just about ready to set out, when Captain James Robertson from the Virginia settlements on the Watauga River walked in.

Chota was the Peace Town, where anyone needing haven could stay until he had fixed the wrong that sent him there, and no Cherokee was allowed to take any revenge or do anyone any harm in Chota. That's why there was never a guard at the gate. If it had been any other town, there would have been a warrior on watch and any warrior would have split Robertson's skull right then and there.

As it was, The Raven and Dragging Canoe lunged at Robertson and the man he had brought with him, and they were about to take their hair off, when Atta-kulla-kulla jumped up and started pulling them off. Now, Atta-kulla-kulla is just a little fellow, hardly as big as a budding girl, but he is Dragging Canoe's father, so he still has a lot of power to push Dragging Canoe around. And he shamed him, too. He shamed us all.

"Here we are," he yelled at us, "in our Peace Town, and a man comes to us in good faith. Even if that man is the enemy, he deserves to be treated the right way in a Peace Town. It won't do for us to kill a man here."

Of course, he was right. We didn't like it, but we couldn't stain Cherokee honor that way; we wouldn't dare make ourselves so blue as to take revenge on a man who came with a white flag. If we met him in battle, we would have to kill him, but we must not so much as bend one of his hairs while he is our guest.

We all felt a little ashamed for The Raven's and Dragging Canoe's temper, even as we agreed with their passion. But they took the shame like good warriors and stood aside.

Robertson and his helper laid out a blanket in front of Oconostota and Atta-kulla-kulla and put down on it a bunch of things they had brought. There were silver arm bands, mirrors, knives and hatchets, beads and buttons of many colors, shiny white plates like the Virginians ate off of, pewter cups, and other things. Robertson picked each one up and talked about it while we watched. Then he told us he had three horses outside with more of these things on their backs.

He was pretty well-spoken, too. John Watts and The Bench, who were sons of two of Raven's daughters and their English husbands, stood beside Oconostota and said in Cherokee what Robertson was saying in English. He said he understood why we were so angry. If it had happened to him, he would have been angry, too. We had every right to be furious, and he understood why we felt like we had to go to war. "But before you go on the war-path," he said, "I want to tell you some things that maybe you don't know.

"The man from Wolf Hills who shot Raven's son is named Crabtree. He isn't a good man, even among the Virginians. He lies to his own people, cheats and steals when he can, is always getting into fights and hurting people that have done nothing to him to deserve being hurt. He is just a frontier ruffian, a bad person. We ought not to blame all the Virginians for what one bad man did."

Robertson said the Virginians at Watauga agreed: "Crabtree ought to be caught and punished for shooting The Raven's son. The law among the Virginians requires that when Crabtree is caught, he has to be put to death, because killing another human when you aren't at war isn't permitted in Virginia, any more than it is permitted in the Cherokee Nation."

The Virginians at Watauga were outraged, just as we Cherokees were. They were our brothers in this. They were on the warpath against Crabtree and all like him, just as we were. Robertson and the Virginians did not want to go to war against the Cherokee, who were not their enemies; they wanted to go to war *beside* the Cherokees, against bad people like Crabtree. "And we are doing it," he shouted. "I promise you, the Virginians promise all the Cherokees: when we catch Crabtree, we will give him his just punishment."

That took a lot of anger out of most of us, for what he said was honest. And Robertson obviously had a lot of courage to travel the hundred and fifty miles from Watauga to Chota, alone, and stand before a Cherokee war council. He seemed like a good warrior. And he was saying he was on our side. He would have made a good Cherokee, a man you could take by the arm in trust and friendship, because we like warriors who face the trouble before them squarely and speak the truth.

Robertson then turned to the goods he had laid out on the blanket. "The people of Watauga want to express their friendship to the Cherokees," he said, "and have sent me here with some gifts for you."

He picked up a silver armband and tried to give it to The Raven of Chota, and another to Dragging Canoe, but they wouldn't take them, because accepting them would mean they accepted what Robertson was saying. Robertson just held onto the armbands for a while.

Then he turned to Oconostota and Atta-kulla-kulla and said, "You Head Men know better than the Virginians how to distribute these gifts. We will leave that to your wisdom." And he reminded them that there were more gifts on the horses outside.

Of course, neither of the Head Men accepted the gifts.

The Virginians, Robertson said, felt very sorry for the family of the slain man and had sent some special gifts to them. He brought out a satchel that contained some silver spoons, which our warriors like to drill holes in and wear in war, and a fist-sized bag of silver coins like the Virginians use in trade. He told the family how they could use these coins when they came to the Watauga settlements. In exchange for the coins, the Virginians would give the family blankets, deerskin jackets, trousers, axes, enough powder and lead to hunt with, whatever the Cherokees wanted and whatever the Virginians could get from their cousins at the ocean.

So we Cherokees discussed Robertson's talk a while. Some were satisfied with his straight way of speaking and wanted to get some of the gifts that were laid out. Some still wanted to go to war. Some wanted to forget the war, but take Robertson and his helper outside the walls of Chota and give them what Raven's son got, and then they'd feel that the crime had been righted. That would satisfy the law of blood.

Atta-kulla-kulla was, of course, horrified at that idea. He jumped up and gave us another speech. "If a man were harmed while he is in a Cherokee house and accepting Cherokee hospitality, it would cast Cherokee honor into the dirt and crust it over. I, for one, will never allow that kind of thing to happen. I am a friend to Robertson, now, and anyone who raises a hatchet to harm Robertson will have to take Atta-kulla-kulla out of the way first."

And, of course, no one in the tribe, not even The Great Warrior himself, could even think of doing any harm to Atta-kulla-kulla.

Na'nye-hi stood up with him and said that she was now Robertson's sister, too, and that his wife was her sister. Na'nye-hi owned a whole herd of cows over in South Carolina where she had been married to a trader named Bryant Ward for many years. She told us, "I am going to bring my cows to Cherokee territory and ask my sisters at Watauga to teach me to make butter and cheese and those other good things my sisters know how to cook so well." She went on and on about how good Cherokee life would be when we have learned the new ways that await us in tomorrow's dawn.

Her half-breed daughter, Betsy Ward, who was almost big enough to get married, said she would help her mother. Betsy said she was living proof that a Cherokee could live like an Englishman and still be a good Cherokee.

But what convinced most of us was Robertson himself. He stood up again and said he realized Cherokee honor had been thrown in the dirt and crusted over. But he wanted us to know that the Virginians' honor had been thrown in the dirt, too. They wanted to pick up their honor and wear it again the way an honest people is supposed to. "The only way the Virginians can pick up their honor again," he said, "is to be allowed to pick up Cherokee honor, wipe the dirt off it, and hang it again on the Cherokee breast where it belongs." He begged us, he begged Oconostota to let them wipe their honor, and ours, clean.

When he finished, there was a long silence. Oconostota looked around the council, but no one else wanted to say anything. Finally, he leaned over the blanket and took up a red button for himself. Then The Raven and Dragging Canoe accepted the silver armbands that Robertson held out for them.

Such a decision, of course, required a celebrating ceremony, so we all prepared to go to the water. Old Taska-ya, the Conjuror of Chota, was our highest priest, so he was the one who had to lead the ceremony. We sang the preliminary songs and did the required dances, then we all ran out and down to the Little Tennessee River. We Cherokees felt ecstasy chilling our bodies as we rushed toward the water. Long Person, the river spirit, was a potent source of power. In His flowing was creativity, insight, the power to cleanse, forgiveness, regeneration.

Taska-ya could hardly flip off his ceremonial clothes before he dove in and began reciting the Sacred Formulas under the water. He knew they sounded like bubbles and burbles to those on land, but the formulas were not intended for them, but for Long Person himself. *He* heard them under the water.

Seven times, Taska-ya immersed himself to recite the seven parts of the prayer:

Now! Listen! Ha! On White Pathways I will be making my footprints.

There will be no evil: for in front of me lightning will be going, and behind me coming.

For my body, you Seven Clans, is beautified by my Provider, and I will fade into the Red Tobacco with which I am clothed.

Where the Seven Clans are, I have appeared: I am beautified.

In the very middle of the sunrays, I stand: in the middle I continue to stand, facing the sunland.

Now then, you Seven Clans, and those of you who founded the Seven Clans, you have wealth near the water which I have just come to choose.

You are not to keep it: if it can be borrowed, I greatly wish to borrow it! Look at me, all of you! My name is Cherokee.

Sometimes, Long Person in the river would temporarily take the spirit of a priest into the other world during these recitations, which was why the assistant priest was in the water, too. Sometimes, he had to hold up the head of the main priest until his spirit got back from its visit to the other world. Then, when the main priest came back and said he had made contact and the time was right, all the rest of us could dive in, cleanse our spirit, and partake of the propitious moment.

This time, Old Taska-ya had to be held up a long time. When he came back from his trance, he stood there in the water and told us of his visit with the Long Person of the river.

"Long Person talked to me in a dream under the water. He said, 'See, the white people came to us down the rivers from the east, just as the dawn and creativity came to us down those same rivers.'

"He said, 'See, the white people have aroused in you the suspicion that is necessary for a cautious decision.'

"He said, 'See, the white people will bring you blankets and knives and iron pots, that you may live in the arms of plenty for a thousand years.'

"He said, 'See, the white people are the doorway to the new age, the promised age of peace, prosperity, and happiness.'

"He said, 'See, the Virginians are the White Dawn people, the children of the Dawn Chief himself.'"

We all knew what he was talking about, of course, because of the prophesy, almost as old as the Cherokee people themselves, that some day there would arise a White Dawn Chief out of the ocean to the east, and he would usher in a new age. He would dissolve all differences between people, mold them as one, and start them on a long age of peace and prosperity.

That was what Taska-ya's divining stones had been trying to tell him when the white, red, and black stones came up all mixed.

When we heard Taska-ya say that, we shouted with glee and all jumped into the wealth of Long Person. We whooped and screamed, splashing the holy water on our bodies and rubbing it in.

We cupped water over our heads and faces. It was wealth. We could feel that. It thrilled us to the backs of our stomachs. As the water trickled through our hair and down our faces, we felt Long Person was trying to speak to us. We felt tears spring up in our eyes as Long Person trickled down our hair and into our ears. If we could only discern what Long Person wanted to say!

Taska-ya was facing upstream, toward the sunrise, toward the mountains over which the whites had come. We saw that as a sign. The Virginians came down the river courses. In a sense, Long Person had brought them to the Cherokees.

Yes, yes, we cried inwardly. We were understanding.

We could feel the power and thunder flowing into our arms, stronger even than the feeling one gets in re-making tobacco. Yes, yes, it was power. It was clean. It was knowledge.

In their forges where they shaped their plows was the spirit of Fire and Thunder, the Ancient Red who had shaped the first Cherokee.

In their tame cattle and herds of pigs was the spirit of Kana-ti, the Ancient Hunter and provider.

In their log cabins walked White Woman, the nurturing mother of the south, who brought us the food we love.

In the paths of their villages and in their laws is embodied Uktena, the Seer, the giant serpent in whose jeweled horn gifted men can read the future.

We Cherokee felt a whirring in us, like a hummingbird's wings, soft and iridescent, radiating outward, past the moon, stars, sun, into the seventh heaven itself. For a moment, we held it all in our mind. For a moment, we understood divine purpose.

"Yes, yes," cried Na'nye-hi from the water, for she had followed close behind Taska-ya. "I can see it now. We can all see it all now. The whites *are* the very wealth the Cherokees have prayed for.

"Yes, yes, they *are* the blessing the Cherokees have purified themselves for.

"Yes, yes, they *are* the Old Traditions that lay down White Paths wherever Cherokees might travel."

"Yes, yes," we Cherokees echoed. Our White Brothers are the children of the Dawn Chief.

On the shore, Dragging Canoe stood silently. He had not gone to the water with the rest of us. Behind him were some twenty or thirty of his strongest allies. He was not accepting what we saw. He was not part of what we now knew.

Into the loving hands of our White Brothers, we Cherokees might commit all, for all came back, even as the child puts himself into the hands of the father and gets all back as the gifts that we love.

Whenever we go to hunt in the far forests, whenever we go to war with our enemies, whenever we go to trade for the goods that we need, the White Dawn Children will be with us.

We will feel their power running through our arms. We will feel their knowledge in our hearts. We will see in their example our way to act, our way to think, our way to be. They will fix our place on this brown earth and in the Seven Layers of Heaven.

So we'll let them live at Watauga, and we will take them by the arm in friendship, for they will bring us gifts and teach us to become like them.

In our deepest spirits, that's what we want. And it's good to know, in the shivering power that runs down our souls, that the Ancient Spirits of our Ancestors who live here want that, too.

Tell Them We Have Started the War

On the bank of the Keowee River in South Carolina, the Terrapin of Seneca listened quietly as the messengers repeated the story. A band of rascals from the white settlements near Augusta had captured Alexander Cameron's black boy again and made off with Cameron's cattle. They were the eight cattle the servant was supposed to drive across the Nantahala Range to Chota on the Little Tennessee River.

Terrapin touched the secret spot on his breechclout where he had sewn a bead of corn pollen, and he tried to imagine its smell. Silently, he uttered the curse to make enemies powerless.

> *You wizards! I am such a wizard as you!*
> *Dayii!*

He looked around at his followers, who were waiting expectantly. "Well," he said at last to Second Man of Seneca. "Call all the people to the council house. We will hear the news when the sun is straight above the smoke hole."

The messengers nodded their agreement, knowing the need for the ceremony. The delay would provide time enough for everyone in the village to hear the news before it was officially delivered. That way, the people could talk it out and be ready with a response when the news finally arrived beside the sacred fire in the town's council house.

Second Man walked beside Terrapin as they strolled away. "Well, what do you think, Old Head Man?" he asked.

Terrapin looked at a distant spot where the sky dipped behind a beloved mountain. Little cloud boys were playing with the ridge. "I think the white man's voice is like the water; you turn your back, and it disappears. Either into the dirt or the air, who knows? But it is gone. It was but twelve days ago, when Mr. Wilkinson buried this matter. But some wicked snake has dug it up again."

"Yuuu!" Second Man grunted his agreement. "Scotchie will not like losing his cattle again."

"I think we will have to go out and get them back, don't you?" Terrapin asked. "Scotchie is our brother."

They paused to let an interval pass. Terrapin was a strong, ruddy-complected man, shorter than Scotchie, but taller than Little Brother. He kept both sides of his head shaved, leaving only a broad scalp-lock in the middle, which was braided and hung down his back. Four eagle feathers were fastened in it, for Terrapin was a good warrior and had been successful in many battles.

Second Man was slightly taller and much younger, hardly as old as Terrapin's own sons. He had thicker shoulders, which were scarified and tattooed black and red with his private war symbols. He wore a pair of the white man's broad-cloth trousers.

As they walked toward the center of the village, they could smell the women's fires and occasionally a whiff of fish cooking, or hominy in the making. Boys who had been playing stopped and stood at the corners of their mothers' hewn log houses, watching. Terrapin and Second Man nodded to the boys, smiling and noting which ones had grown since they noticed them last, which ones were developing muscle and grace.

"Did the messengers say what the rascals did with the black boy?" asked Terrapin, though he knew Second Man had heard the same report as he.

"What are you thinking?" asked Second Man.

"White men like to take money for black people and send them to some island in the gulf."

"Ooof," said Second Man, "Scotchie would not like that. The black boy belongs to him."

"Yah! The black boy would not like it, either. He loves Scotchie like the rest of us. The white men used to sell Cherokee and Creek people to the gulf islands, too; did you know that? They liked the women, because they could make them clean their houses. But the men would not work until they sweated, like the black white men do; so they killed most of them. Some escaped to come and tell us. The whites would steal our people yet and sell them, if their head man in Charles Town had not made them stop."

They paused again, to think about it. They both knew that the head man in Charles Town was no longer head man. He had been tarred and feathered, then put on a prison ship in the harbor. Rascals were sitting in the head man's chair now.

"Ooof," said Terrapin, at last. "White men hardly know how to run their own towns."

"Yuuu!" agreed Second Man.

"And they certainly don't know how to take care of slaves."

Terrapin looked at Second Man, who did not answer. They were avoiding the real issue. Certainly Scotchie would not want to lose his property, either the cattle or the black boy. And certainly, since Scotchie was their friend and clan-brother, it was the same as if they, too, were losing property. They, Terrapin, Second Man, and all the warriors of Seneca, would be duty-bound to get Scotchie's property back. But if it had been that simple, they would already have solved the problem.

The white man's behavior confused them. Not more than twelve days ago, they had tried to take care of the matter in the traditional way. They had gone down to Wilkinson's commissary and observed that the cattle belonged to Mr. Cameron, and that the black boy was doing only what he had been told to do. Mr. Wilkinson had reacted as he was supposed to. He had saddled his horse, ridden away, and two hours later the cattle and servant were released.

But, now, Mr. Wilkinson's word and deed were gone, like the morning mist, but Wilkinson was still there. The Cherokees were honor-bound to protest again. But, if they went to him and complained, they would be saying that his voice was soundless, his acts without substance, and his intentions as blue as the winter storms that came down from the north. How could they insult a man, like that? Unless he were recognized as an enemy.

The Terrapin of Seneca was hesitant to call a man blue.

A man from the North of England, named Hamilton, operated a trading yard near the central plaza of Seneca. He was a lip-service loyalist and a pocket-book politician; both those traits had bred distrust and dislike among his Cherokee associates. Terrapin avoided him as much as he could and always walked especially fast when crossing in front of his yard. He touched the pollen spot on his belt and uttered a silent incantation for speedy and safe passage on the trail, but it didn't work this time. Hamilton came out, yelling "Si-yo." He was followed by a Cherokee man named Laskigitihi.

"Terrapin! Terrapin, old friend! They are trying to get me," called out Hamilton without prelude or a polite pause.

Terrapin turned toward him and waited. At least, his Cherokee wife kept him from stinking like a white man.

"You've got to help me, Terrapin," Hamilton went on. "They're trying to take me out of the nation. I'll pay you. You've got to protect me from them."

When Hamilton paused for breath, Terrapin asked, "Who? Who is trying to get you?"

"The rebels from the New Broad River," said Hamilton. "They

don't like me, because I'm a Friend of Government. They think I'm selling the Cherokees too much ammunition, so they want to take me out of the nation. They may even want to kill me. You've got to help me, old friend."

"Where have you heard this? Who told you this news?"

"Laskigitihi. Laskigitihi, here, just told me. They hate me. They want to do me harm. I'll pay you. I have money, goods, ammunition. Just say what you want, and I'll pay you."

Terrapin looked at Laskigitihi a moment. He was a noted warrior from the Overhills who had killed men in battle. He was married to a woman of Seneca, so he spent a great deal of time with his wife and children in Terrapin's town. He was noted for his honesty, but was also known to play tricks on fools, especially white men. Because of his honesty and his ability to repeat long speeches with accuracy, he had been sent to Chota as Terrapin's deputy, to hear the talks of the Northern Indians, when Cornstalk had poured vermillion on the wampum belt and invited the Cherokees to enter an all-out alliance against the whites. He traveled a lot, went many places, and understood English. It was just possible that he had been to the New Broad settlements and overheard some threat to Hamilton. Terrapin studied him a moment, but Laskigitihi gave no sign, dropped no glance nor made any gesture that would affirm or deny Hamilton's report.

"It's happened before," Hamilton was saying. "Those rascals have killed honest men, who did nothing at all to them. They come in a group, you know that. They work like a pack of wolves. Will you let me hide at your place? Will you protect me? Please, old Terrapin-friend."

"Well, I don't know," said Terrapin. "There may be too many of them when they come. They may be too strong for me to do anything. I may not be able to command enough warriors."

"We'll pay them, too. Just tell them that. Tell every man: a looking glass and two yards of ribbon to every man that saves me from the rebels. I don't want to be taken out and killed."

"Perhaps you should move to the Overhills settlements," said Terrapin. "That would get you well away from their paths." He saw a flicker of a smile on Laskigitihi's lips. "I know!" shouted Terrapin, as if he had just discovered a perfect solution. "Why don't you get Laskigitihi to take you to the Overhills settlements? Let him take you to live with his relatives at Tellico. They will surely protect you and enjoy your company. They will probably let you live with them, even without pay."

"Do you think so?" said Hamilton. "Do you think so? I'll go right now and write Mr. Cameron a letter. I'll ask him if he thinks that's what I should do." Hamilton turned and trotted toward his shack, without saying goodbye or thank you.

As Terrapin turned to continue, he saw Laskigitihi suppressing a smile at him in admiration and appreciation of the way Terrapin had turned his trick back upon him. Laskigitihi fell in behind Terrapin and followed him toward the council house.

When they got to the council house, Terrapin and Second Man found the Warrior of Tellico and Ninituca waiting a respectful distance from the entrance. Terrapin nodded and invited them in. He knew what they wanted. Ninituca's brother had been unjustly put to death for the murder of a white man in Virginia, and Ninituca wanted a white man's death in compensation. Cherokee justice, honor, and family pride required a death for a death.

The council house, like all Cherokee council houses, was a huge log dome. The interior had eight sides: one for the entrance and one for each of the seven clans. Around the walls were several rows of raised benches, enough to seat about 250 people. Eight tree trunks held up the log roof and separated the benches from the open area in the center, where ceremonial dances were performed and where the sacred fire burned. The seats of the head men were placed at the end of the dance area, away from the entrance, and covered with buffalo robes. Outside, the council house was covered with dirt and grass, so that from a little distance, it looked like any other mound, with smoke coming from the hole in its center.

Terrapin took his white seat and motioned the others to sit. Each sat in the segment that belonged to his clan. The air smelled of dust and old ashes.

After a respectful pause, the Warrior of Tellico spoke: "We are already at war. They have killed our people."

Terrapin did not respond. Instead, he turned to Second Man. "The messengers from Chota," he asked, "did they say the Cherokee are now at war?"

"The Northern Tribes brought war belts that were covered with the blood of their people," said the Warrior of Tellico. "And they presented them to the Cherokee Head Men. I was there. I saw it."

"And Dragging Canoe took up the belts?"

"Yes," said Ninituca. "And Old Abram, and the Warrior of Chilhowee, and Ostenaco, though he will not lift his war axe because he is so old. Laskigitihi was there, as were the Warrior of Tellico and myself. We will all tell you that only the oldest Head Men would not touch the belts."

"Yuuu!" agreed Laskigitihi. "Dragging Canoe wants the war to start now. He does not want to wait for Oconostota to set the date, for he knows that the old men will say we should wait two moons or more. He says there is no point in waiting. We all held the belts and screamed our war oaths. We will have to go sooner or later. It might as well be now."

"So Oconostota and Atta-kulla-kulla would not take the belts?"

"No."

"And Scotchie? Did Scotchie take the belt?"

Second Man turned toward the Warrior of Tellico, silently inviting him to respond. "Scotchie will not go to war against his own people," said Ninituca.

"His own people?" said Terrapin. "But the Cherokee are his people. He is one of us."

"I have learned not to trust any white man," said the Warrior of Tellico, "and I am coming to distrust anyone who does trust them."

Terrapin fingered his welt of corn pollen and silently uttered a chant for protection and friendship. This open confrontation was not a Cherokee way. The whites had taught the people too much of this sort of thing. Even those who hated the whites had allowed their hatred to teach them whiteman ways.

"Scotchie will fight, when it comes time to fight," said Terrapin in his friend's defense.

They were interrupted by a messenger at the door, who said there were two white men at the edge of Seneca asking permission to cross Cherokee land. Terrapin and the others went out to question them. They stunk like white men, even from three or four paces away.

"They's a bunch of us, back there in the woods a ways," said one of the white men to Terrapin's interpreter. "They's waitin' in a clearing. We's heard thet thar's some bad white men livin' in Little Chota. This here Mr. Steel. And a Mr. Pritchard. We hear tell they're bad men, and do bad thangs to the Cherokees. We wanta go in there to Little Chota and take 'em away."

"Yes," said the other. "We hear they are obnoxious to the Cherokees, as thorns in the flesh. Like good friends, we would go and pull out the thorn and make the wound smooth again."

Terrapin was not fooled. Steel and Pritchard were honest men—and fair traders. These rascals wanted to take them out and paint them with tar, because Steel and Pritchard were Friends of

Government, loyal to the King, and supplied the Cherokee with powder and shot when they could get it.

"Second Man," said Terrapin, "have some of our warriors hold these men in our council house. We will go and talk to the leaders of that party. Laskigitihi, will you go with us? And you, too, Warrior of Tellico? And Ninituca?"

Some fifty Cherokee warriors of Seneca, arriving to hear the messengers repeat their news about Scotchie's cattle, joined the party. They all carried their weapons, muskets and flintlocks, sabers and spears, arrows and sinew-backed bows.

"Let there be the blood of our enemies on the ground where our footprints have been," said the Warrior of Tellico.

"Yes, by all means," agreed Terrapin. "If we have any enemies."

Not all them are the Cherokees' enemies," said Nathaniel Gist to Alexander Cameron and Henry Stuart. "There ought to be a way to get them off to the side."

They understood him to be talking about the Tories in the Nolichucky Valley. Henry ran his fingers through his red, bushy hair and sighed. This whole mess was getting harder and harder. When he had started out four and a half months ago, it all looked fairly simple: a few words here, the right presents there, assurances of loyalty and brotherhood; then, when the time came, they could form a proper and effective army that would successfully discipline the revolutionaries. But the longer he worked on the fabric of an alliance, the more unraveled it became.

Captain John Shelby of the North-of-Holston settlements and Captain James Robertson, the militia leader at Watauga, had taken a party of armed men and forced some seventy Nolichucky families, at gunpoint or tar pot, to sign or mark an oath of neutrality.

"Ye dinna think our friends'll feel themselves bound by those oaths, do ye?" said Henry. "Them being forced to sign, as they were?"

Gist got up, walked around the settee in Cameron's living room, and sat down again.

"We canna just go and fetch them back here," said Henry. "A start to the war that would be. Those scamps at Watauga'ld think them an army. And t'wouldna be long till the shots started whizzing."

"Aye," agreed Cameron. "The Cherokees 'ld see 'em as joining their army; and we canna want that."

"We still need a way to get them off to the side," said Gist. "They's nice folk among 'em. People who don't mean nobody no harm or hard times."

They were all silent for a time, trying to think the puzzle through.

"Look," said Gist at last. "I'm on your payroll, right?"

Henry nodded. At Chickasaw Old Field, he had asked Gist to return with him as an official scout and interpreter.

"And you ain't had much fer me to do, yet."

Again, Henry nodded.

"Tell y' what. If you c'n find three or four others that we can trust, men who know the woods, 'n maybe a Cherokee 'r two that can speak English, we could make up a little advance party."

"That assumes we canna stop the Canoe from going out," said Cameron. "And I think there's still an Irishman's chance in London of stoppin' him."

"Well, maybe so," said Gist. "Then, this plan will be all off. But, if he does go out, let's have a little advance party of friends ready. We can go ahead into the settlements at Nolichucky, gather those families that are thinking right, and pass them through the lines to back here. Out of harm's way. And in safe keeping. When it comes time and the King's outfit comes through, they'll be a good number of the men and boys that'll put on a uniform and do you good service."

"By the bonny prince, I think he's right," said Cameron. "And I think I know a couple of men we could trust in the job. Isaac Thomas, for one. And Jarrett Williams. Maybe a couple of others. The Tish of Tellico and his nephew would be good linguisters."

"That'd be good," said Gist. "If they's five of us, say, we'd be able to protect each other as we're coming up to a house. Then we c'd conduct 'em back through the Cherokee lines, or give 'em little white flags, or something."

"Aye," said Henry. "But, let's all keep this quiet and amongst ourselves. If we can talk Dragging Canoe out of his war, we wonna need the plan."

"Aye," agreed Cameron. "But I just hope this snake we're pulling out of the basket don't turn and bite our own breasts."

Terrapin and his followers found the party of white men in the clearing where the envoys had said they were. Terrapin quickly counted: there were twenty-four of them, mostly young and gangling, with eyes dull like dry river pebbles. He saw Wilkinson moving behind another man, to stay out of sight. All of them carried long, flintlock rifles. Their horses were tied at the far edge of the clearing, beside their baggage.

Terrapin had most of his warriors remain in the woods, behind the trees that surrounded the meadow. He, Second Man, his interpreter, and the Warrior of Tellico walked out to talk to the white men.

They had just halted halfway to the group of whites, to wait for their leaders to advance the other halfway.

Dayii, sang a bullet through Second Man's chest. He stood a moment, his eyes going out of focus; then he crumbled to the ground. Terrapin and the others dropped to the grass, as the fusillade of Cherokee bullets began to cut the white men down. It was like breaking icicles from a fence rail. Almost at once, the air was thick with acrid smoke.

Terrapin immediately sang a war chant at the top of his voice, both for protection and to tell his warriors to charge:

> *Red Lightning! Ha!*
> *You will be holding my soul in your clenched hand.*
> *Ha! As high as the Red Treetops,*
> *Ha! My soul will be alive and moving over there.*
> *Ha! It will be glimmering here below.*
> *Ha! My body will become the size of a hair,*
> *the size of my shadow!*

As the Cherokees fired again and began coming out of the trees to fight, the white men began to run toward their horses. But several Cherokee warriors who had gone around the clearing came out between the white men and their supplies. The whites turned to the side and ran into the woods.

Instead of pursuing the white men, the Cherokees ran to get the horses and the baggage. Shouting with triumph, they found four kegs of gunpowder and several pouches of shot. The Warrior of Tellico and Ninituca ran to two of the fallen white men to get their scalps. Terrapin had seen five white men fall and a number of others dripping blood.

Terrapin watched as his kinsmen peeled the scalps from two of the white men. Another of the fallen looked familiar. It was young Hiram Hampton, brother of Preston Hampton, whom Scotchie had taken prisoner just twenty days ago at that dumpy little cabin up behind Sugar Town. Scotchie had administered an oath of neutrality to Hiram and left him with Terrapin. As Scotchie had instructed, Terrapin had released him after five days, with his rifle and enough hunting supplies to get him back to the white settlements.

When Terrapin came to Hiram, he saw that he was paralyzed, but not yet dead. Hiram lifted his head slightly and looked at Terrapin. "Ah meant to hit you, you old bugger."

Terrapin hardly needed a translator. He drew his knife, cut around Hampton's hair line, set his foot on the body to keep it from moving, and slashed the whole scalp off, with the ritching sound of flesh ripping. This scalp would be skinny payment to the relatives of Second Man, but it was all Terrapin could manage right now.

Then he set his foot on Hiram's face to keep him from slipping from his grasp and sliced his throat from side to side. The blood spurted out on his hand, as Hiram's eyes went blank.

The Terrapin of Seneca stood up in the meadow near Little Chota, the enemy's blood dripping from both his hands. As the gunsmoke began to clear, he could smell the blood. He looked to the sky and sang out,

> *Ada-wehi Tsalu!*
> *Ani-aga-yunli, in the Seventh Heaven!*
> *You are now dining on his saliva.*
> *It is great to kill in battle!*

The sun was shining in a clear sky. Far off down the hollow, he could hear the nineteen white men yelling to each other as they crashed through bramble and thicket, making their escape. "Laskigitihi," he called, "take one of the prisoners from our council house and go at once to the Overhills. Tell Scotchie that we will go and get his cattle back, but he must now paint himself black and touch the Shawanee war belts. We have started the war for Dragging Canoe."

Hiss-Til-Toyoo

Lieutenant Paul deCamp and the other young officers at old Fort Chadbourne were always happy to see Chief My-la-que-top and his band of Comanches set up camp outside the fort. For one thing, it meant the Cavalry didn't have to be out chasing them. But more than that: the Comanches loved horses and were, perhaps, the best horsemen of the plains. They loved to steal horses from the Mexicans and Texans, just for the fun of it. But even more, they loved to race. They would race their horses against any and all comers.

However, there was one big thing they liked even more than horse racing. And that was betting on horse racing.

The officers at Fort Chadbourne were proud of their racing stock, too. They had brought in long, lean stock from Kentucky, horses that had been selectively bred and carefully trained, horses that knew almost no work but racing. The officers had built a long paddock along the back wall of the stockade, and they had scraped off a big oval track all around the fort, which served the triple function of a parade ground, a race track, and a clear space where enemies could not creep undetected. It was a little over a half mile long.

In early summer, 1872, the Comanche women had hardly finished setting up camp just outside the finish line, before Lieutenant deCamp and a few of his fellow officers strolled out to offer their first challenges. "W'all, Hi, Chief," said Lieutenant deCamp, "Y'got any good racin' stock this here year?"

That was much too direct for My-la-que-top's taste. He wanted to visit for a while first, get a chance to look the man in the eye while he wasn't watching and figure out when he was lying. "Good winter," said My-la-que-top. "We stay at Big Spring. Antelope thick, like fleas on dog. Many skins."

"You're kiddin' us, Chief," said deCamp. "We've had our scouts out that far, and they say they ain't no stock to speak of roaming the prairies."

"Deer gone," he agreed. "Buffalo, not many. Antelope, shy like young girl on wedding night." My-la-que-top saw in deCamp's quick glance at his eyes, then quickly away, that he had touched a spot of interest in the officer. It was good to know where a man's weaknesses lay.

"W'all, yawl wanna race some t'day?" asked deCamp.

"We dance first. Tonight. You come. See squaws dance."

"W'all, I dunno. Y'got any fresh meat?" Paul grinned at his fellow officers, thinking he had put a double entendre over on Chief My-la-que-top.

"No," said My-la-que-top. "All, dry as my first wife."

The other officers got a good laugh, at Paul deCamp's expense.

"We stay seven days," said My-la-que-top, turning away to see that his wives had chosen the best spot for his tipi.

The second and third days, My-la-que-top seemed no more interested in racing than he had the first day. Some of the young Comanches raced with each other. Everyone came out to watch the officers when they exercised their racing horses. Not that there were a great many secrets. The Comanches got news from many sources and knew pretty much what was going on all over the prairies of Texas and the Oklahoma Indian Territory.

On Saturday, the Colonel ordered a parade, as usual. He mounted his own horse, and with his staff at the finish line, reviewed his troopers as they rode past in two's and four's, at a cantor and a gallop, in dress uniforms, though ready for battle. Behind him, in little bleachers, sat the women, children, and civilians of the Fort and Abilene village. Across the track, My-la-que-top and his sub-chiefs sat on their horses and reviewed the parade from that side. All along the track, Comanche men, women, and children watched the government horses with interest. Everyone knew these weren't fast horses, but horses meant to travel long distances, to hold up all day and be ready to travel again the next.

As soon as he had passed in review, Lieutenant Paul deCamp and three other officers raced their cavalry horses to the paddock and exchanged them for racing stock. Then, as the parade ended and the troops wheeled to become spectators, the Colonel drew his sword, flashed it high so that the three young officers on the quarter-mile starting spur could see, then brought it down in a fast chop. They were off and running.

The horses ran in a clump, neck and neck, for most of the way. The little crowd in the bleachers cheered and screamed encouragement to the racers. In the stretch, Lieutenant deCamp urged his mount forward and finished a half-length ahead of the second, who was a neck ahead of the third. The Comanche crowd clapped in appreciation, imitating the white people's applause.

DeCamp wasted no time in the winner's circle, but rode quickly over to My-la-que-top.

"Nice horse," observed My-la-que-top.

"This old chicken?!" exclaimed deCamp. "Why, I bet he cain't even run as fast as some of your ponies!"

My-la-que-top nodded.

"But," continued deCamp, looking off at the distant sky nonchalantly, "I'll bet he can outrun that goat yo're settin' on."

My-la-que-top did not respond at once, but sat, also studying the interesting, distant sky. "How much you bet?" he asked at last.

"How about a nice pair of boots?" said deCamp.

"My size?" asked My-la-que-top.

"Well, ya c'n try 'em on, if'n y' like."

When they had determined that the boots would fit My-la-que-top, he countered with his offer: "Six skins. And we run whole ring around fort." His wives, seeing that the betting and racing were about to begin, had brought out a stack of prime antelope hides.

"Why, where'd yawl get such good hides?" exclaimed deCamp.

"Good season at Big Spring," admitted My-la-que-top, picking up a skin and flexing it in his hands. "Comanches make many fine skins. Soft. See? Make good lady glove."

"Awright, yer on!" said deCamp. "It's a bet."

"We race," said My-la-que-top, taking off his ceremonial feathered headdress.

Again, the Colonel acted as starter. Again, the crowd cheered their favorite. And this time, Lieutenant Paul deCamp came in a length behind.

"W'all," he complained, making excuses, "Y'cain't really expect a horse to win more'n one race in a day."

"You get better horse. I get better horse. We race again," said My-la-que-top, pulling on his new boots.

With that, the general races were on. Usually, they ran six horses in a heat, three Comanche horses and three garrison horses, though usually the betting was on particular pairs. Some races were a quarter or half mile, some three-quarters, some twice around the track. Both sides did a lot of switching around while the horses were in the pre-race line-up. Comanche warriors, thinking they had a good chance of beating the horses being shown, would trade or buy places from the other Comanches. The garrison officers just smiled; they were having fun, and there was no particular hurry in winning everything the Comanches had.

On Sunday, My-la-que-top and Lieutenant deCamp raced a half mile again. My-la-que-top had lost his stack of antelope skins; so the stakes were the horses they were riding. DeCamp hired the sutler's son to jockey his horse, which won by a length and a half.

My-la-que-top was dejected to have lost such a good horse. He retired to his tipi and did not come out until Tuesday. Then he walked right into the garrison and challenged Lieutenant deCamp to a showdown race. "My best pony. Your best pony," he said.

"You mean, you want to race your best horse against my best horse? And you want the horses to be the stakes in the bet?"

"Yes," said My-la-que-top. "And I want other pony back. He good horse."

"W'all, I cain't jist throw him in. Not fer nothin'. What 're you willin' to bet for him?"

My-la-que-top had no immediate answer. He had lost all his skins, his second best horse, everything that Lieutenant deCamp would think was worth taking as a stake.

"Tell ya what, Chief," said deCamp at last. "How about that purty little woman that carries your skins around—when you got skins to carry, that is."

"My third wife?" said My-la-que-top, surprised.

"Yeah. That one. Tell you what, Chief. I'll bet you my best horse against her. And we can bet your best pony against that one I won from you yesterday."

"Good. You lose both horses!" said My-la-que-top.

The track was cleared and everyone in town and tribe was ready an hour before sundown.

My-la-que-top, stripped to a breechclout, was going to ride his best pony. The sutler's boy in a green sateen shirt and cotton jockey pants was going to ride deCamp's horse. Once again, the Colonel served the starting signal, and they were off and running.

My-la-que-top took an early lead, but he could hear and see deCamp's horse only a half-length behind. It was not a time to slack off and coast. He kept his horse at full run. He looked back, to see deCamp's horse fading in the backstretch. He smiled to himself. Such an easy race!

But then he heard deCamp's horse coming up again at the turn into the home stretch. He glanced back. The sutler's boy was cracking his whip on both sides of the horse's haunches. The horse was running crazed, nostrils flaring, eyes as big as turkey eggs. My-la-que-top kicked his horse more, hoping to get a bit more out of him, but it just wasn't there. In the stretch, deCamp's horse nosed ahead and won the race by a neck.

Thus, Chief My-la-que-top lost his best racing pony and his third wife to Lieutenant deCamp. She was his youngest and favorite wife, and—what was worse!—she was lost to a Texan. It made his mouth taste bad. "Don't you worry," he told her. "I'll come and win you back. Real soon."

"I guess this'll teach you t'fool around with the racing stock at Fort Chadbourne," Lieutenant deCamp gloated. "Don't yawl know we get real thoroughbreds in here from Kentucky? Y'ain't got a fiddler's chance in hell of beating our horses, Chief."

My-la-que-top took deCamp's taunts bravely, then walked off toward the Comanche encampment. The next morning, the Comanches began breaking camp.

My-la-que-top was disturbed. There just had to be a way to beat these damnable, pale-faced soldiers. He asked everyone close by, "How. Can I beat the pale-face?"

"Sure," said the medicine man. "Just get a faster horse."

So Chief My-la-que-top temporarily became a tax collector and went among his Comanche warriors. He didn't take anything of value—just the coins and paper bills the Texans used for money. "Look on it as an investment," he told them. "You'll get it all back in winnings." He collected $1500.

The next day, the Comanches rode away, making a big cloud of dust.

The soldiers laughed, relieved to see them go. True, there was less trouble to correct around Abilene when they had their women and children with 'em, but, just the same, it would be good not to have them in the doorway. The Comanches wore such hangdog, ragtag expressions, that the soldiers just had to tease them.

"Yawl c'mon back when y' wanta lose yer skins!"

"If y' got any skins t' lose, that is!"

My-la-que-top and the Comanche warriors didn't even look back.

"That's right," My-la-que-top told a skinflint trader at Fort Sill, showing him the money. "You get me one much fast quarter horse. Bring to me at Big Spring. Comanches go there now to hunt antelope. Make skins and get away from soldiers."

A few weeks later, the trader brought a horse to My-la-que-top. It wasn't much to look at. He was hardly breast high, and he had a broad, round back, like a sheep. His long, shaggy winter coat was coming off in woolly patches. But My-la-que-top could see muscles coiled in his legs, like rattlesnakes, and he liked what he saw. So did the Comanche warriors.

My-la-que-top hopped on the pony, the pony stuck his tail straight up, and they dashed away for a trial ride. When they came back, My-la-que-top gave the trader the $1500 and named the pony Hiss-til-toyoo, which translates roughly as "he sticks his tail up."

Hiss-til-toyoo promptly disappeared—or seemed to, as far as any non-Comanche could see. No one saw him that fall of 1872, nor that winter, nor the next spring at the powwow with the Arapaho at the Big Spring, where the Comanches had some good horses which showed signs of rigorous training and competition. The Arapahos saw the signs and would not bet much. The Comanches won most of the races.

Then, in early summer, 1873, the Comanches again encamped outside Fort Chadbourne. "We come to sell skins," My-la-que-top said, indicating the pelts on their ponies.

"Hey, Chief! Yawl wanta race?" came the call.

My-la-que-top turned away slowly.

"Aw, c'mon now," said Lieutenant deCamp. "We all know yawl got some pretty good horses. We heard how yawl beat all the Arapaho ponies up at the Big Spring."

"Comanche ponies run good at Big Spring," admitted My-la-que-top.

"But y' ain't got nothin t' put up against our Kentucky breeds, eh?"

My-la-que-top shrugged, as if to say that remained to be proven.

"I guess yawl know, they ain't a racing string at any of the garrisons around these parts that kin do anything but eat our dust."

My-la-que-top nodded. The Comanches were quite familiar with all the racing stock within hundreds of miles. Though My-la-que-top may not have seen any new horses they had, he knew from the moccasin grapevine what they looked like and what their capabilities were.

My-la-que-top gave a signal, and his first and second wives came forward, carrying a bundle of buffalo, antelope, and beaver pelts. "We come to buy back third wife," he told Lieutenant deCamp.

A smile spread across deCamp's face. "Well, now. I don't know that I want to sell her. Been mighty good t' me, y'know. Brangs m' slippers an' fixes m' dinner. 'N keeps me company through th' cold nights." He paused, letting his taunt grow to its full effect. "No sirree, I don't believe I want t' sell her . . . but I might bet her on a horse race."

My-la-que-top did not take the bait. "Kaintuck horses run much fast," he observed.

"Tell y' what," said Lieutenant deCamp. "We won't insult you by offering t' race our scrub stock against yawl. After all, we heard y' got some pretty good ponies. So, here's what we'll do: I'll bet yer beloved *third* wife against yer pile o' skins that our *third* best horse'll turn his tail to anything y' got."

My-la-que-top paused, looking back toward his warriors, as if asking advice. None seemed to make a move. At last, the Chief turned toward Lieutenant deCamp again and said, "We race."

"Yippee!" yelled deCamp. "That's what I like to hear, Chief. C'mon, let's clear the parade ground, and let me take those skins off yer hands."

The garrison's third best horse was brought out. He was a fine gelding, long-legged but thin in the haunches. High-spirited, he pranced and champed at the bit, knowing he was about to race and ready to do his best.

Then from the back of the Comanche herd, a warrior brought up Hiss-til-toyoo.

Colonel Richard I. Dodge, who was on temporary duty at Fort Chadbourne, wrote in his diary that the horse was "a miserable sheep of a pony, with legs like churns, three inches of rough hair all over, with a general expression of neglect and patient, helpless suffering, which struck pity into the hearts of all beholders."

The pony was to be ridden by a muscular young warrior who was carrying a big heavy club. One of the sutler's boys was to ride the tall, lithe garrison horse, giving the garrison horse a weight advantage of about forty pounds.

All along the line of spectators, Comanche warriors and women were anxiously making side bets with anyone who cared to bet. It looked like the Comanches had gone crazy and were trying to get rid of all they owned. But the soldiers considered winning a bet, however one-sided, more honorable than stealing, even from the Indians; so all bets were quickly covered.

Before the race could start, My-la-que-top had one more bet to make. The sutler's boy was wearing a bright green sateen jockey shirt. My-la-que-top wanted it for one of his sons. Hardly a thing could be put up against it, but, finally, deCamp grinned and suggested, "Tell y' what, Chief. I'll put this boy's shirt up against that war-club yer jockey is carryin."

With that, the race was on. They were racing on the big oval track, a little over a half mile long, with the start and finish right in front of the Fort gate. At the starting signal, the sutler's boy leaned forward in his stirrups, let his horse have the reins, and they streaked out, smoothly and powerfully. The Comanche rider gave a high-pitched yell, tucked his knees up against the pony's shoulders, and lay down along Hiss-til-toyoo's shaggy neck. With a squirt, Hiss-til-toyoo pricked up his tail, lifted his ears, and started churning his legs. He caught the garrison horse within a hundred yards, passed him, pulled away steadily, then dropped back. At the finish, his tail was still in the air, like a flag, and he was ahead of the garrison horse by three-quarters of a length.

The cavalry officers looked on in amazement at the shaggy dog that had just beaten their third best horse.

The Comanches collected their bets amid laughter and shouting. My-la-que-top hugged his third wife and said, "See? I told you I'd win you back." She was tear-eyed with happiness to be a Comanche again.

The cavalry officers just scratched their heads and looked back and forth from their sleek Kentucky horse to the shaggy Hiss-til-toyoo. "Whut happened?" they asked the jockey. The sutler's boy insisted he had run a good race, but couldn't explain how Hiss-til-toyoo had gotten ahead. "Didja see how he was fading toward the end?" said one. "It jist had t' be an accident," said another. "Bet he couldn't do it again," said a third.

Within minutes, they had convinced themselves that the win was just a fluke. So they proposed another race: the garrison's second best horse against Hiss-til-toyoo, even though Hiss-til-toyoo had just run a race and was still breathing hard.

Again My-la-que-top turned away and looked at his warriors, as if asking advice. "Pony sweating much," he said.

"Okay, we'll give him a half hour to cool down," said deCamp. "In the meantime, we can make our bets."

Finally My-la-que-top turned to deCamp and said, "We race."

Betting was quick, heated, doubled, and redoubled. Even My-la-que-top's son got into the betting—his new green sateen shirt against the sutler boy's patent leather boots.

The second best horse at the garrison, a well-muscled mare belonging to Lieutenant deCamp, was brought out. My-la-que-top inspected the mare appreciatively. "Nice legs," he said.

"Y' damned right, they's nice legs. They gonna carry her across that finish line, too."

My-la-que-top looked at deCamp as if that remained to be proven. Then he offered to bet his second wife against deCamp's second-best mare.

"Hell, Chief. She ain't very pretty," said deCamp.

"You no worry," said My-la-que-top. "No win her anyway."

That infuriated deCamp, and the bet was on.

The horses were brought to the post and the signal given. Again the Comanche rider gave a yell, tucked himself tightly against Hiss-til-toyoo's neck, and let the pony squirt ahead. In the backstretch, the Comanche rider looked back and let deCamp's mare almost catch up with him. In the home stretch, the two horses were neck and neck. At the finish, Hiss-til-toyoo was ahead by a length.

"Well, we cain't let a thang like this happen," said the cavalry officers, almost as one man, and they brought out a fine Kentucky mare with pure Lexington breeding—their best horse.

"Tomorrow," said My-la-que-top. "Cain't expect a horse to win three races same day."

The next day, the Comanches quickly consented to bet everything they had won in the first two races, even though the soldiers now had little to bet with but money. Still, money sometimes came in handy when dealing with traders; so all bets were taken.

This time at the starting post, the Comanche rider threw away his heavy club, gave his high-pitched shout, and Hiss-til-toyoo made away, two yards to the mare's one, his tail waving like a tornado. In the back stretch, the Comanche rider flipped his legs over the pony's rump and, riding backwards, made a horrible face at the other rider, all the while waving his arms and beckoning the Kentucky mare and her rider to come on. In the home stretch, he lay down against the pony's neck again, and they finished almost four lengths ahead.

The Comanche warriors collected almost $1500 in winnings.

"By the damn, Chief," said Lieutenant deCamp as the Comanches were collecting their bets. "What'd you say you call that pony?"

"Hiss-til-toyoo."

"His tail to you? You puttin' us on, Chief?"

By My-la-que-top pretended he did not understand.

The next day, the Comanches were mounted and ready to travel again. My-la-que-top and his third wife were on Hiss-til-toyoo, his first and second wife were on the mare that used to be Fort Chadbourne's second best horse.

"By the damn," said deCamp, staring again at Hiss-til-toyoo. "I never seen anything like it. There must be a way to beat that goat."

"Sure," said My-la-que-top. "Just get a faster horse."*

---

* This anecdote of old Fort Chadbourne is told in General David S. Stanley's *Personal Memoirs*, and in Richard I. Dodge's *Diary*.

Rough Creek, Texas—1888

When Cindy bolted around the corner of the house, yelling, "Momma! Indians killed the Johnsons!" she came face to face with her mother and four Comanches at the porch step. The Comanches wore baggy pants, but no shirts, and they carried big knives in their belts. Two of them held old rifles. The Johnsons' horses were grazing in the yard.

Della, Cindy's mother, was struggling with the leader of the Indians. She held her forearms up before her defensively and grasped the handle of his axe with both hands; the Indian pushed at her wrists with his other hand and tugged at her cuffs. Startled by Cindy, he jumped back, lunged for her, and swung his axe. Cindy had not stopped running, so she slid through the downward swish of his arm and into the circle of Comanches. They were all reaching for their knives or lifting their old rifles. Della immediately pushed through into the circle also, stuck her hands up in the air, making fluttering gestures, as she cried out, "*Tsu-ta-gu ... Gun-e-sti ... Atsila.*"

The Comanche leader stopped his axe in midair, surprised, and gazed at Della. The others stopped, too.

Cindy felt herself peeing, wetting her underpants and ruffled dress, then she stopped suddenly, shocked, and gazed at Della, too. She had never heard her mother say such words before. It was like another language. Somehow, Cindy knew that Della had just invited the Comanches to eat.

The leader seemed to understand. He turned to Della and said, experimentally, "*Ada-sta-yu-huski Tsu-ta-ga?*" Cindy could tell by his awkwardness that he only knew a few words of that language.

Della could not make her hands stop fluttering, but she kept nodding and smiling desperately at the Comanche. "Yes, *Tsu-ta-ga!* Chicken! *Tsu-ta-ga!* Chicken!" she repeated.

Confused, Cindy let her eyes drop. Mary Beth Jewel's long, blonde hair hung from the leader's belt, her mother-of-pearl barrette still fastened in the hair. At the end of it was a wad of blood. A moment more and Cindy's hair would have been hanging there, too—her coarse, dark hair.

"Cindy, don't—don't just stand there," said Della, her voice catching. "Go snag f-four chickens. K-kill and pluck 'em."

"Momma, they ki—"

"I know that," snapped Della. "Go on and catch, and catch those chi-chickens! Quick!"

"Which four should I get?"

"Any four. The best-best you can can find."

Apparently, one of the Comanches understood a little English. "Best," he repeated, then he spoke in Comanche. The others murmured appreciation.

Cindy's younger sisters, Emma and Anna Lee, were standing in the open doorway, staring. Her older brother, Allen, was standing beside Della, protectively, but his eyes were spread wide as if he were trying to see at night. He kept staring at Mary Beth's hair.

Cindy caught four chickens with the poultry hook, but she didn't check to see if they were the best she could find. *Where'd she learn those words?* kept running through her mind. She wrung the chickens' necks and threw them on the ground to flop and kick around till they were dead. *It was another language.* She couldn't manage to break the neck of one chicken, so she went to the wood pile to chop off his head with the axe. As her axe came swishing down, she realized, *Those were Indian words!* As if it were real, she felt an axe swishing through her head, felt her hair hanging from a belt. The chicken was flopping around, its wings mixing its own blood with the sand. In her mind's eye, she saw Mary Beth flopping around like that. "It wasn't me!" she cried, then got a hold on herself. She had killed chickens dozens of times.

In spite of herself, she broke down crying. She sat on the chopping block, stuffed her hands between her knees, and cried. Mary Beth Jewel was her best friend. Big tears dropped on her arms and the ruffle near the hem of her thin, cotton dress. She could hear Della saying, 'Now, Cinda Rilla Nelson, don't you start crying. You've got to try to help out. You can't do anything if you're blubbering. So don't cry.' She blinked her eyes dry. But she whined in grief in spite of herself.

She pulled herself together. She had to do something, something to help out. She gathered the chickens and pulled off the feathers as best she could. Most of the small feathers came off easily enough, but the large feathers were almost impossible to get out without hot water to make them slip. Patches of skin came off with the feathers. She flung them away, hysterically, and broke down crying. She could hear those Indian words with perfect memory— *"Tsu-ta-gu gun-e-sti atsila."* And she still saw her dark-haired mother's hands fluttering up.

When Cindy came back with the chickens, the Comanches were putting big rocks around a fire in the yard.

Della was more at ease, but she still had trouble saying the things she wanted to say. "Tsiski," she said, then corrected it to "Uni-tsiski ge-tsa-di?" Her fluttering hands made motions toward the gray, clapboard house. Cindy had never noticed before how prominent her mother's brow ridge was, nor how piercing her eyes.

The Comanches each took a whole chicken and held it over the fire with a stick, though none of them ever laid down his gun. Soon, the chickens were dripping grease that splattered on the fire and sent up plumes of sharp-smelling smoke. The chickens turned a golden brown. Their feet burned off, but the Comanches just left the black curls of them hanging.

The Indians sat around the fire, laughing and chatting, but Cindy could see they were keeping a close watch on the whole family. Once, the spokesman turned to Della and called, "Amo-atsila!"

She did not understand.

He repeated, "Amo-atsila! Amo-atsila!" angrily, so that Cindy felt herself dodging. Then he said it in English: "Whiskey!"

"N-no," stammered Della, her teeth chattering. "No have amo-atsila."

They turned back to their roasting chickens.

When the chickens were cooked, the spokesman pulled off a drumstick and offered it to the little girls. Both Emma and Anna Lee shrank back, too bashful and frightened to accept anything.

"Take it," said Della, urgently. "Do whatever they want. Don't hang back." But the little girls were scared and could not make themselves accept the chicken. Cindy held her breath. Allen caught on, took Anna Lee's hand, and led her to the spokesman. She still wouldn't take the chicken leg, but the spokesman did not object when Allen took it from him and handed it to her. She looked at Allen, he nodded, and she started eating it. The spokesman grinned at her. Cindy began breathing again. The Indian offered a wing and some breast meat to Emma. She took it, but just held it in her hand.

Anna Lee chewed her chicken leg and glared at the spokesman. Cindy could see that Anna Lee had the same hard, dark eyes as he did. Della and Cindy also had those eyes and heavy brow ridges, though Allen and Emma had the soft, brown eyes of their father. Daddy should be home, Cindy thought, instead of being in Granbury on his butter and egg route. No, he shouldn't; then they'd just kill him, too, the way they had killed the whole Johnson family. They had even killed all of the Johnsons' cows: lifted their noses and slit their throats, so they died walking and blubbering. Cindy kept comparing her mother's slightly dark complexion with the spokesman's ruddy chest. They weren't at all alike.

When the Comanches had eaten their fill of chicken, they belched, wiped their hands on their thighs, and abruptly decided to leave. They caught up the Johnson horses, got on them, and rode away toward Rough Creek Hollow, where the trail led to Comanche Peak and the Wilderness Route. The spokesman turned and waved to Della, calling, "O-si-yo, Tsa-la-gi ulunita."

"Ga-si-yu," Della yelled. Then she added, "Wa-dan!" as she walked toward the departing Comanches, waving. Almost under her breath, she muttered, "Cindy, get the children in the house. Quick and quiet. Don't let them think you're rushing." All the time, she continued strolling and waving to the Comanches.

Cindy and the children rushed into the house, just barely before Della burst through the door, slammed it shut, and swung down the bar. She turned to face the room; her eyes were big and unseeing, her mouth still gaping open. Then she slumped, flowing like water down the face of the door, her arms and legs jerking as if she were having a fit and her teeth chattering uncontrollably. Halfway down, she fainted and sprawled side-long into the room.

Cindy lifted her mother's arms and helped her walk to the plank table, where she helped Della sit in a cane-bottomed chair.

"They're gone," said Allen, who was peeking through a window.

"Momma, where'd you learn them words?" asked Cindy.

Della was unable to talk. She quivered. Her breath came in whoops, as if she had something wrong with her chest. She looked at Cindy, then burst out laughing and crying simultaneously, hysterically. She hugged Cindy and the little girls in turn, her tears wetting their faces. She even hugged Allen, though he was already fifteen years old.

Emma and Anna Lee gazed at their mother, quiet because they didn't understand. "Them Indians had Mary Beth's hair," said Emma.

"Hush, Emma," said Cindy. "They killed all of the Johnsons, and probably Mary Beth, too. They came here to kill us."

Anna Lee, the youngest, couldn't seem to understand. "Then, why didn't they kill us?" she asked.

"Momma, are we Indian?" Cindy demanded.

Della glared at Cindy. She nodded 'yes' ever so slightly. Then she found her voice. "I thought we'd outlived it." She immediately broke into a fit of coughing, so she had to get a gourd of water from the drinking bucket. She spilled water into the lap of her gray, cotton dress, trying to put the dipper to her mouth. "I thought you'd never have to know," she went on, shivering again. She went and looked out the window.

"Lord-a-mighty," said Della, trying to understand. "This is 1888, after all; it's not like we were in the frontier still." She looked at her son and three daughters. "I thought we'd never have to live with it again."

"Live with what?" asked Allen.

"What kind?" insisted Cindy.

Della just gazed at Cindy.

"Momma, I'm twelve years old. I've got a right to know."

Della stared at her children, one by one, and pushed a stray hair back from Anna Lee's face. Her hands were shaking. Suspicious, she went to the window again, pulled aside the curtain, and looked out.

She came back and sipped from the water dipper. "We're Cherokees," she said with too much emphasis. "Grandma was a full blood. Over in—"

Backing away, Cindy protested softly, "No! No!"

Della coughed, but forced her voice to go on. "Over in Rusk County. She lived with the Texas Cherokees. They were all massacred— Oh, God! Those Comanches!" She ran to the window and gazed out again.

Cindy felt something as hairy and as big as a mountain lion jumping at her from the darkness.

Della went on, as if explaining to herself, ticking the points off one after the other on her fingers, as if to get them straight in her own mind. "Grandma wasn't massacred because she had married Grandpa Hart. He was a hotel keeper and lived across the river from the Cherokee territory. Mother was half-blood, but she was white enough to pass."

She paused, gazing into the dipper. Cindy stepped backward, shaking her head in denial.

"Yes,"—Della rubbed her hand over her eyes, trying to understand—"Mother was white enough to pass. She hid in that as long as she lived. I've been hiding in it, too."

Rough Creek, Texas—1888

Cindy stared at her, amazed, horrified, confused. Then Della began talking rapidly, urgently.

"After Momma and Daddy died, I stayed mostly with Grandma. E-di-li-sa—that was Momma's Cherokee name. But she called herself Ada-Eliza. She taught me those sentences. That saved—"

She grabbed Emma and Anna Lee, compelling, forcing them to listen. "You've got to learn those words. All of you. I hated being Indian. Hated those trips to Indian Territory. Everybody was so poor and dirty. I hated being Indian. But I'm not going to hate them anymore. Thank God, I remembered those words! I hadn't thought of them in twenty years. Cindy, I want you to learn those words. Allen, you too. You've got to know something about your Cherokee—"

"No!" shouted Cindy, backing away, around the table. "No! I won't do it! I'm not an Indian. I didn't do any of it. It wasn't me!"

Della gazed at Cindy. Her eyes were hard and dark, demanding allegiance to the blood.

"No!" shrieked Cindy. She turned, unbarred the door, and ran out of the house.

Della ran after her, but stopped at the door. "Cindy, you come back here! You hear? Those Comanches may come back."

Cindy whirled around, expecting a Comanche knife in her chest. Nothing was behind her but the house, and her ruddy-complected, dark-eyed mother standing on the covered porch. "No! No!" she shouted, running toward Rough Creek Hollow.

Briar knives on the path and hatchets in the bushes ripped at her dress, and she heard screeching sounds all around. She ran, tree branches swishing down across her neck, like tomahawks, until she collapsed, out of breath.

She sat up at once, looking around furtively. She felt helpless, her useless hands fluttering in the air before her, just waiting there for them to come back. She had nothing to protect herself with.

Creeping under the thick foliage of a big wild lilac bush, Cindy found the trunk of a small bois d'arc tree. It had died in the thick shade when it was a little over an inch thick, then something had broken it off about twenty inches from the ground. She could see herself swinging it like a club and hitting a Comanche on the chest or in the stomach. She pulled it up easily. The root ball was the size of a baby's head and had three short jagged roots. She hit the ground to test it. After the rotted parts fell away, it was strong and sound. The jagged roots cudgeled the ground. She hit the ground again, for the feeling of safety. The club felt clean and smooth.

At the edge of the lilac bush, Cindy could see a small swarm of fireflies, little phosphorescent spots, hovering. If you went near them, they went out. That was their way of hiding. The hollow was full of life that hid by pretending to be something else. Armadillo families rolled up in little hard balls. Snakes lay like rotted sticks. Bobcats slipped away like water in the sand.

The grandmother Cindy had never known had hidden in pretense; Della had hidden in a secret. But the secret had saved the family. Cindy realized that the Comanches had not killed Della and her children because they recognized that Della was Indian. And now, for a different reason, Cindy was hiding, too. She felt rotten and hard and as transparent as water. She stopped herself from beginning to whimper.

An owl screeched in the hickory tree overhead. Thinking, *It's them, they've come back to scalp me*, she burst from her hiding, screaming, smashing through the bushes and vines. She wasn't going to let them catch her. Crashing, smashing sounds—the murderers were right behind her. Her side hurt from the running, and her lungs were about to burst. Desperate and out of breath, she turned and lifted her club at the last moment to face her attackers. There was nothing there.

She slumped to the hollow floor, exhausted, unwilling to go on, unwilling to go on standing, but she hopped up again at once. She had to get out of the darkness of the hollow. She couldn't stay there. Cautiously, she went on, watchful, silently creeping through the undergrowth along the Indian path, and came out at the Jewels' house.

Mr. Jewel's naked body was tied to a post down by the barn. Under him, ashes and a few stubs of fence planks still smoldered. The cooked flesh of his legs stank so that Cindy caught her breath. His leg bones stuck out white, except where the curls of his feet were black, down by the fire. His body was a big naked blister.

As Cindy stared at him, he lifted his head, barely conscious.

"Comanches," he rasped. "Get help." Then he fainted.

"What?" she cried, surprised that he had been able to speak. Then she realized she had to do something. She dropped her club, untied his hands and shoulders, and laid him down as gently as she could, putting a burnt stub of fence plank under his head for a pillow. *Butter for burns*, she thought, then ran to the milk house and found butter in the cooler. She remembered to take him a dipper of water.

When she lifted his head to give him a drink, a patch of skin came off his neck and stuck to her hand. She slung it away, dropping the dipper and letting his head bang down again. He was unconscious and couldn't drink. She smeared butter on the burns on his face.

She whirled around suddenly, certain that something or someone was behind her. She grabbed her cudgel again. The barn door yawned open. She dropped the butter and ran toward the house.

Mary Beth's younger brother lay on the ground, right outside the back door. Cindy stopped, gazing at him, standing on her tiptoes because she had almost stepped on him. Three, four, five knife wounds gaped at her from his chest, and part of the skin on his head was peeled back. She could feel the wounds, two, three, four, popping open on her chest and the flap of her forehead slicing back. His face was whole, but blood had splattered all over his arms and body. He had flopped and kicked around like a chicken in his death throes, making 'angel wings' in the blood and sand. *An axe in her hand came down on a chopping block.*

She jumped frantically over him, ran into the house, and latched the door. In the dim light, she saw that Mary Beth's sister, her mother, and the baby were dead in the house. They had all been stabbed several times and scalped, except for the baby, who didn't have enough hair. Mrs. Jewel's tongue had been cut out, and her back was broken. The baby had been beaten like a whip against the table.

Cindy gazed for a moment, paralyzed, her back pressed tight against the plank door, her tongue feeling like it was being cut out. She couldn't make her knees be still, and she heard someone whimpering. It was herself. She realized she couldn't stay in a room with three dead people in it. She couldn't just wait for the murderers to come back and kill her, too. She burst out the front door and ran.

Mary Beth was lying in the open yard. Her belly and chest were swollen with gas and stretched the seams of her dress. Cindy kneeled beside Mary Beth and picked up her cold hand before she noticed that the top of Mary Beth's head had been taken off and her skull had been cracked open. Cindy could see Mary Beth's brain. Blood had dried in its ripples.

Cindy's stomach leaped as she felt the swish of an axe pass, not passing this time, but catching her skull, taking away part of it as easily as if it were a melon. No, it didn't swish past. She had grabbed the handle with both her fluttering hands, turned the handle and swung the axe at her attacker's chest, sliced through a neck, sliced also through Mary Beth's skull. "No!" she shrieked. "I didn't do it!"

One side of Mary Beth's face was mashed in, so the eye on that side gawked up at the roof, accusingly. The eye was glazed over and dry, like a slaughtered pig's. "I didn't do it, Mary Beth," she cried. "I didn't do it." Mary Beth's dress wasn't even torn, nor bloody.

Cindy felt sweat break out on her lip, on her stomach, behind her knees. She wiped her lip with a shaking hand. She whirled around, but there was nothing behind her. Still, she knew she had to get away. She turned toward Rough Creek Hollow, but she couldn't go back that way; it was still a wilderness. She heard mountain lions screaming, as they often heard them screaming in the night, as the big cats traveled through the hollow and up the Wilderness Route. She jumped up and ran all the way around the house, looking for a place to hide.

Cindy fell on her knees beside Mary Beth again. "I'm sorry, Mary Beth. I'm sorry. I didn't know."

Cindy dropped the club. It fell against Mary Beth, who resounded with a hollow thump, like a drum. She stared, wide-eyed, at Mary Beth's belly and at her club. She could see herself, drumming in the night beside a bonfire, singing in screeches, while others danced in delighted frenzy. As if hypnotized, she picked up the cudgel and thumped Mary Beth twice, deliberately, listening for the tum-tum, then again and again, beginning to get a curious pleasure from the sound.

Cindy looked around. There was no one in sight, no one to see her.

Suppose she were Indian. What would that mean? Would she want to plunder through the settlements, stealing chickens and killing white people for their scalps? Would she want to howl and dance around a fire in the hollow, parading the bloody scalps at her belt? Would she love that?

Deliberately, she lay the root ball of her club against Mary Beth's cracked skull. She rolled the club head into the wound on Mary Beth's head and gazed at it. It kind of fit. *In another time and place,* Cindy thought, *I might be able to crack open a person's skull and beat out the brains. Maybe it would be easy—no more problem than killing a chicken. Just draw back your club and let fly. There might even be a satisfying crunch when the club head went through the bone.* Cindy raised her club into the air and tensed the muscles in her arm.

Mary Beth's gotched eye was staring directly at the club head.

Cindy stopped. Mary Beth had caught her in the act. She shivered, for worms seemed to be crawling all over her arms, slimy and red, waving like hairs. Some were sliding down her arm, toward her club, as if wanting to help her lift it and swing it. She flung the club against the house, screaming, "I'm not an Indian!" Then she whimpered, "I'm not an Indian, Mary Beth."

Maybe it would be bullheaded and wanton of her to hide from the facts, but that would be better than feeling dirty and indecent. Maybe it was contrary of her, but that was better than being perverse. Cindy stood up and looked around—at the barn, the house, the trail to Rough Creek Hollow—as if she were recognizing for the first time where she was. She turned all the way around. "Cinda Rilla Nelson," she said, "You are not an Indian. You're never going to be an Indian."

She ran and grabbed her club, crusty and dirty as it was. Swinging around, she slung it as far into the pasture as she could. Then she ran after it and slung it again toward the hollow, shouting, "I'm not an Indian! I'm not an Indian! I'm never going to be an Indian!"

Coming back to the yard, she felt the tension drain from her body. She began to shake, like Della had when she barred the door. Now Cindy was scared, for herself, for Mary Beth, for the Johnsons, for her family. "Aaaaiiiieeee!" she began crying, screaming, wailing all at once. Gasping with sobs, she lay her head on Mary Beth's bloated chest, crying, "I'm sorry, Mary Beth"; sobbing, "I didn't know, honest"; whimpering, "I'm not an Indian. I'm not even an Indian lover."

A Hunting Story

"A hunting story, eh? But I don't know any hunting stories."

"Sure you do, Pah-pah. You always know a story."

"Oh—Well, there was one time. Taught me and Billy a lesson, though I didn't realize it at the time. Well, I'll tell you about it; maybe it has a chance of making a difference in your life, though it didn't make any difference to your daddy or my other sons.

"We were livin' under the cap rock on Double Mountain Fork of the Brazos River. Grandma Quahada-ne was still with us. Her name means 'Antelope-person,' you know. She was well over sixty, but, you see, she didn't go in to Fort Sill with Quanah and the rest when they went in. She had married my grandad before that, so she stayed with him. At first, they lived pretty much the way Our People had before—huntin', you know—but since Grandad was white, that was okay; nobody bothered them. Then the hide hunters had killed all the game, so Grandad preempted a farm in the canyon about thirty miles below Lubbock and filed a claim, and everthang legal the way you're supposed to. Good bottom land, too. Good soil, lots of water. Got flooded now and then, but there was a lot of underground water, so his corn and beans and squash made good crops. Dad's brothers and sisters married Anglos and moved to town, to Lubbock, but Dad stayed 'cause he'd married a half-breed from the reservation. I and Billy were born out there in the wild, just the way kids were a long time ago, among Our People. Billy and I had just gotten our first gun—a kid's gun—a single-shot .22 rifle. Not one each, you understand, the way kids demand these days, but one between us. We were supposed to keep down the rats and gophers, and keep that prairie-dog town down the valley from gettin' any closer."

"Were you a good shot, Pah-pah?"

"I was all right. Billy was better. But I never let him know I knew. He died before I had the courage to tell him that. I'll tell you, Charlie; when you know something for true, and you know in your heart it's right, you'd better act—"

"Come *on*, Pah-pah. Hunting. You and Billy went hunting. "

"Well, yeah. Summers, we'd pretty much keep the family in fresh meat. All small stuff, you know. We'd bring a prairie dog or something home, and Grandma Quahada-ne would cook it. She could make a feast out of something that Momma had no idea how to use, cause she'd only learned home economics in the reservation school. Grandma knew the right way to make good use of the world. 'We can't hardly help killin' a little of the world,' she'd say, pointing a crooked finger at us, 'cause our everyday livin' does that, but we ought to make good use of it when we do. We ought not to let it just lay and rot.'

Well, once when I and Billy were up on the plains, keepin' the jackrabbits busy, we spotted three antelope. I was about your size, I reckon, about ten or twelve, but I'd never yet seen a real live antelope in the wild. 'Course, I'd heard about 'em all my life and heard 'em described, so Billy and I both knew what we was lookin at. There were three of them—a skinny old doe, a buck, and a yearling.

"'Les jist watch 'em fer a while,' said Billy.

"'Naw,' I said. 'Les see if we can't hit one. Les get a 'lope for Grandma.'

"'They're too big fer us,' said Billy. 'No way we could carry one.'

"But I wasn't goin' to let any of his excuses stop me. The three antelope had spotted us, probably before we spotted them, and they were just a-watchin', prongs up about as high as they'd go. I took the gun from Billy, even if it was his turn to shoot, but he didn't make no fuss. I could bully him sometimes into givin' me two turns to his one. Well, he didn't really give up his turns; I just took 'em. And Billy learned not to beller, 'cause, when he did, Dad took the gun away from the both of us. I pulled off a shot, but it just scared the three antelope. They all darted off like a preacher goin' to supper, as Grandad always said.

"They have this way of bouncin', like they're not very interested in gettin' very far away very fast. They bounded about three jumps away and then turned to stare at us again. The yearling even took a few steps in our direction.

"I gave Billy the gun and said, 'Here, you hit that yearling in the head.'

"'I can't do that,' said Billy.

"'Sure, you can,' I said. 'You can pop the head off a quail nine times out of ten. I know you can hit that yearling between the eyes.'

"'We're too far away,' said Billy.

"Well, I realized he was right. And I realized why my shot hadn't gone anywhere. 'Okay,' I said. 'We'll sneak up on 'em.'

"I took the gun from him, and we started toward those antelope. 'Course, I realize now that we were about as quiet as a railway engine, and about as hidden as the noon sun in a bald sky. So those antelope would bounce off and turn. We'd creep toward 'em, and they'd bounce off and turn.

"'We'd better go back,' said Billy. 'We're gettin' awful far from home.'

"'Geez, you're such a panty-waist,' I said. 'Don't you want to get an antelope, or don't you?' I knew he'd have to defend his manhood at that.

"'Course, I want to get one,' he said, grabbing the gun out of my hands. 'What d'you think I am, anyhow?'

"So we crept up, and the antelope bounced away. Pretty soon, we came to a little gully, which reminded me of a story Grandma used to tell about how clever hunters could lure antelope within range. 'Here,' I told Billy. 'You get down in this gully and move as fast as you can toward them antelope. I'll stay here 'n keep 'em entertained.'

"Billy had heard the same story, of course, so he ducked into the gully and crept away.

"I took off my shirt and started wavin' it to keep the antelope lookin' in my direction, while Billy was slippin' up on 'em. I even found a stick and threaded it through my shirt sleeves, so I could wave it like a flag.

"Well, that antelope family was plumb flabbergasted. They reckoned they'd never seen the likes of a half-naked boy wavin' a flag on the high prairie. So they started steppin' a little bit in my direction, like they wanted to get a closer look. They were real casual about it, you know. They'd play like they were grazin' on the buffalo grass for a bite or two, then look up as if to say, 'What in the world is goin' on over there?' I figured Billy was within range by that time, but I didn't want to yell at him to shoot, 'cause I knew the noise would scare 'em again.

"I waited the longest time and kept up my antics. The antelope came up to within thirty yards of me, so I figured Billy was maybe as close as fifty feet. He could hit a gopher just peekin' out of his hole at that distance, so I figured we as good as had us an antelope. Us, I was thinkin'. We were a team, so whatever happened, we had both accomplished it. I don't think I'd ever felt so close to Billy. We were more than brothers. We were two arms of the same thought, if that makes any sense.

"But Billy wasn't shootin', even if he was in range. I figured he could practically count the ticks in their armpits by this time. I wanted in the worst way to yell at him, 'NOW!' 'Do it!' 'Shoot!' but I still held my tongue in my teeth, 'cause I knew they would spook.

"Finally, I saw Billy creep up out of the gully by a big clump of blue-stem grass. He was right beside the antelope family. They just turned toward him and gawked, as if to say, 'Lord have mercy! There's *two* of them!'

"By that time, I was tryin' to send every signal I could to Billy, except yelling, of course. I aimed my stick like a gun and 'shot' it over and over. The antelope weren't even interested in me. So I shook my fists at Billy and waved my arms and gave the old tomahawk chop, tryin' to tell him the time was ripe. Hit the anvil while the work is hot, or you'll never make a horseshoe, our grandad always said.

"Well, finally I saw the little puff of blue smoke come out of our rifle, and then I heard the shot. The antelope broke and ran, all three of them, seriously this time. Land o' Goshen, he missed! How could he pop the head off a ground hog at thirty or forty yards, and miss an antelope? They raced down the gully and over the cap rock and down into the canyon off the escarpment.

You couldn't get down off the plains just anywhere, because the cap rock made a cliff. But every so often a gully would cut through and form a sort of streambed about as steep as sand and rock can be stacked. In our area, they all ran down into Double Mountain Fork. The antelope darted off down one of those arroyos.

"'C'mon,' I yelled to Billy, pullin' my shirt on as I ran. 'Les don't let 'em get away.'

"'We'd better go back,' he yelled. 'It's gettin' late.'

"I turned and went back to where he was. I jerked the gun out of his hands, sayin', 'Crap, Wilhelmina. You go on back if you want to. I'm goin' to chase those antelope.'

"'Course, he couldn't give up when I'd said that to him, so he followed me and the antelope off the plains and down into the canyon.

"Well, it didn't take either of us very long to realize we were lost. I don't mean we were *lost*; we just didn't know where we were. I mean, we knew which way to go to find the way home, 'cause all these canyons ran into Double Mountain Fork, so we weren't in any real danger, but it was new territory to us. We didn't know where the trails or the drop-offs were.

"We kept chasin' after those antelope, and the farther we went, the later it got. And the later it got, the darker it got in that canyon.

So we realized pretty soon that we were goin' to spend the night there. That wasn't too big a problem; we knew how to take care of ourselves overnight away from home. We'd done it often enough. We always carried a few matches with us, and we both had kid-type pocket knives. Dad had given me a good knife, one that would take an edge and stay sharp, but I'd lost it in less than a week. Kid knives, I never seemed to lose. Up in the attic in my Dad's old trunk, there's a cigar box half full of 'em. Must be twenty or more in there. Broken blades, sprung hinges, rusty springs. You only seem to lose the good stuff when you're a kid.

"We picked a fairly flat place under an overhanging rock ledge to spend the night. We broke dead wood in the fork of a post cedar and made a fire to keep us company, but, to tell the truth, we were both pretty tuckered, so it didn't take us long to curl up together and go to sleep.

We woke up before the dawn star rose, 'cause both of us were about as cold as Christians. Luckily, we had some firewood left from the night before, so we got thawed out pretty soon, and I gathered more wood by the light of the fire.

"A good while before dawn, Billy said he was hungry, and I was glad he said it first, 'cause my stomach felt like it was about to cave in. About first light, I took the gun and went lookin' for a wide place in the canyon where some grass might grow. I figured there'd be rabbits out nibblin'. I got one with the first shot, and I wedged his head in the fork of a scrub mesquite, cut around and down his neck, and just pulled his skin off like it was a glove, the way Grandma had taught us. I fixed the hide to take home to her. She could make a rabbit skin as soft as a shammy cloth. We roasted his hind quarters over our fire, and ate them without salt. That was some of the best food I ever ate. You know how that is, don't you? Hunger always makes the beans taste better.

"We waited till the sun had warmed us a little, and then decided we'd better get on out of that canyon and head for home. We found a trickling spring and drank a little—not much, 'cause the water tasted bad. We decided our best route would be to work our way on down the canyon till we came to Double Mountain Fork, then work our way up it to home. That'd save us having to climb the cliff back up onto the plains above the cap rock.

"We hadn't gone far before we saw that skinny old doe antelope that had made wild geese out of us the day before. She was still pretty stiff from the cold night, so she didn't seem to even notice us. We were almost right on her.

"I rolled the breechblock back, slipped in a cartridge, and rolled the breech closed. I lifted the gun and shot at what I thought would be her heart. We heard the bullet hit—wump!—like a frog landin' on a bass drum. The doe humped up her back, like she was tryin' to get her breath, and then she bounced off down the canyon.

"'You gut-shot her!' yelled Billy, and I heard in the tone of his voice that he had deliberately missed that yearling up on the plain the day before.

"'At least I hit her,' I said, tryin' to make him feel like he wasn't worth taking huntin' at all. 'C'mon,' I yelled. 'We gotta track her down.' I put a new cartridge in the gun as I ran. I dropped the rabbit skin, but I didn't stop to pick it up.

"I found the trail of blood right away and raced off after the doe. I wasn't sure whether Billy was followin' or not.

"I came up on the doe, not more than a hundred yards away. She had taken shelter in a clump of cedars, but she acted like she wasn't seein' or hearin' anythang around her. Her back was hunched way up, she was frothin' pink at the mouth, and blood was drippin' red right behind her foreleg. I had hit her in the lungs.

"I was still standin' there sort of dumbfounded when Billy came up beside me. He held the rabbit skin in his hands. 'She's in the throes of death,' he whispered. 'You ought to finish her off.'

"I tried to hand him the gun, sayin' 'Your turn to shoot.'

"'I don't want to,' he said. And he vomited suddenly. I saw half-chewed chunks of rabbit in his spume.

"That gave me a sort of courage. 'Well, goddam, Daisy,' I said. 'Don't put yourself out any.' I raised the gun, took aim, and shot the doe between the eyes. She dropped like a duck, rolled down the hill, and wedged against a mesquite.

"Then I vomited. A flood of hot saliva whooshed in and brought with it my rabbit breakfast. I felt dizzy and feverish and couldn't stop vomiting. I saw that Billy was in the same fix.

"Almost like twins, we jerked our pants down and had diarrhea. 'Gol-dang,' I yelled, 'that water we drank was gyp water. It's given us the scours.'

"'I don't feel good' was all Billy could say.

"I was reeling so much and so feverish that I couldn't stand up, so I crawled into the clump of cedars to get out of the sun. 'C'mon into the shade,' I called to Billy, but he was so dizzy he couldn't even lift his head. I think he drank more of the water than I did.

Somehow, I managed to get a hold on his shirt and dragged him under a cedar. He was still hanging on to that rabbit skin. Then I must have passed out. Both of us must have passed out.

When I woke, it was dark again. At first, I didn't know where I was, or what scrape I was in. Then I remembered. My bowels felt like someone had pulled a wire brush through them. My throat was burnin', and my stomach was a hard knot. I felt my forehead. I was sweatin' like I was the headwaters of a river. Then I remembered Billy was in the same predicament.

"'Billy,' I whispered. 'Billy, are you awake?'

"There wasn't any answer.

"'Billy,' I whispered again. I would have called out loud, but I didn't seem to have any voice. 'Billy, are you there?'

"In the starlight, I began to make out his form. I reached over and touched him. He was hot with fever, so I knew he was still alive. I let him rest, thinkin' being asleep was a favor to anyone goin' through what we were goin' through.

"The next morning, we woke at about the same time, probably disturbed by the same thing—the flappin' of buzzard wings. The sun was halfway up the sky and broiling everthang. Our doe was bloated and already startin' to rot. A dozen of the big birds were gathered around, anxious to pick her bones. And ours, too. I was so weak, I couldn't even lift the gun to shoot at them.

"We heard a shot down the canyon. It was Dad, lookin' for us. I waited until the echoes of his shot had died away, then the necessity of the situation gave me strength enough to pull the trigger on our gun. The buzzards all flew up and started circling. I hoped Dad could see them. They were showin' him right where we were. Every ten minutes or so, I made up the strength to put another cartridge in our gun, fire it at nothin', and send the buzzards up again.

"'You oughtn't to have killed that doe,' said Billy.

"I knew he was right, but I wasn't goin' to let him have the satisfaction of hearing me say so. As heavy as she was and as far away as we were, there was no way we could have gotten the meat home before it spoiled.

"'I don't mean just that,' said Billy, as if reading my mind. 'I mean you killed more than that doe. You killed a part of the world.'

"I knew what he meant, 'cause I could sort of read his mind, too. I had killed more than a part of the world; I'd killed a part of ourselves, a part of what we had been taught, and what we stood for. But I bluffed around that. 'Shoot!' I said, 'You don't mean to tell me that old doe was with fawn, do you? She's much too skinny to be carryin' a fawn.'

"'No, I don't mean that,' said Billy. He held up that rabbit skin that he was still carryin' for Grandma, as if it was a sign of something.

"Not long after that, Dad found us. He gave us water from his canteen and carried us out, one on each arm ... like we were little babies ... born again ... and brought us home, safe ..."

"Geez, is that all, Pah-pah?"

"No, not quite all. Grandma Quahada-ne used to tell me that when she was a girl you could walk from Prairie Dog Fork all the way to the Big Spring and never be out of sight of a herd of deer or antelope. Now, you can drive back and forth a dozen times and not see a half dozen. Instead, you see roads and towns everywhere. Those are about the worst use of land I can think of, except maybe cemeteries and golf courses. Golf courses are pretty bad.

"Geez, Pah-pah. That's weird."

"Yes, I reckon I am. But you don't see any deer and antelope, do you?"

"So what? We can go to the zoo when we want to see wild animals."

"Yes ... Yes ... I reckon you can."

"I'm going out, now, Pah-pah. I want to find Billy Birdlove and see if we can get up a baseball game over at the school yard."

Maria Has-Red-Shoes

Maria was born a few miles downstream from the Pine Ridge Agency and named for the Blessed Virgin, but her name was not then Has-Red-Shoes. It was Mahpiya Shunka-sha, *Sky-Horse-Red*. This is how she came to be called Maria Has-Red-Shoes.

Her mother died soon after Maria was born, because there was not enough food in her body for both her lung sickness and the baby. Maria was left with her Lakota grandmother while her father went to Boise, because he had heard there was a man there who would let an Indian work. Five years later, he was killed in a gunfight in a tavern called "The Wild Horse." Her Lakota grandmother wailed and keened, then took a knife and hacked off a joint of her index finger. From the wound, the grandmother caught gangrene and lay dying. "Survive, little Mahpiya Shunka-sha," said the grandmother. "You are the last of the Sky-Horse-Red family. That is why you were given your grandfather's name. Mahpiya Shunka-sha must pull the People's travois now." Then she died. The assistant Indian agent brought Maria to the orphanage that was run by the Church of the Immaculate Conception. She could not speak English.

The matrons fed her a thin potato soup, the church auxiliary supplied her with cotton sack dresses, and she grew to be a skinny, knob-kneed girl of twelve, hardly thicker than a needle, with big, brown, doe-shaped eyes. Though the other children liked her and included her in their talk, she never laughed, and she said little to anyone. During this time, the nun told her her name was Maria MacArthur and that she was to grow up to be a good Christian citizen. She spent most of her time withdrawn in some safe niche, watching what was going on around her, because Sally Benton, one of the older girls, had told her in Lakota, "If you don't watch and learn, you won't survive."

The children were forbidden to speak Lakota, but they whispered it to each other anyway—behind the woodshed, in the toilet, on the edge of the prairie.

She and Sally were walking in the dusk, a little distance from the orphanage. The earth lay before them like a buffalo hide before the food was spread. "All this is yours and mine," Sally had said.

Maria had just watched and waited.

"My grandfather told me once, long before I came here, that the Grandfather of Time had given the world to all of the people. The earth is a big *Umane*, a buffalo hide like a big tablecloth, with tassels going off into the half-directions where the legs are, like northeast. Those tassels are like rivers, and everything—birds, sticks, pebbles, the smallest things—flow into the *Umane*. The meadows that grow food, the game animals, the water in the streams, the air in the sky. And the beauty that is draped over it all. 'All this is yours,' said the Grandfather of Time. 'All this is yours to share.' So, don't you see, Maria? We are wealthy." Sally had taken Maria's thin shoulders into her hands at this point and looked directly into her eyes. "Even if we are hungry, we are wealthy. And that is why we must survive."

Maria had nodded her head, gravely, because her Lakota grandmother had told her that sharing and survival were intertwined: "Learn their language; give whatever you must; but survive. The Lakota must survive." With both her mother and father gone, with Sally so urgent, the only thing Maria could conceive of was to survive.

As soon as she could scour a pot, Maria was put to work in the kitchen of the priest's house, between the orphanage and the church. It was strange. There were chicken bones on the plates and gravy in the pans, but the children of Immaculate Conception did not eat chicken and gravy. But Maria said nothing, not even to Sally, because she already understood that such information changed nothing.

One March night, Sally Benton took two blankets and the priest's long underwear and disappeared into the dark. Maria saw her get out of bed when the two o'clock moon came in the window. Maria raised up on one elbow to watch. Sally made the motion to be silent, looking at the same time toward the end of the room where Mrs. Wallthorn lay snoring. Maria watched Sally put her dress on over her night chemise and push her feet into her ragged tennis shoes. She tied knots in the legs of the priest's underwear to make pockets and began stuffing them with her things. Maria silently drew a pair of socks from her hiding place under her pillow and handed them to Sally. Sally looked at them a long moment, as if to wonder where and how the socks came into being and how Maria came into possession of them, then accepted them because she knew all the orphans had some secret that helped them survive. She sat on her bunk, removed her shoes, and put on the socks and shoes. The socks would help her get across the chilled prairie in the biting night. Sally leaned down and kissed Maria on the cheek. Then she gave Maria a fingernail file and a comb from her own secret bag.

Maria watched Sally stuff her extra dress and a tablecloth into the priest's underwear. Swinging toward the door with a blanket across her shoulders, Sally stopped, turned again, and made signs to ask if Maria wanted to run away also. Maria rolled away, toward Mrs. Wallthorn's bed, so that when the priest would ask her, "Did you see Sally go?" she could honestly answer, "No." She would miss Sally, but she did not want to go with her.

She knew well enough why Sally was leaving. In the summer, when the evenings were long, they were sometimes finished with their work and could walk on the prairie to watch the sun set. One day, when they were out of sight and sound from the orphanage, Sally had put her hands on Maria's breasts, which made little sharp cones the size of plums in the front of her dress. "These are a girl's worst enemies," she said. "As they grow, so does the lust of the Brothers and Father Joseph. Soon, you will not be able to keep them away from you. I have seen them watching you already. They will transfer you to the laundry. And then they will have you deliver Father Joseph's underwear to his rooms. He will look into your eyes, give you food and soft words, and he will grab you like this." At that point, Sally seized Maria's hand, shoved it into the neck of her own dress, and held it against her bare breast. Sally's breasts felt hard and round, like ripe peach halves. Maria was startled, pulled back, then allowed Sally to put her breast in the cup of Maria's hand.

"He will say that to hold a breast is a lovely feeling. And that she who serves a servant of God serves God. And he will take off your dress. When he moves his cassock, you will see that he has no underwear on. He will press against you. And you will have no way of resisting. If you cry out, he will beat you, but there will be no one to hear your screams. If you cry in pain, he will say that adversity is a good service to God. If you tell the nun, she will pretend that you have said nothing. I cannot stand it, Maria," she said, releasing Maria's hand. "Either I must run away, or hang myself from the pipes in the toilet. I will go and look for my mother's brother, who used to live near Fort Robinson."

"No, Sally," Maria cried. "They bayonet people there!"

"I know," said Sally, "but that's better than killing myself."

Maria grabbed Sally and hugged her desperately, as if she would never let her friend go. For Maria was well aware: she had no relative near Fort Robinson, nor anywhere else.

Sally hugged her in return. "Whatever will happen to us Indians?" she asked. "Father Joseph likes to have the lay brothers start the girls, so that the first sin does not lie with the priest."

Maria tried to break away and run, but Sally held her tightly. "I know," she said. "I know. It happened to me, too."

"Mister Bruno?" asked Maria.

"Yes. Mister Bruno," answered Sally. "The dumbest, stupidest little bear in the world."

Maria said nothing. Mister Bruno was one of the few people in the world who had held her gently. She wanted to be with him now.

When Maria was eight, Mister Bruno, who swept floors, repaired harness, and taught woodshop, had been attracted by her big beautiful eyes. He offered and was assigned to help her with her catechism. He had taken her to the saddle room behind the laundry, where the nun had no business. He gave her candy and sweet biscuits for right answers.

Then he began holding her on his knee or his lap and putting his arm around her willowy shoulders. His tenderness was new to Maria; she could hardly remember even her grandmother's touch, and she liked the sensation.

At night, she lay awake, letting her mind live it again as he spoke her name and took her in his arms. She heard again his soothing voice.

"You do like me, don't you, Maria?" Mister Bruno would ask, and she would nod, her eyes big and honest, because very few people had ever called her by name. And there were sandwiches, sometimes a chicken wing, even a fragment of sweet cobbler or pie. He seemed to delight in holding her on his knee and watching her eat while he drank an amber liquid from a fruit jar. The nun was pleased with her progress in English.

There was no great change when he put his hand on her bare leg and moved it up under her dress. She had stopped eating when he did that the first time, but he said, "It's okay. This is what people do when they like each other."

Maria accepted that. She had never loved anyone, except her Lakota grandparents, and they were both gone, and no one had ever liked her. She didn't know what she was supposed to do. And it felt good to be touched on the bare buttocks by a big warm hand. She quivered with a feeling she couldn't say was pain or pleasure when he rubbed her between the legs. She only knew she wanted more. So when he pressed his thumb into her, the pain was mixed with a shuddering thrill that made the pain okay.

She lay in her bunk at night, letting the memory of his hand move over her, lift off her dress, felt his lips kiss hers, heard her own body scream like some distant hungry wolf that would not be silent until she pressed her hands between her legs and her finger into herself.

For over three years, she had rushed to the tack room at her lesson time to hop astraddle the prone Mister Bruno. She could hardly wait for the tingles to run fish-like all over her body, and she would do anything he asked her to. She agreed each time he told her, "Now, don't tell anyone at all about what has happened here. God may strike you dead if you tell a single soul." And she would nod, her big doe-silent eyes open. For the first time since she had come to the orphanage, she was not alone.

She was twelve when Sally left. Mrs. Wallthorn came and searched around Sally's bunk. "That ungrateful wench," she muttered, not noticing Maria, "that—that harlot! And during Holy Week, too! Stole bread and blankets from the priest's room, before skulking away like a common thief."

Maria had quickened and blushed before she could get control of herself and her eyes. Of course, Sally would need food, but Maria had not seen the bread. Its presence astonished her. She hoped she had not given away the secret.

But Mrs. Wallthorn was focused upon her own sense of outrage and victimization. Then she noticed other children. "That girl— Let us never again speak her name aloud. That girl has committed a terrible sin, and I forbid you all to ever pray to Almighty God for her forgiveness or redemption. And now, let's get on with our work. Sally Benton never existed."

Alone, in the light of the two o'clock moon, Maria touched the comb and fingernail file under her pillow and felt again, in memory, Sally embracing her there on the edge of the prairie, asking of no one, "What in the world will become of us Indians?"

Sally had predicted accurately what would happen to Maria. She was taken from her job in the kitchen and put to work in the laundry, washing clothes on contract for the Chinese laundry in Rapid City, clothes which no Indian children wore, red dresses with pleated skirts, blue dresses with gathers in the sleeves, pastel dresses with matching belts and round white collars trimmed with ric-rac or lace. She did not know the girls that worked in the laundry, and some of the boys that couldn't work in the fields were there as well, but she dared not ever glance at them, much less speak. For Sister Magdalene was meaner even than Mrs. Wallthorn; she would thwack the girls and boys across the back with her walking cane—so that Maria was again lost in a world of plenty she could not taste and activity she did not understand.

Mister Bruno had not sent for her since Sally had run away. She lay in her bunk at night, crying softly so as not to disturb Mrs. Wallthorn's snoring, praying to the two o'clock moon that Sally was safe, and visualizing herself and Mister Bruno lying together under a buffalo robe in some warm lodge safe from enemies, some great good place where Sister Magdalene and Mrs. Wallthorn could not send even their wicked imaginations.

One day at lesson time, Maria slipped out the back door while Sister Magdalene was beating Tommy Turtle-back with her cane. She gathered her skirt above her knees and ran barefooted like a warrior.

But when she got to the tack-room door, she heard a voice and stopped. She put her eye to the crack in the door. Elizabeth Yellow Bird was sitting on Mister Bruno's knee, his hand was under her dress, and Mister Bruno was saying, "You do like me, don't you, Elizabeth?" Elizabeth nodded gravely, waiting for what was next.

Maria caught her breath before she cried out with the wound. She lifted her skirt again and ran like a hunted doe to the edge of the prairie where she and Sally had embraced out of sight and sound.

"Oh, Sally, Sally," she cried, big tears wetting the front of her dress. "He doesn't want me. He doesn't love me. I could have gone with you; I should have gone with you."

She wanted to inflict pain upon herself, as if that would compensate the loss. She beat her face, her chest—if she had owned a knife, she might have cut off a joint of a finger. But nothing would do. And through it all, Sally's plaintive voice kept asking, "What in the world will become of us Indians?"

"Nothing will ever happen, Sally," Maria cried out. "There is no future for Indians. The women cannot live without food, the men cannot live without work. And they will let us have neither. There is nothing for us to do."

Then Maria realized that Sally had refused to accept the future they had planned for her. Had she survived? Maria looked across the prairie. Had Sally gone that direction? Had she found her mother's brother near Fort Robinson? Was she safe in some good place where bayonets could not reach her?

Sally was the only person in the world who would speak hard with her, but never lie. Maria looked at her own plain, thin dress and bare feet and wanted desperately to be with Sally. Should she try to find Sally anyway? Should she start across the prairie with no bread and no blanket, not even a pair of tattered shoes? She sank back, even before she started, for she did not even know in which direction Fort Robinson lay. She was as lost as the lonely afternoon moon.

Tommy Turtle-back found her there at dusk. "They've sent everyone out to look for you," he said. "Sister Magdalene has caned everyone, because she didn't know where you were."

She looked up at him, her doe-like eyes still full of tears. He was a pudgy, bookish boy of fourteen who could not run fast like the other children, and he fell off horses; so Mister Anthony, the boys' ranching teacher, had sent him to Mister Bruno to learn woodshop, but he spent most of his time working in the laundry. He was as lost as she was. "Whatever will happen to us, Otuhan Maka?" she asked in Lakota, thrilled and ashamed that she had spoken his name for the first time.

He shrugged his shoulders, not knowing quite what she was asking. "We will get beaten, and they will feed us potato gruel," he said in Lakota.

"No, I mean, what will happen to us Indians? What will happen to Indians who do not even know the way to Fort Robinson?"

He shrugged again. "I don't know."

The sunset had spread a red cape across the evening sky. "All this is ours, Tommy," she said in Lakota, sweeping her hand across the western sky. "All the air, the water, the earth, the sun. All this is ours to share."

"Come back with me," said Tommy, switching to English. "You will be beaten, but— If you let me take you back, the rest of us will not."

Maria did not move.

"I'll give you my pocketknife if you'll come back with me," said Tommy. "Half of the blade is broken off, but part of it will still cut. And I have a book you can read."

Maria opened her eyes and gazed at him. She was no longer crying. Tommy leaned toward her, a pocketknife with celluloid handles in his cupped hand.

"I'll get each of the others to give you something, too. It's like a trade. We'll each give you some thing, and you'll save us from a beating."

Maria reached up and folded the pocket knife back into his hand, then allowed him to help her up and lead her toward the orphanage. "When we get in sight of the orphanage," he said, "I'll throw my arms around you, like I am bringing you in by force."

Maria nodded and leaned against him. She wanted him to hug her now.

Both Sister Magdalene and Mrs. Wallthorn beat her with switches when they got back. To save the cloth, they took off her black dress. They hacked, whacked, and red welts ricracked her back. Tommy backed to the shack door near the tack room, watching them thwack her, wanting to rack her in his slack arms and comfort her. Through her tears, Maria saw him staring at her plum-like breasts. He was trying to smile. The clacking attracted Father Joseph, who came in and stopped the matrons. "Here, here," he said, "Stop beating this child." He looked at her big, tear-filled eyes, her nubile breasts. "Such a pretty child!"

"But, Father Joseph," said Sister Magdalene, "she was trying to run away."

"Really?" he said, picking up her dress and starting to straighten it. "Were you trying to run away, my dear?"

Maria shook her head.

"Did you know when Sally Benton ran away in the night?"

Maria nodded.

"But you weren't running away?"

Maria shook her head again.

"Well, Sister Magdalene, the matter is closed. Such a pretty child," he said again, slipping her dress over her head.

Not long after that, Mrs. Wallthorn caught Maria and Tommy Turtle-back fornicating. From her window in the girls' dormitory, she had seen Tommy carrying a ragged Double Wedding Ring quilt toward the creek one day. And, some minutes later, she saw Maria slip from the laundry and race toward the creek by a different route. She took Sister Magdalene with her, and they knifed through the grass to surprise the lovers.

Maria and Tommy had found a side arroyo high in the cutbank of the creek, where several bushes hung over the drop-off. They had fashioned a bed, a great good place sheltered from the sun and almost impossible to find.

The matrons dragged them back to the orphanage for punishment. Again, they stripped Maria and whipped her with willow switches, raising criss-cross welts on her back. Father

Joseph, hearing the switches whistling and Maria screaming, came in to investigate.

When told about the matter, he put Maria's dress back on her and led her away toward his room, saying, "I will discipline her myself."

Father Joseph stood her beside his day bed and questioned her. She told him everything he asked. "And you have been—have been fornicating—for three years?" he asked.

Maria nodded.

"Well," he said, "that certainly calls for some discipline. Take off your clothes." He lowered his head in prayer.

"Father Joseph," said Maria, drawing the dress over her head. "Can you make Sister Magdalene and Mrs. Wallthorn quit beating the children?"

Father Joseph lifted his head and looked at her. "What?" he asked. "What do you mean?"

"The matrons," said Maria. "They cane the children too much. Can you make them stop? A little?"

"No, no, child. We have to have some means of maintaining discipline. It's all tit for tat. The children misbehave, and the matrons punish them."

"But they're so cruel," said Maria. "They beat us like they hated us. Like we had done something mean to them."

He opened his arms and took her onto his knee, touching the welts on her shoulders.

"We give them all we can," continued Maria. "We have nothing left."

He ran his cold hand down her back and across her dirty panties. She had no welts there. He repeated the move and passed his hand over her thigh. Watching his hands, Maria suddenly knew what she had to trade. She turned toward him abruptly, so that his other hand passed over her puffy nipple. "You can make them stop," Maria suggested. "I'll give you whatever you like, if you'll make them stop."

Slowly, carefully, he said, "You can, perhaps, imagine that a job like mine often gets lonely." His voice sounded moist and warm.

Maria nodded, her big, silent, doe-like eyes wide with anticipation.

"We often want someone to touch us, too," he said.

She nodded.

He lurched back against his pillow, pulling his cassock halfway up his thigh, as if by accident.

Maria Has-Red-Shoes

"I will touch you, Father Joseph," said Maria.

"Do, child. Do so, please."

She lifted his cassock. As Sally had warned, he was wearing no underwear. She put her hand on his leg and shifted her body so that she was standing on her knees. She moved her hand along his thigh. He leaned back and looked at the ceiling.

"Please, Father Joseph. Make them quit beating the children." He was silent; Maria began to pull his cassock down again.

Father Joseph looked at her a long moment. "Alright. Alright," he said at last. "I'll tell them to be more sparing of the cane."

Maria pushed his cassock up again and touched him. He felt like a small cucumber. Father Joseph squirmed and sighed. She moved her hand back and forth. He began to whimper.

This was what Sally had run away from. It was either run away to Fort Robinson, or hang herself from the pipes in the bathroom. Or survive, by living through it, survive by giving what you must. Maria shucked off her panties, crawled up, and threaded herself down onto him. She felt the thrill quaver once in her body and die, but she kept moving the way Mister Bruno had liked. She wondered if Mahpiya Shunka-sha would ever feel the trembling again. She wondered if she would feel it when she took Tommy Turtle-back to the edge of the prairie again, out of sight and sound.

"And tell the cooks to give the children part of the real food from the kitchen."

"Yes, yes," he said, twisting. "Real food. My God, you're so good."

"Remember, now," said Maria, leaning toward him. "No whipping, and we get some real food."

"Yes, yes," he said. "I swear it. Before God, I swear it. No caning, and real food."

She felt him throbbing and his heat passing into her insides. Then he lay back, sighing. Maria understood that she could stop moving.

After a while, he looked at her again. "Thank you, dear child. Where did you—" He broke off, then, after a moment, continued on a different track: "I must go to Omaha."

She waited, not moving.

"To buy supplies," he added, hastily. "Would you like to go with me, my child?"

Maria hesitated, watching him in silence.

"We could dress as farmers," he went on, "and go as father and daughter."

He was fair, and she was dark. *No one would mistake us for father and daughter,* thought Maria, but she waited, sensing that the time was not yet right to strike a bargain.

"We could stay in the same room. To save money, of course."

"Oh, Father Joseph," said Maria, finding words to trade, words she never knew she had. "I cannot go like this. I want a blue dress with a belt and a white collar trimmed with lace."

"You shall have it, my dear," he said.

Maria squirmed on him again. "And I want some red shoes," she said. "Red shoes with a buckle across the top."

"Oh, yes, my child," he said, making the sign of the cross over her forehead and beginning to writhe inside her again. "Oh, yes, yes. You shall have your red shoes. Two pairs of red shoes, if you like."

Tommy Turtle-Back

1

The winter Tommy Turtle-back turned fifteen, he was moved from his job in the orphanage laundry to work with Brother Bruno in the woodshop; it was time for him to learn a trade. He was studious and intelligent, but did not understand horses and harness—he was always in the way when he was told to help out in the stockyards—and he riveted leather straps, like reins, in the wrong place. "I'll swear," Brother Bruno would say, drinking a clear liquid from a fruit jar, "You're about the dumbest thing I ever saw, Tommy. I'd have to get as drunk as three Indians to do things as bad as you do them by nature."

Tommy always wanted to look down, at the floor, to hide his face, but he had already learned enough about interpersonal relations to know that the white men would not allow that. He was forced to look them in the eyes. So he had developed a way of hiding with his eyes open—looking straight at a man, but not seeing or hearing any more than if they were a horse or a steer. That way he did not have to deal with their invasion of his personality.

"Look at me," said Brother Bruno. "I'm talking to you."

Tommy gazed at him silently.

"Don't you understand, Tommy?" said Brother Bruno, taking him by the shoulder. "You can't stay here in the orphanage forever. You've got to learn how to make it on your own. You've got to learn to take care of yourself."

Tommy still just gazed at him silently.

"Answer me," said Brother Bruno, shaking Tommy's shoulder. "D'ya understand what I'm saying."

"Yes," said Tommy, realizing that some answer was required.

"Well, that's good," said Brother Bruno. "Tony says you ain't worth a shit for farming or ranching. Can't keep your head out of a goddam book long enough to learn anything. So I'm s'posed to teach you some woodworking. You gotta learn how to act in the outside world, and support yourself, and all. Here, have a drink. You 'n me 're going to have to be buddies, if we're going to pull this thing off." And Brother Bruno pushed the fruit jar into Tommy's hand.

Tommy drank a big gulp of the clear liquid, thinking it was water. It burned his throat; he sputtered, coughed, retched so hard his stomach muscles hurt; tears formed in his eyes, tingeing everything with starbursts of light. He tried unsuccessfully to remain impassive, thinking unaccountably, realizing that *the priest, nuns and brothers that ran the Orphanage of the Immaculate Conception could simply murder the Indian children if they liked, and no one on the outside would ever know it—or care.* He was outraged and amused by that irony.

Brother Bruno was tickled by Tommy's reaction. "Kinda gets to you, don't it? You'll prob'ly learn soon enough to drink your booze without sputtering."

Tommy looked at the ground.

"Well, come on," said Brother Bruno, getting down to business. "Les see if you can saw a straight line. We've got to make three coffins for the Pine Ridge agency. Seems they's a lot of Indians dying this winter, and we got to make the boxes to plant 'em in."

Brother Bruno set up a pine board on a sawhorse, showed Tommy the angle to hold the saw, and gave him hints on how to make the stroke. "Y' have to saw on the bias and the angle at the same time. That way, you c'n make a corner that'll hold water."

The shop was unheated, and, during blizzards, little feather-shaped deltas of snow formed in front of the cracks, so it was difficult to work in heavy coats and gloves. But, in spite of the cold, Tommy began to feel warm. It began in his stomach, where the burning drink grappled with the burning walls of his stomach. He began to sweat on his upper lip and the soft parts of his eyelids. Hot saliva bathed his tongue. Without warning, he vomited, spewing sour liquid on himself and the pine board under his knee.

"Geez! Watch it," said Brother Bruno, scooping up sawdust to put on the board. "That lumber costs money; we can't afford to waste any of it."

Tommy reeled and plopped down on the floor on his butt, unable, it seemed, to keep his head above his shoulders. He was unaware of the board, uncaring. But he felt better almost at once. His stomach rejecting the liquor had allowed it to accept him again. He felt a curious glow, a tingling in the nerves that ran across his shoulders, down his back, into the outsides of his legs. He got up and helped Brother Bruno throw sawdust on the pine board, a smile running up only the right side of his face.

"You may think it's funny," said Brother Bruno, "but it ain't. If the stink don't come out, we won't be able to get it past the priest, or the BIA agent. We can't waste the board."

"Wash it," said Tommy.

"Now, that's a good idea," agreed Brother Bruno. "You run around to the laundry and sneak us a wet rag. If we wet the whole side of the board, the stain won't show. You got a good head on your shoulders, Tommy. That was quick thinking."

When they had cleaned the board, Brother Bruno offered Tommy another drink from the fruit jar, saying, "Now, don't drink so much. Jist sip it, okay?"

When Tommy sipped this time, he was ready for the burning, but he was not ready for the rushing tingle, both hot and cold at once, across his shoulders, down his back, along his legs. The right side of his face burst into a smile.

"That's better," said Brother Bruno. "Someday, you'll make a pretty good drunk, Tommy Turtle-back."

2

When Tommy Turtle-back graduated from the orphanage high school, it was obvious to everyone that he ought to go to college. About the same time, Father Joseph discovered that Maria Has-Red-Shoes was pregnant, so he quickly arranged a marriage in the orphanage chapel and got the board of directors to award Tommy a small scholarship to a state college in the farm country north of Denver. He himself drove the newlyweds to Rapid City, put them on a Greyhound bus, and blessed their journey.

In Greeley, Tommy was delighted with the college. Each subject was a new world to be discovered and he was a voyager out collecting continents. He especially liked sociology and economics and the poetry part of literature.

But he and Maria soon discovered they had no money. The priest had even deducted the costs of their bus tickets from their already tiny stipend. Rent for a room and a dinky kitchenette used over half of what remained, and food soon took the rest. Tommy quickly saw that his token scholarship would hardly get him through the first week of classes, so he would have to find work.

He got a few odd jobs around Greeley: pitching hay, feeding cows, working in the corn. But at each job, the farmers soon learned that Tommy was both uninterested and incompetent, and they fired him. Maria suggested she could help out by turning tricks, which, reluctantly, Tommy agreed to. There seemed no other source of income.

Maria's business was confined at first to the weekends, but soon expanded to every night and a few afternoon appointments. She started bringing home half-filled bottles of liquor that had been left over from her trysts. A drink, she discovered, helped to dull Tommy's outrage. Still, they quarreled, often screaming at each other in Lakota. Tommy would sometimes stop their fights with: "Look, Maria. Look what the goddam system is doing to us! We're not mad at each other!" And they would kiss and make love.

As compensation and insulation, Tommy buried himself in study. He read incessantly, not only the assigned texts, but many of the works the instructors mentioned only in passing. He wrote excellent, perceptive term papers. He began writing angry, protesting free verse that no one else thought was poetry.

When Maria's bulging pregnancy began hurting her business, Tommy realized that he would have to go back to work. Through the college placement office, he got a job with a carpenter, because he could say, honestly, that he had been an apprentice in the orphanage woodshop for three years.

The carpenter put Tommy to work on the framing crew. But Tommy bent the big nails, and he could not saw a board squarely. He realized that he had been taught to saw only on a bias and angle, and a saw set squarely on a board seemed abnormal. The carpenter moved him to the roofing crew. But Tommy was clumsy and fell off the roof. The carpenter put him on the insulation crew, but Tommy got sick on the fiberglass dust that the workers had to breathe. Finally, the carpenter threw up his hands in disgust and fired Tommy.

At last, Tommy was forced to apply for welfare. But, since both he and Maria were Indian and had never had Social Security cards, there were many delays. A Salvation Army soup kitchen kept them from starving, and Tommy started begging on the street corner. He found he often needed a drink to put his misery out of his mind.

Maria had the baby in their dinky room on dirty sheets. Tommy knew enough to wash her with warm water and keep her clean. In a few days, Maria and the baby girl were doing well. They agreed that Tommy should go to Denver and look for work. Maybe he would have a better chance there.

In Denver, Tommy skidded through a series of worse and worse jobs. There was not much demand for a carpenter who only knew how to make tapered coffins, which the grave diggers preferred because they required less digging. No one recognized that a man who had learned to saw both on a bias and an angle at the same time could be taught to make a pretty tight cabinet. When he went back to Greeley, he discovered that Maria had taken the baby and gone to Fort Robinson, looking for an old school acquaintance. And so Tommy drifted downward, until he skidded onto Larimer Street.

3

Tommy Turtle-back rammed his grimy hands into his pockets to see if he had any money left. Thirty-eight cents. Not enough for another drink. Not even enough for a bottle of Thunderbird. Even if he found someone who had a few cents and they put together enough to get a bottle, he'd have to share it with the bastard. He leaned against the building for support and gazed down the street. In the liquor store on the corner, a Budweiser sign flashed on and off. They had iron bars on the windows.

Fuckers! he thought. *They must think we're gonna sneak in and drink their sign.*

Along the street, several men were sprawled in doorways—blacks and chicanos, mostly, but also several Indians and a few white men. Some of them would have a bottle in a paper sack. Maybe he could find someone who was willing to give him a little drink. He stumbled along to the first one, holding onto the building for support.

"Hey, Buddy. Share a little with a friend?"

"Buzz off, Muthafucka. Git yer own boddle."

"Ain't got but thirty-eight cents." Immediately, Tommy realized he should not have said that. Some people would follow a man with thirty-eight cents and roll him. Maybe even do over his teeth or eyeballs.

But the man acted like he had not heard.

Clever bastard! thought Tommy. *He'll let me go on a ways, and think I won't suspect him, and then—wham!—he'll bend my skull.* Tommy stopped a few yards down the street and pretended to lean heavily against the building, so he could sneak a peek at the man.

The big black was lifting a paper sack to his mouth.

In the alley, Tommy saw three men sleeping on the asphalt in pools of their own urine. He knew there was no sense in asking them. They weren't even awake enough to understand what he said. He went through their pockets, but found nothing.

In a doorway further on, he came across someone he knew: Oscar White Owl. Oscar was clean-shaven, his hair was combed, and he had on a clean shirt. "Hey, Chief," said Tommy. "You been to church, or sumpin?"

"Salvation Army Mission," said Oscar. "They do this sort of thing to you. But damn! I need a drink. You got anything?"

"Not a thing," said Tommy. "A few cents in change."

"That's me," said Oscar. "That patent-leather Ojibwa gimme seventy-five cents at the mission. I'm supposed to get sumpin to eat. But, shit! How can a man eat, when he's as sober as I am?" Oscar scooted over, so Tommy could sit beside him on the step.

"At least, you're clean. Fine citizens passing won't curl their lip when they catch a glimpse of you."

"Yeah, and I smell funny, too. That goddam soap stays with you."

"Makes you smell like a customer," said Tommy.

It took Oscar a few moments to realize that Tommy was getting at something. "Go on," he said.

"Well, y'see. You go in that liquor store. And you browse around, like you can't find what you're looking for. And finally you ask the clerk for something that ain't on the shelf. And insist he go in back and look for it in the storeroom. As soon as he turns his back, I boom in and grab the first case of whatever is closest to the door. I zoom around to the back of Dempsey's Drugs and hide in their dumpster. Then you come and join me when you get rid of the clerk."

"Shit! What'll I ask for?"

"I don't know. Something that ain't there. Peach schnapps. Or some Manicheviez."

"Suppose he finds what I ask for?"

"Play persnickety," said Tommy. "Turn up your nose. Or say you don't think it's worth the money he's charging."

"Shit, Tommy. He'll see through it."

"Hell. Buy a pack of cigarettes. Or a candy bar. That'll restore his faith in his good, red-blooded, Indian customers."

"I don't know," said Oscar. "Seems awfully risky to me."

"Shit, you're just an innocent bystander. If they catch me, you don't know me. You've never seen me in your life. You'll be Joe College, as they haul me off to the pokie. At least, I'll get a meal and a bed. Maybe even a home for six months. It'll be just like home to me; it's been six years since I left the orphanage."

4

One midnight, in Grand Rapids, Michigan, Tommy Turtle-back climbed into a dumpster behind the College Arms to get out of the blizzard. He was surprised to find plenty of room. Out of habit, he felt around in the junk to see what he could find. Several cloth things: he tugged at something that seemed to be a curtain and spread it across his shoulders. God! It was good to sense a little protection against the cold!

He felt something like a broomstick, except it was soft and greasy; no, it was waxy. It felt like a candle. He lifted the hinged lid of the dumpster to take a look in the light of the street lamp. It was! It was a candle! He had a book of matches in his shirt pocket. If only the gusts from the crack around the dumpster lid didn't blow it out, he could have a little light. Maybe even a little warmth.

He managed to hold a match in his freezing fingers sufficiently firmly to strike. He lit the candle.

As the light drove back the darkness, he began to see what he had stumbled into. There were several small pieces of furniture: a small endtable, a chair with a fabric seat, a hooked throwrug, several textbooks (*Introductory Sociology*—he had already read that one; *The Story of Philosophy*—high schoolish; *The Little World of Don Camillo*—he'd never heard of that one; he set it aside to take with him), three drawers from a chest of drawers, and the broken chest in the far corner, a pillow, a blanket with a cigarette burn in it, various pieces of girls' clothing, including a pair of panties with holes in the seat. *Now, that cracker can really fart,* he thought.

Then he understood. It wasn't all just coincidence. Some nice girl had just graduated at the end of fall term and was moving out of her apartment—probably going home to Daddy for Christmas—and she threw away everything that wouldn't fit in her TRX. There would probably be food, still fresh from her refrigerator, if he looked deep enough.

Since he had been making his living at dumpster-diving, he had seen it happen a lot in June. But he hadn't seen it at Christmas time. It always bothered him that they were so extravagant in their waste. Didn't they know the Salvation Army would come and pick up usable things? Or Goodwill? A lot of people on the reservation could use things like these; there ought to be a way to get them from where they weren't wanted to where they were needed. *Shit, they could just take them to the inner city. There'd be plenty of people there to use 'em.*

Tommy pushed the chair upright and worked its legs down through the garbage. He could make it sit pretty straight. He sat down tentatively, half expecting it to tip and send him sprawling. Three-quarters of the things in his life had sent him sprawling.

He righted the endtable, dripped a little candle wax on it, and set the candle in the puddle, so he wouldn't have to hold it all the time. He cupped his fingers around the flame to get a little warmth in them. 'Oh, the weather outside is frightful,' he hummed.

He worked the blanket with the cigarette burn loose from its tangle and wrapped himself in it. Just like home, home on the range. He was an Indian again, wrapped in his blanket, but he didn't have a peace pipe to wave around when he gave his counsel. *Maybe the girl had thrown away an unfinished pack of cigarettes? No, she would have taken such necessities along!*

He flattened out the garbage on the floor of the dumpster and spread out the throwrug. He was practically ready to receive guests.

He pushed aside the curtain rods and the torn jeans. A broken bottle of hair conditioner, some shampoo, cosmetics, a compact with a broken mirror. And then he saw a box with bottles in it. He had to lift two of the drawers from the chest and push away the old toilet seat before he could get the box free. He set the bottles out on the throwrug: a 1.75 litre bottle of vodka, still three-quarters full, a bottle of peach schnapps, still unopened, a half bottle of seltzer water, and another of diet tonic. Something brown, but the label had been soaked off. *No cocktail glass?* he thought. "You inconsiderate bitch," he muttered, half aloud. "Why didn't you have the decency and foresight to at least throw away a cocktail glass?"

He opened the diet tonic. It was dead. The idea of seltzer in vodka didn't sit right with him. He opened the peach schnapps and took a sip. It was sweet, but also burned like hell. He hadn't felt a burn like that since Brother Bruno had given him his first drink. He smiled, wondering if a big gulp would make him vomit as spontaneously as he had that first time. Probably not; he'd poured a lot of shit across the cobble-stones of his stomach since then.

He opened the vodka and sniffed at it. It was all right, but he wished he had something to cut it with. He couldn't take vodka straight. No, he corrected himself, he didn't *want* to take his vodka straight. He poured some of the peach schnapps into the vodka bottle. *Bitch,* he swore, *where's the goddam orange juice?*

"Why don't you just ring for it, Tommy?" he said aloud to himself. "Let the butler or the maid bring in the orange juice. Use the silver bell on the mantle, but, gently please, I have a headache."

Yeah, he thought, *then the drink would be as fuzzy as Miss Rich Bitch's navel!*

He paused for a moment, thinking about her. He scratched around and found the panties again. He sniffed the crotch. Yeah, sure as hell, she had worn them. God! How long had it been since he had had a good screw? Too long. He lifted the vodka bottle and drank deeply, drank deeply to a good screw.

The liquor hit his empty stomach with turmoil, and he thought for a moment he was going to throw up. *Need some food,* he thought, feeling the smile go up the right side of his face. Naw, Oscar White Owl would say— *how long has it been since Oscar died? Only a year?* Oscar would say, 'Why ruin a fifteen-dollar drunk with a fifteen-cent sandwich?'

Tommy held the vodka bottle up and made a toast to Oscar: "Spoken like a serious drinker, Oscar." *God! Perforated liver!*

Not that he blamed Oscar. Neither of them had ever had a chance in this life. No one he knew had ever had a chance in this life. Except maybe the fucking priest. He had it dicked. Anything he wanted, he had it dicked.

"Holy shit, Tommy," he said aloud to himself. "You have a real talent for depressing me. You have a real talent for depressing everybody! Can't you think of anything cheerful?"

"The bird is on the wing, the poet says; drink to the happy bird."

He lifted the bottle and drank long and deeply again.

He had begun to feel the buzz of the booze, so the dumpster didn't seem as cold as it had. He placed the bottle on the endtable, carefully, so it wouldn't topple. What was he going to do with his life? Why hadn't he ever had a chance? Why had he run out on Maria and the baby? He had heard she was in California, making commercials for television. Wearing a doeskin dress and ersatz eagle feathers and selling—What was it, she was selling? He couldn't remember.

"Drink to your fucking success!" he yelled, grabbing the bottle again and jamming it into his mouth.

It wasn't a bad drink. He was getting to like it. He noticed that the level had gone down quite a bit in the bottle. He poured the rest of the peach schnapps in and tried it again. Yeah, not a bad drink. Maybe he'd invented something. Maybe he could sell the idea for a small fortune. He drank again. "Hey, ya, ya."

He lay down on the throw rug and drank again. Then he spread the curtain over him and doubled the blanket over his body. He felt snug. Like one feels in a great, good place. He hadn't been this warm all winter. He drank again. There was only a cup or so of liquid left in the bottle. *Maybe I should save something for breakfast,* he thought idly, then passed out. The candle sputtered, guttered, and died.

5

The next morning, Tommy was still comatose when the garbage

truck maneuvered around, ran its huge metal horns into the sockets on either side, and lifted the dumpster up over its head and back. It dumped all into the pit in the top of the truck. Then the hydraulic ram smashed back the trash, to make room for more.

When the truck was filled, the driver headed for the landfill area. The hydraulic rams pushed the garbage, untouched by human hands, out of the truck, and a bulldozer fourteen feet wide covered the debris almost at once with fresh dirt, to keep the seagulls from Lake Michigan from picking over the edible bits.

How Beans Make Decisions

Eddie NightWalker, a graduate agronomy student at the State Agricultural University, was stimulated by Professor Johnson's soils course. The old man obviously knew dirt. It's true, Eddie smiled with the others when Professor Johnson got poetic about the streaks of a tulip or the potency of a compost. But Eddie had grown up in the Qualla Boundary, near a crossroads and general store called Cornstalk; so he knew what Professor Johnson meant when he talked of the way a good soil would crumble in your hands, and he knew the feel of fecundity in it. Eddie understood the language of moist dirt.

Eddie was delighted when he learned that they expected him to do research, to add to the world's fund of knowledge, but even Professor Johnson smiled wryly when Eddie told him he wanted to study how beans make decisions.

"You talk like they were sentient," said Professor Johnson. "I mean, intelligent, like they had minds of their own. They're just beans."

"No. Yes," said Eddie, whipping his forelock back. "I mean, they know what they're doing. They don't sprout just anytime, but only when they've read—when they've determined that the circumstances are right. They know what they're doing ... and how to get it done."

Professor Johnson was not convinced.

"Look," said Eddie, his Adam's apple bobbing around uncomfortably. "All plants act like their basic motivation is to produce seeds to propagate the species. I mean, it's uh—it's their purpose in life."

Professor Johnson nodded.

Suddenly, Eddie could see, as surely as if he could touch it, the network of forces that drive the juices in beanstalks—the genetic magnetism that directs which nutrient to become which leaf, which bean; the cosmic magic of maturity and reproduction. And his nervousness was gone. "When we pick a crop of green beans," he said, "the plant promptly sets on a new crop of beans. The bean doesn't think it's feeding any starving children in India; it just thinks it's doing what it's supposed to be doing: making seeds. If the farmer doesn't pick a setting of beans, the plant will let the beans ripen and the vine die, because it thinks it's done its job. We depend upon the indomitable, ethereal will of beans to make beans."

Professor Johnson just stared at Eddie.

"You taught us yourself, Professor Johnson, that beans must have their elements. Each plant must have its earth, its oxygen, its nitrogen, its quantity of carbon dioxide. Each plant must have its warmth, its light from the sun, its water to live by, to tickle the chlorophyll into synthesizing plant food from mere air and dirt. When we loosen the ground with a hoe, we are talking to the beans. When we spray water from the sky, when we shade the bean patch or plant it near the exhausts of the freeway, we are talking to the beans. Everything we do is a message to them. I am determined to know the language of beans. For then I will know how beans make decisions."

"Sheeeze, Eddie," said Professor Johnson, shaking his head in acquiescence, "you might have become a good farmer, if you hadn't've got mixed up with beans."

Eddie acquired his passion for beans in his American Lit general education class, where the instructor awakened him one day by saying, "I am determined to know beans." Quickly, Eddie drew up his lanky legs and tried to reconstruct what was going on. The writer was Henry David Thoreau, who isolated himself in the woods around Walden Pond, where he planted thirty-four rows of beans, and the instructor was saying Thoreau's excuse was: "I am determined to know beans."

That night, Eddie pored through *Walden*, looking for the sentence. He never found it. So, after the next class meeting, he asked the instructor to point it out. "Oh, I don't think it's in the book," said the instructor. "I think it's in one of his diaries he was keeping at the time. Or maybe in a letter to Emerson. It's probably the source of our saying 'So and so doesn't know beans about such and such.' I'll look up the source for you, if you're really interested."

Eddie shook his head, letting the instructor off, for he had already discovered the meaning of it. He had read the book a second time and read it again that night, sensing his way by degrees into Henry's values: how Henry had gone to the woods to live deliberately; as determined to know life as completely as he was to know beans; convinced that to live was to suck the juice out of every experience, every piece of knowledge; to live as completely and as naturally as a bean; to know, when it came his time to die, that he had lived, lived truly, and had not been walking around his whole life dead.

In the library, Eddie looked up Thoreau's diaries, his other works, his letters to Emerson. As Eddie read those stirring commandments toward independence, knowledge, honesty to self, the continents and planets of his inner world began to stir and look for their orbits. Then, one day, the image of Emerson in a photograph opened its mouth and spoke to him, not with words, but with images of the farthest orbits of roots in their soil, the tendrils of stars in their places, and the spider webs of gossamer connecting them all.

Now, as Professor Johnson described a good friable soil, Eddie could feel the gossamer web of connections in the earth crumbling in his fingers, yet not being destroyed; he could smell the rich organic power, see along the tendons of its mere chemistry to the roots that thrust, parry, grunt, and cry with jubilation. Agronomy had given Eddie a whole new vocabulary that the farm where he grew up could not offer, and Thoreau gave him a will to see. Eddie jumped upon each new discovery with an ecstasy far greater than any explorer finding a new continent.

In time, this farm boy from a crossroads named Cornstalk, graduated in agronomy, with distinction, and won a fellowship that aroused the envy of his more urban, more social fellow students.

In a thousand trays of sprouting beans, he learned the temperature, water conditions, light, air, and nutrients that beans most wanted in order to sprout and grow.

In a thousand measuring cups, he mixed the fertilizers and measured the meals for his potted beans.

He ran out of laboratory space, so he lined his apartment with bean cases, then installed ultraviolet vegetation lights and row after row of floor to ceiling shelves across the room, until his apartment began to look like a library of beans.

He walked reverently up and down the aisles, eye dropper in hand, feeding each plant its diet, and he kept careful records.

He began talking to his beans, and they sent messages back to him. Each shining leaf was a message, each tilt of stem, each yellow streak along the leaf that said "I need more nitrogen," each red fleck that said "I need phosphorous," each burnt edge of leaf that said "Give me potash."

Eddie expected his beans to grow toward the source of light, as do all plants. And he was not disappointed. But his beans surprised him when he noticed they grew away from the rock 'n roll, disco, and reggae in the apartment to his right and toward the Beethoven in the apartment to his left. He moved a representative selection of his bean pots to a sound stage and, controlling all other factors, played them various kinds of music. It was true: beans disliked popular music and grew away from it, as if trying to escape. But they liked classical music, Beethoven better than Tchaikovsky, and leaned toward it, as if opening their little ears. They were indifferent to the folk tragedies of country western.

Professor Johnson scoffed and wouldn't even read Eddie's interim report on "The Musical Tastes of Beans." Eddie sent the article to a dozen professional journals, all of which also scoffed, except one offbeat editor who sent a Xerox copy to a friend who edited a literary journal that specialized in satire, *The Put-on Newsletter*, where the article was eventually published with only partial credit to Eddie. Three months later, it elicited a letter from the Bean Institute of Southwestern Colorado (BISWC), inquiring if he had any more such entertaining articles.

Eddie's central analysis, however, was crammed with arcane details, fully substantiated, and his dissertation, *Modus Deliberandi de Phaseolo Vulgari* (without, of course, the chapter "De Gustibus Musicis Fabarum"), was well received. A few people even read it, for it was fairly well written, Eddie having learned some principles of style by reading Thoreau. Professor Johnson even managed to parlay his protege into an entry-level teaching position at the State Agricultural University. "Anyone who can put that many beans in one pot can't be a bean-brain," he quipped, and his joke won over the hiring committee.

To everyone's surprise, including Eddie's, he loved teaching—and he was good at it. He knew agronomy well, and he spoke a language that boys and girls understood, from Cleveland to Belle Fourche, from Calgary to Corpus Christi. Once his initial nervousness subsided, his voice became smooth and his gestures strong. He spoke of the corn and beans, the earth and air, as if they were people with whom he had a personal relationship, as if they were partners to humans—and they came alive to his students. His Basic Agronomy class grew in the second and third weeks of the term until he had no desks vacant. His Soils Chemistry in the second term had to be moved to a larger room. His Bean Culture, a special study the department chair allowed with a snicker, enrolled more students than any special study in the history of the State Agricultural University. At the end of the year, an overwhelming number of students voted Eddie the best first-year teacher at the university.

"That's all well and good," said Professor Johnson, his arm across Eddie's shoulder, as they were on their way to a tête-à-tête lunch, "but you do realize, don't you, that that's not what you were hired for."

"Oh?" said Eddie, not realizing.

"Dammit, man, you've got to— Look," Professor Johnson took another approach, "have you quarried any articles out of your dissertation? I mean, other than that literary joke."

"It wasn't a joke," said Eddie, seriously, his throat twitching again.

"Dammit! You know what I mean."

"Well, no," admitted Eddie. "I sent the whole dissertation to a couple of university presses, but I don't think they publish dissertations called 'How Beans Make Decisions.' Of course, they say they can't print dissertations until they've been revised into a book. I thought mine was already a book."

"So it is. So it is. But that won't satisfy RTP."

"RTP?"

"The Retention, Tenure, and Promotion Committee. Where have you been? Don't you realize you're coming up for review?"

Eddie was silent.

"Look, Eddie. I like you; you're almost like a son to me. I want to see you get on here. So I'm going to tell you: this is the way it's done. You take a chapter or a segment out of your dissertation, write some jazzy introduction so it looks like an independent study; you renumber the footnotes, and send it out to a professional journal. If one of our friends is on the editorial board, they print it, and RTP is happy. Winning that teaching award won't hurt you, much, in the first year, because you're still on probation. But you've got to shape up—and not let it happen again."

Eddie took Professor Johnson's advice and revised several chapters from his dissertation. After a few months, two of them were accepted in third-rate journals, with the proviso that the jazzy introductions be stripped off.

"Well," sighed Professor Johnson, "I guess that's about the best we can do with beans."

Eddie won the Teacher of the Year Award in his second year, and a thousand students submitted a petition to make his Bean Culture class a regular offering in the curriculum and designate it as fulfilling one of the general education requirements in the philosophy of life.

RTP was not impressed, though they did give him an additional probationary year. The chairperson's letter acknowledged that "the committee recognizes that it sometimes takes a certain period of time for some candidates to adjust to academic life. It is hoped that the committee will be able to make a more favorable prognosis next year."

But it didn't happen. Though he continued to be a popular teacher, and though he managed to get two more chapters from his dissertation printed in friends' journals, RTP noted that "candidate has not initiated any new areas of research beyond the material that was in his dissertation" and granted him a "terminal year," a grace period to find another job elsewhere.

Eddie was disillusioned, of course. The only thing he knew was beans and dirt. But where in the world could one sell a knowledge of dirt and beans? Dismayed, he nevertheless continued watering and nurturing the beans on his thousand shelves. There, he could lose himself. There, amid the grunt of bean stems growing and bean leaves slapping the air, he could attain a degree of contentment. And he once again centered the orbits of his internal continents. And there, he began to realize that he had been untrue to himself. A bean never tried to be anything but a bean.

At that point, a middle-aged man in a plaid shirt and blue jeans knocked at his door. "Hi," he said, "Ah'm from Biswick."

"Pardon me?" said Eddie.

"Ah'm from Biswick. Y'know? The Bean Institute of Southwestern Colorado."

"Biswick?" said Eddie, not able to think of anything else to say.

"Yeah. We heard that you've been aholdin' out on us. We seen some of them other thangs you printed in them journals."

"Journals?"

"Yeah. Like this-un. 'Distress Signals that Beans Send.' You got any more little ditties like that?" The man was holding up a copy of a semi-popular journal that had printed one of Eddie's chapters with the jazzy introduction but without the renumbered footnotes. "Say, c'n Ah come in?" asked the man.

"Oh. Yes, of course," said Eddie. "Please excuse me. Excuse my manners."

"Oh, that's all raght," said the man. "No harm—" He stopped suddenly upon seeing the rows and rows of beans in Eddie's apartment. He walked forward, slowly, circling the end of one case, gazing at shelf after shelf of bean pots. "Golleeee," he said at last, "you shore got a lot of pets."

Eddie just shrugged. He didn't want to admit to a stranger that they kept him company on long evenings, comforted him in times of adversity, never asked to be treated as anything but what they were.

The man lifted a bean leaf with an index finger. "Hello, there, little feller. You're alooking mighty chipper." When he dropped the leaf to touch another, the leaf went on nodding. The man walked up and down, between the shelves of Eddie's library of beans, surveying the plants from ceiling to floor. "Yessir. Ah reckon Bill was raght. He ses to me, he ses, 'Jim'— that's me; Ah'm Jim— 'Jim,' he ses, 'Now, thare's a man that knows beans.' Ah reckon he was raght."

Eddie waited, not quite wanting to admit to himself that the man made him feel good about knowing beans.

"Well, le's get down to brass tacks," said Jim. "We know that you've done a whole, complete book about beans. We want to see that—if'n we can, that is."

So Eddie laid a copy of his dissertation on the coffee table, explaining that he himself did not know enough Latin to even re-translate the titles of the chapters, but he could tell Jim his original titles. "I called the whole work—" He paused, brushing his nose with the back of his hand, trying to wipe away his embarrassment. "I called it 'How Beans Make Decisions.' Of course, we can always change that. I've been told it's kinda dumb."

"Don't sound dumb t' me. 'How Beans Make Decisions.' That's kind of catchy. Good title, provided that's what the book is really about." Jim paused, his words hanging like a question in the air.

"That's exactly what it's about," said Eddie.

"Good. That's what Ah like t' hear. Le's quit beatin' around the bush, Mr. NightWalker. Biswick wants to consider publishin' your book as a premium for our members and people that loves beans everwher."

How Beans Make Decisions was printed in a gift edition of 40,000 in less than a month. There, on its slick pages, in language almost as smooth as music, farmers saw their own vague, inarticulate awareness of beans and dirt take root, sprout, and blossom into truths they could talk about. The book generated so much attention that a New York paperback house contracted to publish a trade edition on soy-coated paper, and the publisher asked Eddie to write a book on Zen and beans.

"But—but—I don't know anything about Zen," said Eddie.

"Oh, we think you do" was the publisher's response. "And what you don't know, we'll help you along with. We want you to spend some time with a Zen master we know."

When *Zen and the Art of Bean Culture* was released, the publisher got him a spot on *Donahue*. Again, once Eddie had wiped his forelock out of his eyes, his voice smoothed, then arced out to the remotest corners of TV land, embracing and linking the trajectories and orbits of human yearning, soothing and assuring hearts everywhere that there was purpose in the universe, just as there was purpose in beans and dirt. Twenty thousand people rushed out to buy the book on its first day.

When the book sold out its first edition to solidly appreciative reviews and Eddie had appeared on seventeen more talk shows and book news programs, he got another letter from the Retention, Tenure, and Promotions Committee. They had read his two books, found them solidly informed, as well as readable, and were now offering him tenure and simultaneous promotion to associate professor. "Why didn't you tell us," the chair of RTP added, "that you are a representative of an ethnic minority? This university affirmatively strives to recruit, retain, and promote members of underrepresented population groups."

"You mean you're an American Indian?" cried Professor Johnson, bursting through the laboratory door, where Eddie was feeding his beans. "Why the hell didn't you tell me? That would have fixed everything from the beginning!"

"It ought not to make any difference," said Eddie, after his momentary astonishment had passed. "Besides with a name like NightWalker and an address like the Qualla Boundary, I thought everybody would know."

"Sheeeze," said Professor Johnson. "Eddie, Eddie, Eddie ... And that reviewer in the *Times* said you're a goddam medicine man! A holy man, fer Christ's sake. A seer!"

"That part's not true," said Eddie. "That's just advertising hype." He went on, measuring each bean's diet with his eye dropper, noting in his records the quantity delivered to each.

"Put that stuff down," said Professor Johnson impatiently. "We've got to talk."

"But my beans— I've got to take care of—"

"Eddie, Eddie. Don't you realize you can have a couple of graduate assistants, now? You can hand over this—this— mechanical part of your experiments to others."

"But," said Eddie, feeling that something was tearing at his delicate and personal relationship with his beans. "I couldn't—"

How Beans Make Decisions

"Sure you could. We'll get you a first-rate bean-sitter for your babies."

The next day, a letter from the university president invited him to receive an honorary doctorate and deliver the featured address at commencement.

"I can't do that," Eddie told Professor Johnson. He was packing his books, getting ready to go back to Cornstalk, then on to Colorado.

"But, Eddie. It's your big chance."

"It's all sham. They're so full of hypocrisy."

"Oh, I wouldn't go so far as to say that," said Professor Johnson, rubbing his nose with the back of his hand.

"Tell me, Arnie," said Eddie, his heart hitting a couple of beats harshly because he had never before used Professor Johnson's first name, "Tell me, what makes my ideas different now, from what they were six months ago? Why was my research unacceptable then, but acceptable now?"

"Why, the exposure."

"But they're the same ideas. Exactly the same data, the same interpretations, the same conclusions, the same words. What changed all those votes on RTP? What gets me elected now, that lost me my job six months ago?"

Professor Johnson could only make a helpless gesture. "The reputation, dammit, the status. That makes it possible for you to say what you want to. Prestige is what makes people stop and listen."

"You mean the politics of reputation is what gets me elected? You mean that committee has no way of evaluating on its own, no way of making a decision, until some flag-waver comes by with a bandwagon, and then they all hop on? Don't they have minds of their own?"

"Sure, they've got minds. Some of the best minds of my generation, best minds of any generation."

They were both silent a moment.

"I know what you're thinking, Eddie. But look around, and you'll see art critics that can't distinguish chimpanzee finger paintings from art. Music critics can't distinguish street noise from music. Literary critics can't distinguish word salads from literary art. Why should you expect a group of agronomists to be different?"

"But don't they have an intelligent way of making a decision?"

Professor Johnson did not respond.

"Oh, I see," said Eddie. "When a culture loses its aesthetic and critical ability to distinguish failure from success, it no longer has any way of choosing what is successful. It has to get its decisions from somewhere else. So, there's where the politics of reputation serves. A voter no longer needs to know what is good and what is bad, or what is true; he only needs to know what is popular."

"You talk like they were sentient— I mean, intelligent, like they had minds of their own," he said. "They're just an academic committee."

"Why does it happen, Arnie? You take a group of men and women who are reasonably intelligent, put 'em on a committee, and they're not even as intelligent as beans," said Eddie. "That's why I can't accept—"

"But—but—the honor!" cried Professor Johnson.

"No," said Eddie. "An honor is not honor when it's offered by men and women who have to be lobbied into an opinion, men and women who have no opinion of their own and are incapable of evaluating mine. That's not an honor. That's less than an empty husk that was once a bean pod."

"But, Eddie, you can't—you can't just throw away your ..."

"My integrity?"

"No, dammit. Your chance. You've got a chance to change something now. With your reputation, you could work the system for some good. You could change RTP."

"Oh, I doubt that," said Eddie, turning to leave without saying goodbye. "There's not anything to work with. RTP is not even as intelligent as beans. The whole damned culture is not even as intelligent as beans!"

Ghost-Face Charlie

1

Chay-li stood in the Post Oak trading post behind an old grandmother, examining his knuckles and waiting his turn. He needed some .22 shells so he could hunt cottontails for table meat; he hoped they had hollow points. The grandmother had bought four yards of red and black calico, but kept shoving the change, a fifty-cent piece on the counter, back toward the clerk and holding up five fingers. The clerk had counted the yards out on his fingers, using his pidgin Comanche and saying "one-bit, two-bits, three-bits, four-bits; four bits and four bits makes a dollar." And he would push the fifty-cent piece toward the old grandmother again.

They had been through the routine three times, when Chay-li spoke up. "She wants her change in dimes, so she can give each of her grandkids a present."

"Well, why didn't she say so?" exclaimed the clerk. He put five dimes on the counter and swept away the fifty-cent piece.

Immediately, Chay-li turned his hands so he could look at his palms, but he kept his attention on the women and girls sitting around the hot potbellied stove behind him. They had all stopped talking. Wer-tah-ne, the girl he hoped to marry someday, if he could ever get the dowry together, glanced up, then quickly back down. The grandmother gave no sign of recognition. She tucked the cloth under her arm and turned to take her place at the stove with the other women and girls.

"So, Chief," said the clerk. "What can I do for you?"

Ashamed, Chay-li turned toward the girls to indicate that surely some of them were next in line.

"That's all right," said the clerk. "They're givin' up their turn to a man."

Chay-li said nothing. The girls and women were all looking at the stove or the splintered wooden floor beside it, but he knew they were watching him intensely.

"So you're one of those who've been to school up at Chilocco, hunh? Got a education 'n all, but I see you've let your hair grow long again. You know nobody's goin' to hire you in 1921, lookin' like that, don't you?"

Blindly, Chay-li studied his hands. They were too soft; he needed more callouses if he was going to do any work.

The clerk was getting impatient. "So what can I do for you, Charlie?" When Chay-li did not respond, the clerk went on. "Come on, now. I ain't got all day. I know you talk good English, probbly better'n me. Why, I'll bet you can even cipher up to the rule of threes. They taught you all that up there at Chilocco, di'nt they?"

Chay-li turned away, humiliated, speaking Comanche loud enough for the women and girls to hear clearly, so they could take the report back to Our People. "I didn't learn anything up there. I forgot it all. It was all a waste of time."

He pushed through the door and out into the snow. He'd have to hunt in the old way until he could come back when no one was around. Or maybe he could get someone else to buy bullets for him. He rejected the idea, even before it formed, of having one of the younger boys or old men buy them for him. But, a woman—a woman would work. Maybe he could get his mother to buy ammunition for him. Maybe his sister, Raylene. Or his aunt Elsie Sparrowfoot. She could be trusted not to say anything about it.

In his anger, Chay-li pulled his jacket closer and scrunched his neck down to try to keep warm. The clerk had made him look foolish in front of Wer-tah-ne. She had been to Chilocco, too, so she would understand every word said in both languages.

Maybe he should get out of this part of the country, the way they urged up at the school. Leave Oklahoma. Get work somewhere. Quanah's son who had been to Carlisle did that. Married the missionary's daughter on her condition that they leave. He had built up a good drayage business in Florida, folks said, and made a good living for himself and his family. Of course, he was a quarter white to begin with. He could pass easier than a person like Chay-li.

At home, his mother, father, and sister were getting ready to go to a Comanche Eagle doctoring. "That Oscar Scott's boy, Willie, has the ghost sickness," his mother announced. "He thinks he got it in France during the Great War, but— if you want to know what I think— I think there aren't any Comanche ghosts in France. That boy got caught by a ghost right here in Oklahoma. Comanche ghosts don't have anything to do with France. And they don't have anything to do with anybody but real Comanches. That shows he ain't got no mixed blood in him, if he can get the Comanche ghost sickness."

His father just scoffed, but went out to hitch the team to the wagon anyway. Chay-li went out with him. His dad recognized that he wanted to say something and stood waiting.

Chay-li hesitated because he felt like a traitor. Tentatively, he said, "I've been thinking of leaving this part of the country, maybe going to Oklahoma City. See if I can't find work."

His father said nothing for a long moment, as Chay-li had expected. "You know what your mother would say: you ought to stay right here, find you a good doctor that's willing to train you and pass on some of his medicine. Become maybe an Eagle doctor, like she's wanting for herself and Raylene."

"You know I can't do that, Dad. Besides, you know as well as I that all the real doctors choose their apprentices, not the other way around. I don't believe in all that witch doctor stuff, anyway."

"Hmmpf!" grunted his father. "Is that what they taught you up at that white-man school?"

"No, Dad. You know I—" He broke off, frustrated. How could he tell his father about the logic of cause and effect? How could he tell him about evidence and superstition? How dare he talk back to an elder of the tribe that way?

When his father had finished hitching up the team, he said: "Go help your mother and Raylene with their baggage. She's taking enough clothes and food for us to stay several days. She figures this doctoring will take at least three or four days."

"Don't you have to go to work, Dad? Did you get word to the Johnson Ranch that you'd be away for a few days?"

"Nope. They'll just have to understand that a man sometimes has important things to do, other than work. There's no way I could get out of this doctoring, you know that."

"Mr. Johnson'll say you're just another lazy Indian. Didn't want to work anyway."

When his mother had adjusted her bags in the wagon to her satisfaction and she and Raylene had climbed up on the seat, Chay-li's father motioned for him to come back into the house. His dad went to the cabinet where he kept his liquor, reached around behind the bottles, and brought out a Prince Albert can. He pulled a twenty dollar bill out of the can and handed it to Chay-li.

Chay-li looked at it, amazed. He had seen twenty dollar bills a few times in his life, but he had never held one.

"And don't stop in Oklahoma City," said his father. "Go on to some place where the white man doesn't hate Indians."

Chay-li choked up, tears pressing the back of his eyelids. How could he say thanks? How could he accept his father's secret cache? How could he leave after such a show of love?

"And don't be around here when we get back," his dad went on. "If she even hears wind of this, she'll cedar-smoke you till you can't get your breath."

His dad turned and went out, but paused at the door. "Write the missionary once a year or so. He'll come out and read your letters to us in Comanche." Then he went on, without saying good luck or goodbye.

Chay-li put all his clothes in a potato sack, saddled his horse, and left. He went by Wer-tah-ne's parents' lodge. They were one of the few families that still lived in a tipi, though there wasn't any buffalo skin to cover it. They had pieced together fragments of wagon sheets and sailcloth.

"I've got to get out of here," Chay-li told Wer-tah-ne in English, so her parents would not understand. "I'm going somewhere where I can earn a living, make enough to have decent clothes on my back and keep warm in winter. I want you to come with me."

Wer-tah-ne would not look at him. A Comanche girl did not normally look at or speak to a man not of her immediate family.

"We can get the missionary to marry us on the way out," Chay-li went on, becoming desperate. "We'll leave all this behind"—he made a sweeping gesture to take in the tipi, the wooden shack where his parents lived, the wide expanse and rolling hills—"We'll make a better life for ourselves somewhere."

But Wer-tah-ne would not go. She wanted Chay-li to bring dowry presents to her father, to bargain with him in the old Comanche way that almost no one nowadays kept up. She wanted to dress in a white doeskin dress that had been her grandmother's. She wanted her father to put her hand in Chay-li's and Chay-li to lead her away to the wedding lodge. If Chay-li would not marry her that way, she would just have to wait until another young man came along who would.

2

Charlie snapped off his alarm and lay back on his cot. The pre-dawn light seeped in at the window. Thank goodness, it was getting warmer. The winds off Lake St. Clair were less biting now, and the storms off Lake Huron were fewer. But the freeze and thaw cycles were irritating. No sooner did your body begin to expect a spring warming, than—bang—the world hit you with another freeze. That was the way life was: the world was always hitting you with something you didn't expect.

He sat up and groped for his shirt and pants. He didn't have time to lie back and think. Thinking just got you in trouble anyway. He had to fill his water jug, fix himself a sandwich, and find a piece of fruit, then walk the mile and a half to the assembly plant where he put bolts in the fenders of black Model-T Fords. He had been doing that for over two years. He had only missed two days, once when he had the flu. His foreman said he did good work, and the money was good. He had even sent twenty-dollar bills to his dad three times. He just hoped the missionary had given his dad the money. In Oklahoma, he would never have doubted that the missionary would be honest. But life in Dearborn was different.

He had heard from the missionary only twice: once to tell him that Wer-tah-ne had married Willie Scott, and once to tell him that his father had been trampled to death by a bronco in an accident at the Johnson Ranch. Both times, the loss and despair had given him a pain in his neck that wouldn't go away until he was treated by a rubbing doctor.

His neck was hurting again, right down where it blended into the curve of his back. He hunched up his shoulders and rolled his head around, stretching and flexing to get the pain out. Maybe he'd have to go to that chiropractor again. Get his bones adjusted.

The tension in his neck and shoulders was slow to leave this morning, so he kept stretching and rolling his head as he walked to work. He quickened his pace, then slowed down. Why would a pain in the neck make him think he was going to be late for work? He hadn't been late to work in two years, except those two days he missed when he was sick, and then he managed to stop the black man who lived further beyond the edge of town and sent the foreman word that he had the flu.

Erastus, the black man, had life even worse than Charlie. He lived in a rundown shack with a skinny wife and several children—Charlie had never been able to count them accurately. At work, he sat apart and ate his lunch with the janitors, and said "Yassuh" and "No-suh" to the other workers on the assembly line. But he had a good heart and was honest. When Charlie had the flu, he and his skinny wife had shown up right after lunch. She made strong, hot lemonade, laced it with cheap whiskey, and forced Charlie to drink it all as quickly as he could. Then she wrapped him in a hot mustard plaster and kept him bundled under more quilts than he needed. His head spun, he had hallucinations of an Eagle doctor chanting, and he sweated more than he ever had in his life. But he felt better the next day, and he was able to return to work the day after that.

Funny, that thinking of the skinny wife should remind him of the times he had put on a shirt and tie and taken the bus to Detroit on Sundays and walked along the streets, looking for something to do. The stores had all been closed, of course, so he couldn't as much as buy a new hat. But the people were closed, too. He'd smiled at the men as they came down the steps of their churches and tipped his old hat, the way the teachers had shown him at Chilocco, but he could almost see something—a door, something as big as a garage door—closing in their eyes. The women sometimes acted almost as if they wanted to smile and say hello, but a man in his position didn't dare acknowledge such a gesture in another man's woman.

The pain in his neck was making him dizzy, so he quickened his pace. Maybe he could walk it out. A thin hoar frost lay on the neat yards he passed, and on the roofs, except where the heat from a chimney or flue had melted it. It made the houses seem uninviting, as if the doors and windows were frozen shut. He knew some of the men who lived in the neighborhood, men who worked on the line at the plant. They always joked with him and called him "Chief" at the plant, but not one of them had ever invited him into his house. I probably wouldn't have known how to behave anyway, thought Charlie.

When he got to the plant, he was sweating too much and breathing too fast. The foreman was the only one there. "Geez, Chief. You buckin' for a raise or something?"

Charlie tried to act surprised, to say "Really? Am I early?" But he could hear that his voice came out in a fog. His heart lurched with fear.

The foreman turned then to look at him more closely. "Jeeee-sus, Charlie. What's wrong? If it wasn't so early and I didn't know you don't drink, I'd say you was drunk. What's the matter?"

Charlie could feel the right side of his face hanging limp. He felt himself panting. He could feel his scared heart beating. "I don't know," he tried to say, but he could hear that the words were slurred.

"Come on," said the foreman. "I'll take you over to the dispensary. Doc won't be there yet, but maybe we'll just have to call him in early. Maybe the nurse will have an idea of something to do."

By the time they got to the dispensary, Charlie's right arm was twisted up in a painful cramp. It was bent at the elbow, the wrist was flexed all the way, and his fingers were contorted out backwards. He couldn't move the arm. It and his face were paralyzed.

The nurse took him into an examining room, where his reflection in a mirror shocked him to a standstill. His right eye wouldn't close, and it was watering so much that tears were streaming down his face. He couldn't feel them. His mouth drooped on the right side, slack and slobbery, and his face hung loose, like dead, gray flesh.

The nurse pulled him toward the examining table. "Does it hurt anywhere? Do you feel anything?"

He managed to indicate his neck with his left hand.

"Why there's a knot at the base of your neck as big as my fist!" said the nurse. "It must be pinching every muscle and nerve you've got."

The nurse went out to the anteroom to call the doctor. Charlie could hear her insisting "emergency" to the doctor. The foreman stood by the door, waiting, helpless. Trembling inside, Charlie tried to tell him that everything would be all right, but he couldn't talk plain.

And he wasn't sure that everything *would* be all right. That was a Comanche ghost he had seen in the mirror. His mother was wrong. A Comanche ghost had somehow gotten out of Oklahoma, flown all the way to Dearborn, and caught Charlie by the soul. He was sweating and panting, hyperventilating with the fear.

The doctor arrived shortly. "Yes," he said, and "ummmm," and "I see."

"You were right, Nurse," he concluded. "The muscular cramp and probably the vertebra is pinching the seventh cranial nerve. Bell's palsy, it's called. Usually involves varying degrees of paralysis. No known cause. No known bacteria or virus associated with it. Probably of psychosomatic origin. Usually goes away after a few hours, especially with massage and a calming of the patient. Put a hot compress on the neck and massage his face, arm, and shoulder. Talk sweet to him, so that the hysteria abates."

He went out with the foreman. "Strange," Charlie heard him telling the foreman. "Usually only see these symptoms in soldiers that've been shell-shocked. It's a psychological thing."

The nurse kneaded Charlie's neck through the hot compress and gently stroked his face, occasionally flexing his arm. "I'm going to tell you about when I was a little girl," she said. "I grew up on a farm in

Iowa, where I had the most wonderful parents. I had the sweetest dolls to play with. My dad wanted me to go on to school and make something of myself, but I still wish I was back there on the farm. The sky was so big, the sun was so warm. Nothing ever seemed bigger than you could deal with...."

Slowly, over a couple of hours, Charlie's face straightened up again, his arm relaxed. By lunch time, though his muscles ached with strain, he was able to go back to work on the assembly line.

3

Not much had changed in Oklahoma. The same dust covered Charlie's shoes and pant legs as he walked along the same winding road. His mother seemed to be scolding the same flock of chickens and milking the same old cow. The shack had decayed some: more boards were split or missing; the parts near the ground had rotted a little more. The same sun burned in a bald sky.

He cast his eyes down in shame and deference as his mother came out to meet him in the road. He showed her the knot on his neck. "I've got the ghost sickness, *pia*. I need a good Eagle doctor."

"That one over by Post Oak died," she said. "But he passed his power on to Raylene. I don't know whether she's any good or not. And, of course, we won't know until she's lived past her month-sickness. She didn't *want* to take the power, so that's a good sign."

"I'm sorry," said Charlie. He knew how much his mother wanted the Power to choose her.

"We all just do what we can," she said. "You stand right here. I'll go get some cedar."

After a moment, his mother returned with a wand of smoldering cedar in her hand. Chanting the purification prayer, she puffed smoke across the wand onto Charlie's chest, then moved the wand up and down, along his legs, across his back, under his arms, letting the smoke get at the body and cleanse it. She got him to breathe a bit of it, and he choked. "That's good," she said, "get it all over your soul." Finally, she was willing to touch him and let him touch her. "Welcome home, Chay-li," she said.

"I'll fix up the house some," he said thankfully, picking up his suitcase and following her into the house.

Raylene sat at the table, sorting her medicines and rolling them in small bundles. She got up and put her hand on Charlie's arm. "I'm sorry, Sis," he said honestly, putting his hand on top of hers. He didn't know how to express his feelings. Choosing to become an Eagle doctor meant that Raylene would not marry and would have to live a life of intense training, but she would not be allowed to practice until after her menopause.

"It's okay," she said. "There isn't anyone I want to marry right now anyway. Or maybe I'll get married in a few years, raise a bunch of kids, and come back to doctoring in my old age. That's permitted, you know." With her free hand, she patted his hand on hers. "Anyway," she went on in English, "Welcome back to the land of a thousand ghosts." He put his hand over the knot on his neck, as if it were one of the ghosts.

The next day, he went to the Post Oak trading post to buy .22 shells, thinking he would hunt a little for table meat. There was a new clerk there, a young man about his own age. Chay-li pretended he didn't know more English than a word at a time and a grunt. He pointed to make the clerk understand what he wanted. The women and girls sitting around the cold pot-belly didn't even pause in their chatter, acting as if they did not recognize him. Maybe it was the short hair, he thought, feeling inadequate; he would let it grow again, maybe even long enough to make braids.

Outside, along the street, it was obvious that all the houses and stores belonged to white people. When he looked in at storefronts, he saw that most of the customers were white, too. Both shopkeepers and customers looked at him angrily, like he was a stranger, an intruder. He felt abandoned. There were a few Comanches sitting in wagons, their teams tied to storefront hitching posts. None of the Comanches seemed to recognize Charlie either. Not even the drunks.

Mr. Johnson saw him and made a point of reigning in. "Sorry about your dad, Charlie. He was a good man. A good worker, a credit to his race."

Angry and proud at the same time, Charlie hardly knew what to say.

"Come on around when you get settled in and get ready to work," said Mr. Johnson. "I need a rider that can talk both languages."

"I got the ghost sickness," said Charlie apologetically, rubbing the knot on his neck.

"Pshaw!" scoffed Mr. Johnson. "I thought you were too smart for that kind of crap." He turned and rode away.

In the driveway of the abandoned livery stable, Charlie found Willie Scott. He was drinking. He offered Charlie a drink from his bottle. Repulsed, Charlie waved it away.

"What kind of friggin' Indin are you that don't drink?" asked Willie in slurred English.

"What went wrong, Willie?"

"Nothin went wrong. Everthang went wrong. Whattya mean, wrong?"

"They cedar-smoked you, didn't they? They cured you of the ghost-face, didn't they?"

"Sure. Made me into a real good Indin again."

Charlie was impatient with Willie. "Well, if you don't like it, you could get out. You're a veteran and all. Speak good English. You could cross over. You could go anywhere you want, do whatever you want."

"You think sho? I tried all that. They won't let me haf—have a friggin' job. They won't let me have a spo—lottment of land. They won't let me do any—any thang, 'cept drink. They want me be a friggin' drunk Indin. I'm best damned friggin' drunk Indin in this whole territory. They won't let me be a white man. They won't even let me live at the edge of town."

"Yeah, I know a little about that," said Charlie, patting Willie sympathetically on the shoulder and turning to leave. "But I don't seem to fit in here either."

Walking along the street, Charlie felt his hands shaking, and he was breathing too fast. He walked even faster, for he suddenly had a senseless fear that someone—one of the men in the storefronts, or several of them—was about to run out into the street, his hands splayed in the air, his mouth open and screaming. Or one of their daughters would streak out, naked and shrieking, leap on Charlie, throw him to the ground, and rip his entrails out with her fingernails. And all he could do was howl, "I haven't been late to work. Honest, I haven't been late to work."

By the time he got home, Charlie had ghost-face again. His face was slack and paralyzed, as before. The knot in his neck had swollen, and his hand and fingers tingled. His mouth twisted over to his left side. He was breathing too fast, hyperventilating, sweating profusely, and trembling with fear.

His mother sounded almost happy. "I've been expecting this. I'll call in that Eagle doctor from Medicine Park. He has a good reputation for curing ghost sickness. He uses Raylene as his assistant."

Together, the three undressed Charlie and left him lying on the bed in his shorts. Together, they wafted smoldering cedar wands around his body, until the room was so full of smoke that they all had coughing spells. After chanting prayers all morning, the doctor washed Charlie's face with warm water, then applied his mouth to his cheek, sucking out the sickness. "I'm going to suck that ghost into myself," he said, crooning. "You're going to be all right. Everything's going to be all right. I'll suck that ghost right out of your face and then I'll spit him out. I got the Power, so he won't hurt me. I got the Power, so I'm going to fix him so he can't catch anybody else." He brushed Charlie's face with his eagle feather, coaxing the ghost to the surface; then he sucked gently on Charlie's cheek to pull the ghost out.

He gave Raylene a feather and said, "You rub the knot with that real softly. That'll pull that old ghost right into the feather. And when we get him into the feather, we'll burn that ghost and bury his ashes under a cedar tree. We'll fix him so he can't catch any more Comanches."

Twenty or so families had shown up in old wagons and were camped in the yard and pasture. Charlie's mother kept cooking for them and giving them the news of the treatment. By the second day, Charlie's face was straight. By the third day, the knot on his neck had begun to go down. Raylene and the Eagle doctor were rubbing it right out of existence.

On the fourth day, near evening, some drummers arrived and started a dance. Chay-li was able to put on a breechclout that had belonged to his grandfather and proudly dance the male lead. Raylene, in a doeskin dress, danced the female lead. The whole community fell in behind them and danced around the drum until dawn. The knot in Chay-li's neck seemed to be gone for good. Dancing around the drum in a doeskin breechclout, he felt more like a real Comanche than he had since leaving for boarding school.

All night, Chay-li's mother went among the people, handing out food and smoking them with her cedar wand. "A real Comanche," she kept saying. "Those old ghosts don't chase anybody but real Comanches."

Dillie's Den

As soon as we entered Dillie's Den, the woman from California zoomed to a black-on-black pot in the Maria Martinez style. As Dillie, the shopkeeper, explained Maria's unique process of hand firing, none of us could help overhearing that she spoke excellent English and knew her business well. I smiled at her, trying to convey my admiration. The woman from California decided to buy two of the pots. As she was digging in her plastic purse for money, she said to Dillie, "You speak such good English. Did you go to a white school?"

"Yes," said Dillie, smiling and accepting payment from the woman. "After Albuquerque Indian School, I went to New Mexico State, then the University of Michigan." She rang up the sale, gave the woman her change, plus a business card with "Diligence Ci-yáh-n-ree" printed on it. She started wrapping the pots in corrugated material, packing them for travel.

"My goodness," said the woman from California. "How in the world did you manage all that?"

Dillie paused in her pot packing and looked at the woman, as if trying to decode her meaning.

"I mean," the California woman went on, "Did you get some sort of government subsidy to go to boarding school? My son was turned down, so we had to pay ourselves. It's getting so, if you're not red, black, brown— uh— I mean, a lot of preference is going to minorities these days."

Dillie looked at me— why me? I don't wear any badges of my remote Indian background— as if I could explain the woman; I shrugged and smiled again.

Then Dillie began a roundabout story, in the Indian fashion, which she had obviously told before:

"About eighty years ago this fall— I was five years old, I think— about twenty-five white men came to our pueblo one day. My mother and the other women hovered near their doors, asking each other, 'Who are they?' and 'What do they want?' But nobody knew.

"I remember hanging onto a fold in my mother's dress and peeking out at them. Some wore silver stars on their vests, which frightened me. I couldn't speak any of their language. I had no idea what white men did to people. There were some Indian police with them, but they were Apaches, not from our tribe. Three men in business suits and two women in long, gray skirts were in charge.

"At first, the strangers with silver stars on their chests didn't say anything to anyone. I'm sure that some of our elders asked them why they had come, but none of us knew. The boss man in the suit walked right past our Head man and gave a signal to the police and marshals. He just lifted his arm and waved them on."

Dillie imitated the motion with her own wiry arm. Her body was shriveled, but firm and stringy, as if she worked out on a regular basis to keep herself vigorous, even at her age. Her off-white jersey dress with a single turquoise brooch and silver conch belt called attention to her small waist.

"Suddenly, the U.S. marshals began seizing children and forcing them into the middle of the plaza. The Indian police formed a ring around the children. One of them grabbed me, tore me from my mother's skirt, and put me in the group.

"Some of the marshals began going from house to house, bursting right in, often coming out with another child. They were snatching everyone from about age five, up to fourteen or fifteen."

Dillie looked up, gazing at nothing, as if her eyes were fixed on that scene eighty years before and she were there, not here in Dillie's Den, an upscale, open, well-lit art shop on the plaza in Taos, where the silver in glass cases gleamed with workmanship and the best pottery was displayed on pedestals with individual spotlights. I recognized paintings by Gorman, Begay, and Oliver.

"I screamed for my mother: 'What have I done? What's wrong?' But I couldn't hear if my mother answered. There was so much noise, so many of the children crying and screaming. One of the older boys darted to escape; the police hit him and knocked him down. Then they picked him up and shoved him back into our herd.

"The marshals and Indian police tightened the circle around us, keeping us in and our parents out. I heard my aunt screaming, 'What's wrong? Why are you doing this?'

"I had been separated from all the children I knew well. I thought they were going to kill us. I screamed and peed my pants at the same time. As I wailed, I became aware that someone was shouting to me—calling to me by name—talking loud in our own language above the uproar. I recognized the voice of my grandfather.

"I looked around to see where he was. He was a very old, stooped, bowlegged man in braids and a black hat. He wore baggy white man's clothing and a white dance apron over his pants, but he was standing as straight as I have ever seen a man stand. Carrying a feather prayer fan in his right hand, he stood back away from the circle of marshals and police, not looking toward us children. I realized he didn't want the white men to know he was talking to one of us, even though neither our white guards nor the Apache police knew our tribal language. He acted as if he were shouting at some deaf thing in the sky."

Dillie paused and looked out the window again. I could tell that she was blinking back a tear. "Yes, yes. Go on," urged another lady from Cincinnati. Dillie worked at wrapping the pottery the California woman was buying.

"Grandfather talked loud, so I would hear him above the screaming and crying of the other children and the wailing mothers." She paused, straightened up, and for a moment became that old grandfather.

"'Daughter, the white man seems all-powerful. There is nothing we can do to help you. They are going to take you away and put you in school. They won't really harm you. They want to teach you the white man's way. If you run away, they will chase you and catch you. They will take you back and punish you.

"'There is one way you can defeat the white man. Learn everything well he tries to teach you. Learn everything about the white man's way. Learn to speak his language. Then you will have defeated the white man. You will be as wise as he is in his way; and he won't like it, because you will know also the Indian's way.'

"I stopped my sobbing. I stood up straight, as straight as my old, old grandfather, and I tried to look proud and do as he told me. I never saw him again, but I can see him now, standing there, waving his feathers at the sky and praying for us at the top of his voice."

She worked for a moment at her wrapping table, then looked up, made eye contact with the lady from Cincinnati, and went on.

"They took us by hack and wagon to a railroad station— I don't know where it was— and mixed us in with other Indian children. Then we were put on the train. I was thrown in with an Apache girl about my size and age. We looked at each other a long time, each unable to break the silence. I could see tears forming in her eyes, and I know from my blurred vision that I was about to cry, too.

Then when we did try to speak, we couldn't understand a word of each other's language. I tried combinations containing 'scared' and 'devil' and 'crying,' but none of them made any sense to her. Nor did her words, whatever they were, make any sense to me. We both screamed and cried out when the train lurched and started to roll. She told me later that she thought they were taking us some place to slaughter us.

"Then a matron from the Indian school came by with a basket. She was handing out chunks of a brown loaf and saying 'bread' to each child. I did as my grandfather had told me. I repeated 'pread.'

"'That's right, dear,' said the smiling matron, though I didn't know that was what she said. 'Bread.' She emphasized the 'B'. 'The staff of life.'

"The Apache girl and I took the food and began eating, for we were so hungry we thought they were intent on starving us. I suppose she wondered, as I did, if they were trying to poison us with the bread, but I was so hungry I ate it anyway.

After the first few bites, when the edge of my hunger had dulled, I looked at my travel companion. She was eating fast, too. 'Bread,' I said.

"At first, she didn't respond. So I pointed at my bread and said again, 'Bread.'

"'Pread?' she asked.

"'Bread,' I repeated. I don't know if I got the pronunciation right or not. But she understood.

"'Pread,' she said, beginning to smile.

"I broke off a bit of my bread and gave it to her."

Dillie pinched off some of her imaginary bread, leaned across the counter, and gave it to me. I took the part of the Apache girl and gave her a pinch of mine.

"That's right. She did the same. She gave me a pinch of her bread. And we sat there in silence for a moment, eating the bite of each other's bread.

"'Pread?' she said, reaching over and touching my shoulder.

"'Bread,' I agreed, and I leaned my forehead across to touch hers.

"'Pread,' she murmured and snuggled down against my side.

"We finished eating and huddled together in the corner of the wooden bench; we finally fell asleep from the exhaustion that fear brings.

"When we got to the school, the matron stripped off our clothes and gave us a bath. I had gone naked in public a good part of my life— I was only a very little girl— but this bath embarrassed me terribly. I understood that the matron was scrubbing us with kerosene because she thought we had lice and would spread vermin or pestilence if left alone. She dressed us in little print dresses, and I never saw my own clothes again.

"The matron put my new friend and me into a dormitory room with two older girls, a Lakota from South Dakota and a Comanche from Oklahoma, neither of whom spoke either of our languages. The Comanche girl was sad and sour because she was so unhappy at the school, but the Lakota girl took my friend and me by the hand, led us to the dining hall, and showed us how to eat with a spoon and fork. The matron called her 'Sally,' but I never knew what her Indian name was. The food was some sort of ground cereal—a dumpling that clumped up like mashed potatoes—in a meatless stew. I don't think I could have eaten it, but Sally kept urging us and tasting it herself to show us it wasn't poison.

"In the dormitory room, my friend and I were each given a narrow cot and a couple of blankets. I had never slept alone in my life. I could always count on the warmth and presence of my parents, or an aunt, or an old dog, or someone. I was petrified. I sat up straight in the dark, my eyes as big as my pajama buttons. I was struggling not to cry like my friend and traveling companion, whom we could all hear sobbing in the dark. Sally understood and took us both into her bed with her. She talked softly, in a language neither of us understood, and yet we understood everything she said, including that we would have to learn to sleep alone, that we would have to learn to be strong, that the matron would punish us all if she found us in Sally's bed."

Dillie worked a moment at her wrapping table. When she had control of her voice again, she looked up.

"In time, I learned to speak English without an accent, and I mastered every course they offered me, whether it was home-making or chicken feeding. I behaved properly, and they let me start taking the academic courses. The white people treated me well, always finding scholarships for me when I needed one and encouraging me to go further. I worked so hard the matrons gave me the name, Diligence, but I kept also my Keres name, Ci-yáh-n-ree, which means 'She is Alive.' Like Sally, I was able to help many Indian children adjust to the white man's school."

The California woman reached across the counter, lay her hand on the back of Dillie's, and said, "You must have wished very much that you were born white."

Dillie looked at the woman a moment, as if she were a Spanish Conquistador, stepping ashore for the first time. Then she continued with a hint of fury in her voice. "I got a teaching credential, only to learn that white people would not let an Indian teach in their schools. I got a certificate in bookkeeping and typing, only to learn there are no jobs for Indians in the white man's commercial world. When I got a degree in art history, I decided to go into business for myself, here in my home country. It has been hard to learn the ways of the white man, but I have come to agree that iron pots are better for cooking than earthenware, that carpets are better than clay floors. Windows are desirable for light and ventilation. Medications and health are better than illness and grief. The money I earn and the commissions I pay my Indian artists are preferable to the poverty and pain the white man made our lot when I was a small child."

She picked up the finished package and placed it in the California woman's hands.

"But never—never have I wanted to be a white person. Never have I forgiven the white man for the brutal way they rounded up us children and shipped us away from our parents."

The California woman turned the package to look at it and found it satisfactory. "The tour is taking us out to the D.H. Lawrence and Mabel Dodge house this afternoon," she said brightly. "Do you know if they've got a good souvenir shop out there? I want to buy a plastic tomahawk for my nephew."

A man from Oklahoma, who lived on land thrice confiscated from Indians, put down his intended purchase and stalked out, announcing loudly, "I've had about all I can take of this Great White Father Guilt Trip."

Betjegen

Betjegen wiped the steel drain board once more, glanced proudly at the thirty-two quarts of green beans she had canned that day, and strolled into the livingroom. Erik was leafing through a copy of *Farm Journal*, and Mary Lou, his wife, was looking at *TV Guide* to see what was on. It was Erik who noticed the Indian staring in the window—a short, gaunt face under a traditional red cotton headband. It was Betjegen's brother from the reservation.

Betjegen went to the door, but her brother refused to come in. So she went out to the edge of the lawn and, while Erik and Mary Lou watched from the open door, she and her brother had a short, muffled conversation in Navajo. She turned back to the house.

"What is it, Betty-Jean?" asked Erik and Mary Lou simultaneously.

"My mother," said Betjegen. "She's very sick. They don't expect her to live."

"Then you must go home at once," said Mary Lou, taking her in her arms. "That's what your brother wants, isn't it?"

"Yes."

"Come. I'll help you pack a few things."

By the time Betjegen had found her handbag and put a few clean shirts and Levi's in her brocade valise, Erik had gathered a gunnysack of fresh corn. "And why don't you take some of your beans?" said Mary Lou. "And some packages of beef? We certainly have enough to share a little."

"Well, maybe some of the beans," said Betjegen.

"Don't you want to take some meat? They have a little freezer on their refrigerator, don't they?"

"Yes."

"Then take a few packages."

"You're sure you won't mind?"

Mary Lou wrapped four packages of frozen meat in several layers of newspaper and put them in a small cardboard box, along with five jars of the green beans.

They went outside. Erik and Betjegen's brother were putting the sack of corn in the back of Betjegen's pick-up. Mary Lou put the box of meat and beans beside it. Betjegen stood beside the open door, holding her handbag and valise.

"Maybe I should go with you?" offered Erik.

"No. Silly," said Betjegen. "I must have driven that road a hundred times. I'm not likely to get lost." Erik took her valise, went around the pick-up, and put it on the floor on the passenger's side.

Still Betjegen hesitated. "I was going to hem Carole's dress."

"I'll do it tomorrow," said Mary Lou. "As strict as you are, you'd probably make it too long to suit Carole."

Betjegen swung up into the pick-up, like a person swinging into a saddle. Her brother hurried away, to the back of the barn where he had tethered his rawboned horse. Erik closed her door and kept his hands on the metal sill, looking up at her in the dim light. "Now, Betty-Jean, be sure to get word to us if you need anything, you hear?"

"You're sure it's okay?" said Betjegen. "You'll be able to manage?"

"Oh, sure. No need to worry. We'll make out okay."

As always, Betjegen was warmed by the support of Erik and his family. She had come to live with the Collins family when she was eleven and Erik was ten. They grew up practically as twins. When she finished high school, she took a job as a typist for a hardware merchant and just stayed on with the elder Collinses. She helped with the cleaning, the cooking, the sewing, the canning. After all the Collins children had married and moved away, she nursed many a 'cousin' and many a 'nephew' or 'niece' through one kind of sickness or another. Later, she became a companion and housekeeper to the elder Collinses, who loved her perhaps more than one of their own. They left her the big house, a nice annuity, and a small lump sum in their will.

After the death of the elder Collinses, Betjegen was lost in grief for a long while. Unable to stay in the big house because it reminded her too much of her loss, she moved in temporarily with Erik and Mary Lou. But she had no job, no purpose, and soon felt lonely and out of place.

She went back to her family on the reservation and put herself to work. She helped her father apply for a government housing grant, and she got a subsidy to drill a well. She cleared and planted a garden, then installed the pump and dug the ditches herself, for she was a good mechanic and wrangler. Her sisters' husbands made snide remarks about her work, so that she began to feel like an intruder, and the loneliness of the bald, flat horizon depressed her.

When the small frame house was built, her mother and father refused to move into it, because it was all squares and rectangles. The circle of the hogan seemed more natural to them.

Betjegen again developed the stomach and bowel trouble she frequently had when visiting the reservation and had to move back to town. Erik and Mary Lou took care of her. When she recovered, she became a sort of self-appointed maid to Mary Lou and a hand on the ranch with Erik. She more than earned her own way, but Erik and Mary Lou felt she had no life of her own. They wanted to help her, but she was hard to please.

She owned the big house, but did not want to live in it. Erik offered to help her if she wanted to build a small house of her own, where she could organize her life the way she wanted. He even suggested she select a nice trailer house, which she could take back and forth from the home place to the reservation.

But Betjegen would hear nothing of it.

She was hysterically afraid of living alone.

She heard them singing in the night even before she could see their bodies silhouetted against the fire. Friends and relatives from the whole area had gathered for a medicine dance. They danced in a big square around the fire, moving their feet and swaying to the rhythm of their chanting. The firelight glinted off the cabs of the pick-ups parked around the dance.

In the hogan, a doctor was drumming and chanting over a small sand painting. Within its circle, the four directions and their powers were represented. Betjegen's mother, naked to the waist, was leaning against a roof support. Betjegen could tell at a glance that she had a high fever. She was flushed and sweating more than the little ceremonial fire could account for.

Betjegen waited near the door until there was an intermission in the medicine ceremony. She went to her mother and touched her hand.

Her mother focused her eyes on Betjegen and smiled weakly. She murmured the Navajo greeting and added in her few words of English, "Good. You here."

Betjegen felt her mother's forehead. About 102°, she estimated. "Where is the hurt, mamacita?" she asked.

"Some enemy has shot his pins into my neck and head. And into my bones. It must be that witch that lives on Mesquite Mesa."

"Has the doctor from the Indian Health Service been here?"

No one acknowledged that she had asked the question, as was their way of ignoring a social mistake. Betjegen knew, even in the asking, that they would not answer. Even if the IHS doctor had come and left some medicine, she knew her mother would have left it lying where the doctor had put it down. Such primitivism enraged her. Would they never change?

Betjegen guessed that her mother had some kind of virus and would recover in a few days. About the only thing anyone could do was try to relieve the pain. She dug in her handbag for the box of aspirin she always carried, but she did not offer them to her mother. Instead, she handed them to the medicine doctor. He nodded and shook out two to give her mother, then he waited.

Betjegen understood. "Mamacita," she called out loudly, "I am going out to dance in the medicine square, so that we may drive the pain bugs from your body."

She went out in their silence, borrowed a small shawl from her younger brother's wife, and joined the medicine square. She knew the basic superstition of the dance. One moved to the north to dialog with the powers of the cold, of destruction, but also of wisdom and balance. One danced to the south to get in touch with emotionalism, warmth, nurturing powers, the spirit of the harvest. One prayed to the east for creativity, beginnings, the future; to the west to the powers of death, immortality, the persistence of spirit. The chanting was a dialog with the powers. It was supposed to integrate all variant perspectives upon the present moment.

Her brother's message had hardly been in perspective, she reflected. Her mother was far from dying; the family's impulse was about as unbalanced and destructive as it could possibly be. Unrealistic as usual, her family had jumped to a wrong conclusion. There was no need for her to be here at all.

Still, if it would humor them, she would dance. If they saw it as helping her mother, she would go through the motions. They danced past the dawn.

That afternoon, her mother was better. Though she still felt weak, the pain and fever were gone. The worst part of the illness was past.

In small family groups, the friends and relatives who had participated in the medicine dance went away, and Betjegen was left with her mother and father, her sisters and their husbands and children.

She had forgotten the meat in the flux of arrival; it had thawed and was on the verge of spoiling. It would have thawed anyway, for,

Betjegen discovered, the refrigerator was not plugged in. Her mother and sisters stored flour, cornflakes, and other things they didn't use in it. One glance at the stove told her they hardly used it either, preferring to cook outside on an open fire. The beds and sheets also had been used very little.

The garden she had planted when she was home last had gone to weeds. "Why didn't you hoe the garden, like I told you?" she berated her sisters' husbands. "Don't you understand that you can't get squash and beans if you don't cut the weeds?"

They made no comment.

"The children, then. Can't you get your children to hoe the weeds?"

"They are needed with the sheep," they said.

Her brothers-in-law were silent for a long time. At last, one of them said, "That may be all right for you white people, but how can you expect a Navajo to offend the earth like that?"

It was the same every time she tried to "talk some sense into" her stubborn relatives. Many such incidents had led her to complain more than once, at chamber of commerce picnics, of "those lazy Indians on the reservation that wouldn't do anything but lay around and draw their welfare checks." Frequently, after visits to her Navajo family, she returned to her Collins home with bowels that were sour, not just from the foods and spices she was unused to.

Toward supper time, she gave her sisters the cuts of meat that could be dried and cured in the Navajo way, and she got out the skillet to fry the ground meat. Even though she was exhausted from a sleepless night, she set the table in the house, opened two jars of the green beans, made biscuits from flour she had brought before, and boiled some of the fresh corn.

The family sat at the table, awkward in their chairs and clumsy with their knives and forks. She knew they were trying to please her. They all ate some of the beans, politely, but she could tell they did not like the taste. The beans lacked their kind of seasoning. The biscuits and the greasy, fried hamburger, they ate with some pleasure. The fresh corn, not one of them touched.

When she dressed for bed that night, Betjegen realized that she was the only person in the house. She tried to calm herself, knowing that the others were only a dozen steps away, in the hogan, or in wraps on the ground. She lay, tense with exhaustion, but found herself stiff, straining to hear imagined noises. She put on her robe and went outside.

She murmured the Navajo greeting, "Yah-teh," at the entrance to the hogan, stooped, and went in. Her mother was asleep, but her father was awake in the dark. She sat on a sheepskin, beside her father.

"Papacito. What's wrong?"

"Why, nothing is wrong, little Betjegen."

"Yes, it is. I try and try to show you all how to live better—and nothing ever happens." She was so tired, she could not stop herself from beginning to cry.

"You must be patient with us, little Betjegen."

"I am patient."

"We can change only slowly. We need time."

"Time!" she cried, tears running down her cheeks now. "I've stopped counting the years I've tried to get you to understand about germs—and nutrition—and—and health and comfort. I've tried until I'm sick of trying. And it's always, 'Wait a little, little Betjegen.' Papa, tell me what's wrong."

Her mother was awake and looking at her.

Her father was silent for a long while. He built a small fire in the middle of the hogan floor, a small ceremonial fire. Her mother sat up. Her father drummed on the clay floor with his fingers and chanted part of the Blessing Way—only fragments. Then he stopped and looked at his daughter.

"Why did you send me away when I was little, Papacito?"

"For your welfare," he said. "We were so poor. There was no food. Many children were dying with hunger. Their little bodies just wasted ..."

"Was I like that?"

"Yes."

Betjegen paused and looked down at her hands in her lap. They were fully formed, adult hands, strong hands capable of considerable work. She could almost imagine there the child's hands, scrawny, thin bones and skin, dying with marasmus; not permitted to live, but not having to go through the trouble of living either. She looked up. "I don't know; perhaps it would have been better if I had died. Then maybe—" She broke off, unable to express her ambiguity and frustration.

Her father said nothing. He searched for and found a small drum, then began thrumming and singing parts of a curing ceremony. Her sisters and their husbands heard and came in to take their places in the circle of the hogan.

Her father stopped singing, and they all looked at her in silence.

She understood. It was her chenille robe and nylon nightgown.

It was not just that their smell offended her family; they would have tolerated that in polite silence.

It was not just that they were in the style and taste of the white man; for they, too, wore ordinary clothes from the department stores.

The robe and gown were veils. They disguised the real person. More, they hindered the inner soul from reality. They hindered sensory communion with the spirit of the ceremonial fire, hindered communion with the good feelings of others.

For a moment, the Betty-Jean in her rebelled. Among the whites, she was considered very modest, even prudish. She wore her dresses long and full, her collars high.

Then, softly, she removed her robe and dropped it outside the hogan door. Then the nylon gown. They all watched her, but their watching did not make her ashamed.

Her father built up the fire with small sticks of greasewood, sage, cedar, and oak brush. Then he picked up the little drum again.

He began singing, not an established song, but a murmured sing-song of obvious comments about his actions.

> *I pick up this little bowl, see?*
> *I pick up this little bowl of sheep tallow.*
> *It is light. I pick it up easily.*

He dipped his finger in the bowl of sheep tallow and wiped the grease on Betjegen's stomach. He took a chili pepper and smeared it in the tallow on her belly. He rubbed the pepper across her chest. He dipped his finger in the bowl again and drew the four directions across her brow and down her forehead and nose. He drew a grease circle around her face.

> *You stand in the center of the universe.*
> *In blessing, you stand in the center.*
> *In welfare, you stand in the center.*
> *In beauty, you stand in the universe.*

Then, each member of the family went to her and gave her a part of themselves. The men embraced her arms and legs as Begochiddy embraced the Ethkay-nah-ashi when he moved them in time with the creation; they imparted to her their strength and endurance. The women embraced and shook her, too, breast and womb, imparting to her their fertility and survivability.

Betjegen felt their love filling her. Her heart tingled, and thrills ran down her arms, down her legs. Her body throbbed with a warmth that was the fire and was not.

Her father's voice murmured inside her chest:

"We know so little, little Betjegen. And what we know is known only at the edges.

"We appreciate and love what you intend when you come here, but you must understand that only we are the keepers of our own welfare.

"It is probably true that your boiled corn tastes better than our dried and parched corn. Ours is hard and wears our teeth flat with the chewing. But it is ours. And we like it. It is likely to be all we will ever have. If we taste yours, we may never again taste ours with pleasure."

Betjegen awoke to the thick, greasy smell of sheepskins. Someone had covered her, and her body was glowing with oily warmth. She opened her eyes. She was in the hogan alone. She knew that she had slept there alone and was not frightened.

In the ashes of the firepit, she recognized fragments of her chenille robe and knew that her nylon gown was there also. It did not make her angry.

She sat up and felt her nakedness. It did not make her ashamed.

Her breasts and belly had been smeared with sheep grease, red pigment, and charcoal. It did not repulse her.

She could already hear Mary Lou catching her breath when she welcomed Betty-Jean home with a hug and thinking, *You smell like an Indian,* but catching herself and saying instead, 'You probably want to take a nice long bath.' But she wouldn't hurry that scene.

She needed time to think, to assess what was hers to be content with, to ask where she would fare best, where she could be the keeper of her whole life with most pleasure.

She could not live here, she knew, for her temperament required good kitchens and clean sheets. Yet there was warmth and comfort and nurture here. Perhaps she would talk to Erik about where he thought she could park a trailer house.

She stood up, wrapped the skeepskin around her, and went outside to sit in the mid-morning sun. As the grease on her face absorbed the sun's heat, she became aware of the four directions drawn on her face and the circle of the horizon around it.

From such fragile symbols, her family drew strength. Why couldn't she also? Why shouldn't she combine fertile emotionalism with naive beginnings and sorrowful persistence, and balance them in her life with the chill of rationality? Her father had always told her these perspectives were open to her at each instant of her life. With such directions, she need never be lost, for she stood in the center of her own awareness.

She closed her eyes and turned her face toward the morning sun. She could feel the lines of tallow warming from the inside. She could feel the loving hands of her father drawing the lines. She could feel the sustenance of her sisters and their husbands. And she began to glow with assurance.

Slowly, her inner peace would come.

Surely, no matter where she walked, among whites or Indians, it would come.

Amid kitchens or hogans, slowly she would come to know, as she knew clearly in this moment, that the four directions met in her own eyes, the circle of the shining universe surrounded her face.

Cookies and Milk for Jackie

Jackie Bull-Breath's parents were killed in 1972 on route 666 south of Cortez, Colorado, by a Texan in a white Cadillac. They were making the right turn to Tawaoc on the Ute Mountain Indian Reservation, when the Cadillac struck them a glancing blow, like a rattler hitting a mouse. Jackie was pitched clear of the '53 Ford and gently dropped, as if by some providence, into the sand of the bar ditch, but her parents were thrown ahead of the car, then crushed as it rolled over them. The incident was declared an accident; the Texan was not even given a ticket for speeding. He had to creep back to Cortez to get the dent in his fender popped out and his wheels aligned, but he paid cash, and no one thought to write down his license number.

Moses Frye, pastor of the South Montezuma Lane Primitive Baptist Church, who operated one of the missions at Tawaoc, officiated at the Christian funeral, because Frank Bull-Breath and Comfort Winter-Moon had been members. They were an example and an inspiration. They drove a car no more than twenty years old and paid their own way and washed the feet of their fellow man.

After the burial, Moses went to the tarpaper shack of Billy Tames-Doves, Jackie's mother's brother, and asked, "Is this the eternally sainted, little orphan daughter of Franklin D.R. Bull-Breath?"

Billy Tames-Doves knew enough English to dig a ditch in Cortez, if he hit it lucky, but not enough to decipher the Reverend Frye's verbal gynmastics. He looked at his wife, Daisy Stays-at-Home, who often stood idle two hours or more in the aisles of The City Market, waiting for one of the Ute or Navajo checkers to come on duty, rather than try to speak English to an Anglo. Daisy looked at Jackie. Jackie looked at the puffy, jolly Reverend Frye in his black coat and didn't answer. Of course, he knew who she was; he had seen her at least a dozen times at the mission, when she was reading Jesus stories to the Ute children, because she had learned good English from Frank Bull-Breath's TV and enough phonics in first and second grade at the BIA school to pronounce just about any word in English, even those she didn't understand.

Reverend Frye changed his tone and bent slightly to speak to Jackie directly. She was skinny and knob-kneed, a little tall for a ten-year-old Ute child. "You are to come and live with Christiana and me, now, my little lost lamb."

Jackie looked at Tames-Doves and Stays-at-Home. She could see that they understood, for it was common enough that whites took Ute children away, not always for the few dollars of welfare money. "Why?" asked Billy Tames-Doves in Ute. Jackie translated.

"Because it is my Christian duty," said Moses Frye, bending again to look into Jackie's face. "God, in his infinite wisdom, hath chosen to take your happy parents unto his bosom. Christiana and I will be your earthly family now."

"She has a family," said Tames-Doves, after the translation. "It is the way of the Ute Mountain people, and I am her mother's brother. She will live with me and Stays-at-Home." Billy knew that he had no practical defense, for he and Daisy did not have the marriage paper, even though they had two children of their own in the Ute way of marriage, as well as Daisy's daughter, Helen.

"You have no right," said Reverend Frye, after the translation. "You are not her legal guardian. Suffer the little child to come unto me," he said to the ceiling, "for I will have her." He did not have to add that the court would give him custody if he asked, for Billy Tames-Doves already knew that.

Billy also knew that Jackie would go, regardless of what any Ute wanted. Perhaps she would even benefit. She knew English as well as any ten-year-old and did well in the white man's schools. Perhaps she was one who could find a cozy refuge in the town of Cortez. Perhaps she was one of the few who could find work when she was old enough, earn her own way and acquire a sense of accomplishment, a feeling that the work she was doing was significant. Perhaps she was one who could make the transition and survive in the white world.

Jackie collected her cotton print dresses, worn jeans, and books and sat on the front seat beside the Reverend Moses Frye in his sea-mist green '57 Chevrolet. Her bare legs stuck to the vinyl. "Will I get to go to school?" asked Jackie.

"Oh, yes, my dear," said the Reverend Frye. "And church. And—and—so much more! You are to be my little helper, now."

"Do you have a TV?"

"Oh, no, my dear. They're far too unGodly."

Still, Jackie Bull-Breath was filled with expectation, as she rode to the little white house at 1517 Montezuma Lane, next door to the little white church, whose glass-fronted message board proclaimed: "I have seen the burning bush and it hath cleansed mine eyes."

Christiana Frye smiled and smiled and adjusted her bodice beneath her padded breasts. Jackie saw at once how she pulled back slightly from the crisp-bacon color of Jackie's skin. Nevertheless, Christiana took Jackie to a church rummage sale to buy her some clothes. They found a Judy Garland pinafore and a plain gingham, which Jackie even liked; then Christiana found a green velveteen dress with a red sash. "Oh, look!" cried Christiana. "An Indian dress! It's just perfect for you!"

Jackie was about to tell her that she couldn't wear it, because it was a Navajo dress, but Christiana was too enthusiastic to listen. She held the dress up to Jackie's chest to judge its length and fit. Her excitement and pleasure caused Jackie to hesitate, to feel some of the thrill and enchantment too. Christiana even hugged her momentarily, and Jackie felt such a rush of warmth and need that she had to swallow the bubble in her throat. For a brief moment, pale Christiana seemed to be Comfort Winter-Moon, and Jackie was nestled in the arms of a great, good place, a place safe from all enemies. Jackie closed her eyes to preserve the moment, wanting also to touch Christiana. And then the moment passed; the clerk had turned away. Christiana swished the dress away and moved on to the patent leather shoes.

At school, the teacher walked past Jackie's desk without looking at her, and, when their glances did meet from the front of the room, the teacher's eyes glazed over with a fixed look. Jackie soon saw that the teacher was interested only in the Anglo students, who also pretended she didn't exist, and that the town Utes thought she was a reservation Indian in a hand-me-down gingham, who probably could not speak English. She said little to anyone, because no one spoke to her. Nevertheless, she listened to the lessons and learned. In the reading book, she discovered rural families where mothers baked cookies for their children and served them milk after school; urban families whose fathers arranged weekend outings at the zoo; families with grandmothers, and younger sisters, and dogs named Rover.

After school, Christiana always told her to take off her clean school clothes and put on a print dress she had brought from the reservation. In a dress her mother had chosen, Jackie was so lonely for Comfort Winter-Moon that she felt like weeping. Rather than let Christiana see her cry, she stayed on the back porch or crouched at the side of the house beside a lattice that covered a basement window, where she could wait for the Reverend Frye to return from his rounds. After he parked on the driveway, he frequently put his arm across her shoulder, pulled her to his pudgy side, and asked if anything interesting had happened that day.

Sometimes, when she was sure Christiana had left the kitchen, she crept back inside. Once, she found an opened package of cookies on the counter. She found milk in the refrigerator. She poured a glass of milk and took two cookies. She imagined Comfort Winter-Moon with her, sitting right across from Jackie at the wooden table. She leaned toward Jackie and asked how the cookies tasted. "Fine," said Jackie aloud.

Then Christiana came back into the kitchen. "I thought I heard something in here! What are you doing?"

Jackie looked at the little red squares in the plastic tablecloth. It was obvious what she was doing.

"Get out of here!" growled Christiana. "Those aren't for you." She poured the glass of the milk down the sink and threw the cookies in the trash. "Now, get on out of here. And don't come back until I call you."

Jackie was so surprised that she did nothing. She gazed at the trash can, trying to get a glimpse of the cookies.

Christiana grabbed the flyswatter from atop the refrigerator and slapped at Jackie. She hit her shoulders, her hips, and her calves as Jackie ran outside.

Jackie darted from side to side, even though Christiana had not followed her past the kitchen door. She had to find some place to hide, but Christiana knew her favorite places on the back porch and at the side of the house. She looked at the church, but knew she couldn't go in there; she wouldn't be allowed. At last, she found a gully in the desert sage land behind the church. She crouched there in the Indian summer sun, freezing and alone. *Why?* she wondered. *Why, Why?* She picked at a scab on her ankle, until she made it bleed.

Weekdays, after school, Jackie had to stay outside until supper time. She often hung around the schoolyard, her fingers laced in the chainlink fence, watching the boys play touch football, watching the girls come around in groups waiting to be chased. No one paid her any attention, and, if they accidentally made eye contact with her, their eyes flicked past quickly. No one said, 'Go on home, Jackie,' but she heard it anyway.

Sometimes, she stood there, watching, until it was almost dark, until it was time for Moses Frye to drive up his driveway, change into his slippers, pull her to his side, then sit down to eat his supper.

In the wintertime, Jackie learned to creep quietly, after school and before Moses came home, to the door between the kitchen and the livingroom, where she could watch Christiana as she was reading paperback books with half-dressed couples kissing on the cover, or women with petticoats larger than sofas being kidnapped on sailing ships, or women with ample breasts being introduced to the king. She was careful not to make a noise, for she wanted to watch as Christiana shifted on the couch, heaved great sighs, and sometimes cried, cried apparently for pure pleasure.

Jackie began to imagine herself there on the couch, sighing, crying with pleasure. At night, when the house was quiet, she crept to the livingroom, found the books beneath the cushions, and read passages by the light of the mercury-vapor lamp at the church corner. There, in those pages, men touched women and made them feel thrills; they comforted each other, fought and made peace, cursed and cried and insisted each could not live without the other. It was a lovely, turbulent, and interesting world, that world of Christiana's dreams. But, Jackie knew, if they caught her reading Christiana's books, they would punish her.

Saturdays, Jackie could feel the tension in the house so acutely that she had to get out, even if there was snow on the ground. She put on a coat and warm shoes, then walked along the streets in the shadows, trying not to be seen, wondering if there was a place for her in the universe, some soft, warm place. It didn't even have to be a great good place, if it were her place—and safe.

She often paused on sidewalks, peeking from behind telephone poles and watching, looking into people's backyards. Some of them had dogs and small children. Some had laundry hanging on clothes lines, being whipped by the cold autumn winds. Sometimes, she caught a glimpse of a woman in a kitchen, her hair straying down over her sweaty forehead. *Jackie reached out to brush back the wisps of damp hair.*

She wasn't just watching; she was there in her mind, *in the house with the mother, standing in the doorway to the kitchen, waiting to be told to set the table with plates. Or maybe she could even peel an onion or scrape some carrots. And when the father drove up the driveway, she could go to the front door and open it for him. When they looked at her, they would see her and smile.*

Some evenings, along the streets, she stood behind bushes and searched in windows of other people's houses. She sought people inside, real people; not people in books, but real mothers who tucked their children in bed, kissed their husbands, and curled up with them on the couch to watch *Gunsmoke.*

What would it be like, Jackie wondered, *to have a blanket tucked tightly around your neck? What would it be like, to sit on a couch, eating popcorn and watching TV with a grandfather who could touch you if he put out his hand?*

If someone said, "Jackie, dear, I've brought you some cookies and milk," what would it be like?

On Sundays, Jackie tried especially to please Moses and Christiana. At church, she combed her short, black hair down slick and wore her Judy Garland pinafore, white anklet socks, and her black patent leather shoes. "Isn't she just lovely!" cried the church ladies, then added to each other behind shielding hands, "but couldn't they have done something with that greasy hair?"

At the church door, Jackie heard these same ladies exclaim, "It's such a generous, wonderful thing that you and Reverend Frye are doing! Such a selfless, wonderful thing!"

Christiana smiled and smiled and replied, "It is our duty."

One Sunday, thinking she would please Christiana, Jackie even wore the green velveteen Navajo dress with the red sash to church, but afterward Christiana said, "Outside! And don't come back until dark!"

Then she stood in her black patent leather shoes, among patches of old snow in the barren back yard of the South Montezuma Lane Primitive Baptist Church, and wondered what to do with herself. She picked up a small limestone rock and scraped her arm, but it was too blunt and too soft to cut herself with. She threw it half-heartedly at the back door of the church.

To the southwest, she could see a portion of snowcapped Ute Mountain. Some people said it was a sleeping man, an ancient chief, lying on his back. The butte at the south end did sort of look like his feet sticking up. The mountain was sacred to her people, but they did not tell the sleeping Ute myth; perhaps it had been invented by white men. Directly to the east of the mountain lay Tawaoc, where she was born, where her parents lay buried, where her mother's brother lived.

She walked through the sage and rocks, up the slope behind the church. At the top of the rise, she could see Ute Mountain without

Cookies and Milk for Jackie

the tangle of electric lines that laced the town together. There were places on the high slopes of the mountain where only medicine men were allowed to go, places where white men were prohibited. She tried to imagine herself as a medicine man, *standing on the toe of the Sleeping Ute and saying to a white man, "Go on. Go on outside. You're not permitted here."* Instead, she saw herself petting a dog.

Suppose I walked on over the hill? Where would I come to? Could I walk into the darkness of a canyon and never be seen again? Could I disappear, like my parents who had dropped into their graves?

Ten miles to the east, under a high black cloud, she saw the snowy ridge that was Mesa Verde, where Anasazi people had lived in cliff dwellings in ancient times. *Could I walk into that past? Could I climb a cedar ladder and find a mother who would hand me a corn cake and a cup of root tea? Could I sit on the parapets above the ladders and gaze down the long valleys, watching for the approach of enemies?*

Over the San Juan Mountains to the north, a thunderstorm was booming. She could already feel the first winds of the coming blizzard.

She turned back and walked along streets she had wandered at twilight. She had often admired one family, especially. She liked to pretend that she was a part of that family. The father picked her up, the way he did the other children, and swung her through the air so that her feet swirled above Ute Mountain, above Mesa Verde, above the great good places of the San Juan Mountains. The mother combed out her hair and braided it. The children talked and played with her, and the puppy came to be petted.

She stopped in front of their house and gazed into their picture window. There they were! The father was pretending to be a horse and the children were trying to ride him. They kept tumbling and laughing. The little girl bumped her nose on the floor and cried for a moment, but went quickly back to riding the horsie. The little boy stood, waiting his turn. Jackie stepped off the sidewalk, over the mound of old snow and onto their lawn, awaiting her turn. She could not see the mother.

Then a patrol car stopped on the street behind her and a sheriff's deputy stepped out. The door of the house popped open, almost as if it had exploded, and the mother raced out onto the walk. "You got here real quick, Wilbur. There she is!" The father came out onto the front step in his stockinged feet.

The deputy was confused. "The call said there was an Indian prowling around the neighborhood."

"Yeah. There she is!"

"Geez, Josie," said the deputy. "She's just a child. Hardly ten years old, I'll bet."

"You never know," said the father. The little boy and girl were hanging onto his pants legs, their thumbs in their mouths. Their breaths made little clouds in the cold air.

"We just don't want any trouble around here," said the mother.

"Yeah," agreed the father. "Don't want anything to get started."

"Geez," said the deputy. Then he pulled off one of his fur gloves, bent down to Jackie's level, and asked in Navajo, "What's your name?"

"I'm not Navajo," said Jackie. "I'm Ute."

"See?" said the father. "You never know what they'll do. What's she wearing a Navajo dress for?" He rubbed his shoulders briskly to counteract the chill.

"So what's your name?" asked the deputy in Ute.

"Jackie," she said softly. "Jackie Kennedy Bull-Breath. And I speak English."

"Well, Jackie Kennedy Bull-Breath," said the deputy, "why don't you come along with me? We'll take a ride down to the office."

"Am I under arrest?" asked Jackie.

"Well, sort of," said the deputy.

"Ask her where she got that green velveteen dress!" yelled the mother, hugging her own elbows. "And those patent leather shoes?"

I have never, never in my life, been so humiliated!" cried Moses Frye. "To be called down to the sheriff's office! And on a Sunday at that! She's going back to that reservation today. Right now!"

"Now, now, Moses," said Christiana. "She's just a child. There's no harm been done."

"No harm? No harm! I should have known from the beginning that it wouldn't work!"

"I know," said Christiana. "They just don't seem to respond to anything we do for them. But maybe we should keep trying."

"No, we've done our duty. We've given it a fair chance. No one can say we didn't give her a fair chance."

"No, no one can say that."

"Get your things together," said Moses. "I'll take you back to your uncle."

"Now?" cried Christiana. "It looks like a storm is coming. It may even be a blizzard."

"I don't care. I'm going to do it now. Get her things ready."

Cookies and Milk for Jackie

Jackie hesitated, looking from Christiana to Moses and back again, uncertain what to do.

"Go take off that dress," Moses said toward Jackie. "You can't take that one with you. And not the pinafore, either. It makes you look too—too—"

"The gingham, then?" asked Jackie.

"Yes, the gingham," said Christiana, touching Jackie on the shoulder and moving between Moses and the little girl. "You can have the gingham."

Jackie looked up at her, surprised. Christiana guided her gently toward the bedroom to change.

"And the patent leather shoes," added Christiana. "You can take the patent leather shoes. Lord knows it's little enough."

So the Reverend Moses Frye drove through the gathering storm, taking Jackie Bull-Breath back to Tawaoc. He did not wait to see if Billy Tames-Doves was at home, but turned and drove away as soon as Jackie was clear of the Chevrolet.

Jackie stood in the barren yard, holding her few books and dresses and gazing at the tarpaper shack that was no protection against weather nor law. She saw Daisy Stays-at-Home peering out a foggy window. Daisy came out as soon as the Chevrolet was gone, brushed back the wisps of Jackie's hair, and took her in her arms. She did not know how long it would be before a social worker came with a sheriff to take Jackie away again. She could only survive for the moment. "Come, Jackie, dear," she said in Ute, "We'll have some cookies and milk."

Chitty Harjo

1

Jake Backturn scuffed his shoes twice across the linoleum and knocked on the door to the teachers' lounge, as the note in his hand directed him to do.

Almost at once, the door opened, and Miss Cheryl Hochfleur, the social science teacher at Okemah High, invited him in. She directed him to sit in one of the easy chairs and took a seat right across from him.

"Uh. What's this all about, Ma'am?" asked Jake. "Have I done something wrong?" He didn't know what to do with his hands, so he stuffed them under his knees. He couldn't help but notice her breasts; God! she had a great figure!

"No, not at all," said Cheryl. "I wanted to congratulate you on breaking the scoring record last Friday. Twenty-two goals and four free-throws! You've got something to be proud of."

Jake blushed. "Why, thank you, Ma'am. I was hot, I admit that. But I wouldn't have made half the points I did, if Chitty Harjo hadn't kept feeding me good set-ups, shots he could have made himself. Didja see that time in the third quarter when he faked the whole Okmulgee team out of their shorts and shoved the ball into my hands. That shot was like dropping a puff-ball in a lake; I couldn't miss."

"Yes. Such a display of teamwork. And your shot swished through the net like a whisper. Didn't even touch the hoop. I almost jumped out of my pants when I saw that play."

Jake looked quickly at the floor between his feet, imagining Miss Hochfleur jumping out of her pants. All the guys in the locker room made raw jokes about Cheryl Hochfleur's pants and chest. He scuffed his shoes uncomfortably on the linoleum and waited.

"What do you think of Chitty Harjo?" she asked.

Jake was baffled. He looked up at Miss Hochfleur, but he didn't see any mockery or criticism in her eyes. "Why, uh—, he's okay. Great basketball player, and he can throw a baseball faster than anybody I've ever seen." He smiled, thinking he had satisfied her question, but she sat, waiting.

"Uh—he's a star in his own way, you know. Did you go on the road trip to the Henryetta game? He was the high-point man that night. Thirty-two points! I didn't think anybody'd ever get that many again."

"I want you to make friends with Chitty Harjo," said Cheryl.

Jake recoiled, knowing what she meant, but recovered at once. "Oh, we are friends. Greatest of friends on the court. We're like brothers. This team is a little band of brothers. We don't even have to signal to know what each other is about to do. Sometimes, I thinks he knows what I'm going to do even before I know it."

"I want you to be friends with him off the court."

Jake was caught by surprise and could only mutter, "Uh—"

Then, because she said nothing, but only sat, waiting, he added, "I always say Hi to him when I meet him in the hall. I mean, I try not to be mean to any of them, the way some of the guys are, a lot of the guys are."

"I want you to do more. I want you to quit treating him like an alien. I want you to invite him down to the Dairy Queen and have a shake together. I want you and your girlfriend to go on double dates with him and Betty Spanalghee. I want you to make him a part of your life."

Jake straightened up, folded his arms across his chest, and looked at her directly. So that was what this was all about. Another lesson in social science. It made him a little angry. "What the fu— what the hell do you think the guys would think of me if I did things like that?"

"It doesn't matter what the other guys think," she said. "You're strong. You're popular. You don't have to worry about what the other guys think of you. You can tell the other guys what to think of themselves. You could lead them into making friends more with our Creek students."

"La-de-dah," he said, sprawling backwards in his chair. "Wake me when this is over."

"I'm serious, Jake," she said, leaning forward toward him so that the upper part of her breasts showed. "Life should be played like a good basketball game. We, all of us, ought to be looking constantly for ways to feed each other good set-ups. We ought to make it our business to make our fellow men look good."

"Yeah?" he scoffed. "Whatta you get out of this? What's in it for you?"

Cheryl flinched, pulling her feet back under her chair, folding her hands in her lap, and stared at her knees. "I admit, I have an ulterior motive," she said slowly. "Perhaps you know that I am a Quaker, a member of the Society of Friends."

He squirmed in his chair.

She went on: "When honesty lives for a moment, I am paid. When truth is served and made a part of someone's life, I am rewarded."

"Yeah? And what do I get out of it?"

"Nothing," she admitted. "The same nothing that Chitty Harjo got out of feeding you thirty-two set-ups last Friday night. The nothing you get for knowing that you've done something right, and done it well."

Jake stood up. "Is that all, Ma'am? Can I go now?"

"Yes, you may go. Congratulations on scoring sixteen points more than anyone at Okemah High has ever scored. No one is likely to come near that ever again."

Jake stomped out and slammed the door. Fucking do-gooders! It would be a cold day in hell before he gave Miss Cheryl Hochfleur the time of day again, tits or no tits. Fuck! Make friends with a friggin' Indian! He paid her no more attention than his grandfathers had paid the Quaker Indian agents at Fort Cobb and Fort Sill.

2

Corporal Jake Backturn was awakened by a ruckus in the Quonset two bunks down. A pair of Georgia and Alabama rednecks were picking a fight with a new guy, a replacement for the boy from Minneapolis who had bought it when he stepped on one of Charlie's land mines. Jake yelled, "Hey, you fuckers! Shut up! Can't a guy get a few winks?" He pulled the sheet tighter around his ears. Through the fog of his sleepiness, he heard a voice say, "Jake? Is that you, Jake?"

He recognized the voice, though he hadn't heard it in years. He swung out of his bunk, stalked down the aisle in his G.I. shorts, and peered between the shoulders of the Lookie-Lou's. Sure as shit, it was Chitty Harjo.

Jake peeled open the ring of shoulders and stepped in, grabbing both the Georgia and the Alabama redneck by the scruff of their T-shirts. "Hey, you cock-suckers! Go out and shoot up a bunch of commies if you just have to get your rocks off, but leave this guy alone; he's my friend."

"A friggin' red nigger?!" exclaimed the Georgia redneck.

"Red nigger or not, he's okay," said Jake. "He just may save your lousy ass, someday. He fed me thirty-two set-ups in one game a couple of years ago, but I only made about half of 'em. Go beat the meat in your own shorts, if you just gotta have some home entertainment, but you leave me and my buddy alone. Unless you want a set of dishpan hands."

"Hey, Corporal, can you put me on KP?" rang several voices, almost at once, and Jake realized that the threats and punishments of basic training didn't work in Nam. If you were on KP, you couldn't be out in the bush tripping Charlie's booby-traps, or stopping a sniper's bullet, or taking a bamboo sliver up the ass-hole all the way to your brain. KP was a positive choice.

"I'll put you both on point for a whole month."

Several of the guys scoffed, "Ha." That was one thing about Jake; he was absolutely fair when it came to point and swing. He assigned the duties on a rotation basis, taking his turn like everyone else, even though both the lieutenant and captain told him repeatedly that a good squad leader always walked drag.

"Okay, break it up," Jake said, shoving the rednecks toward the circle of onlookers. "Party's over. Go on home."

Disgruntled, but recognizing that the fray was finished, the crowd began to disperse. Jake turned back to Chitty and offered a handshake. "What the fuck is a nice guy like you doing in an oven like this, Chitty?"

Chitty returned the peace handshake, saying, "Same thing I've always done, Jake: whatever Uncle Sam tells me to do."

"Shit, Chitty," said Jake. "That's no way to have grandkids."

Chitty, Jake, and several others sat in the PX, drinking Japanese beer to celebrate Jake's promotion to sergeant. A big near-giant of a mixed blood from Fort Huachuca, who called himself Josie, had joined the squad several weeks before. He was six foot, six, and so big through the shoulders that the Army had to make his shirts for him special. No one ever thought of calling him an Indian, or kidding him about his feminine name, for, although he had a few small scars from knife fights, everyone was convinced his opponents did not survive.

Josie was one of the first to admire Chitty for his quick eye and fast trigger. Having grown up with guns, Chitty was a sure shot, and he had saved the squad a couple of times from a sniper that no one else suspected.

"Did you see that Chitty?" Josie asked the others in the squad. "Chitty, bang, bang." So members of the squad started calling him

Chitty-Chitty, Bang-Bang. Chitty always lowered his eyes and became silent when the others were talking about him.

In the PX, Chitty got the attention of the others and said, "I think we ought to drink a gulp to our squad leader. I know you all hate it when he calls us out to do drills, or when he takes the dope away from you so you can't smoke, but maybe you've noticed also that we haven't lost a man since Josie joined us, and all the other squads have been coming back bloody. And, shit, we been out more days than a calendar has on it. He's made us into a team that takes care of each other. Nobody ever deserved his promotion more. Congratulations, sergeant!"

Jake smiled modestly and said, "Thank you, Ma'am," before he realized he was thinking of Miss Cheryl Hochfleur. He didn't know what to do with his hands, so he put them under his knees.

"Thank you, Ma'am!" echoed Josie, laughing. "You got that right. Mama's going to take care of us. Not very many of us, girls. Few, but we're a tight little band of sisters. Nobody gets to fuck with us." He laughed and drank, spilling beer out the side of his mouth.

The others laughed, too, and drank from their beers.

Suddenly, Josie started singing one of their basic training songs:

The biscuits in the Army, they say are mighty fine,
But one fell off the table and killed a pal of mine,
   Oh, I don't want no more of Army life—
   Gee, Mom, I wanta go—
   Oh, Mom, I wanta go—
   Hey, Mom, I wanta go—   Home.

The others had joined in the song, but being finished, all became silent and gazed at their beer. About the only way they had seen anybody go home was in a body bag. Charlie's shit was never very far away, and just waiting to hit you in the face.

3

Jake Backturn walked up the gravel walk to the Big Quarsity Baptist Church. The wound in his right arm had healed—a freak wound in which an exploding round had plowed the flesh away for ten inches, but missed the bone—healed, the doctors said, but it still hurt. They couldn't explain why it still hurt. He had to use his left hand to open the door.

Inside, he met a man whose skin was the color of a walnut. "Yes?" said the man. "Can I help you?" His voice was full of hostility, as if he really wanted to say, 'Why are you whites always invading our territory?'

"I'm looking for the Rev—" Jake's throat caught, so he had to start over. "I'm looking for the Reverend Billy Harjo."

"I am Reverend Harjo," the man said coldly. Then, remembering his Christian principles, he repeated more warmly. "I am Billy Harjo."

Jake offered his left hand to shake, saying, "I'm Jake Backturn. I was with Chitty in—" Again, his throat stopped up. He couldn't make himself say 'Viet Nam.'

Reverend Harjo went pale. He still had not taken Jake's hand to shake, but now noticed the wound in Jake's right arm. He backed away softly and sat on the end of a pew.

"I'm sorry about Chitty," Jake went on, his voice wavering with the tears that were trying to break through. "I was with him when he bought— when he got killed."

Reverend Harjo was refusing to look at Jake.

"Chitty saw it coming before any of us did," said Jake. "He hit me like a ten-pound hammer and drove my face into the mud. But that left him standing there as big as a bulldozer. He took a whole volley in the chest. Six of the squad—" His throat gurgled. He cleared it and tried to go on. "Six of the squad caught it at the same time. I only got this." He held up his right arm. He saw Josie holding up a stump of an arm that hadn't started to bleed yet and saying, "Shit! That was my knife hand!"

"I remember you, now," said Reverend Harjo. "You're Jake Backturn. You're the one that made Chitty look so good in the Henryetta game, the year Okemah went to the State Championship. You kept feeding him set-ups that he couldn't miss."

Jake sank onto the pew across the aisle from Billy Harjo and let the tears start. He hadn't realized. He had been interested only in the team; he always fed the ball to the teammate who was in the best position to do the best job. A pain like an exploding shell ripped through his right arm. Chitty always knew who he was setting up, and whose life he was saving.

They sat in silence for a while, both crying and not looking at each other.

"Something else I didn't know until too late," said Jake. "In 'Nam, Chitty was closer to me than any brother ever could be."

Reverend Harjo looked up at Jake, wide-eyed, with horror and hatred in his eyes, thought Jake.

"Anyway," Jake went on, having to go on, "if you have a service—" He forced his throat to go on. "When you have a memorial service, I want— I've got to come."

Reverend Harjo stood up, screamed, "My son! My son!" and, falling on his knees, embraced Jake's legs. Jake did not know if he were screaming in protest to the Gods about the loss of his son, or if he were adopting Jake.

The drums had been beating insistently since a half-hour after dark and the bonfire had been replenished at least a dozen times, but Jake still sat in his wheelchair at the side of the dance circle at the Big Quarsity stomp ground, like an alien. The nurse, Betty Spanalghcc, had negotiated Jake's temporary furlough from the VA Hospital where the psychiatrists were trying to talk him out of the pain in his arm, saying it was all in his head. The doctor's condition was that Jake be under Betty's supervision constantly.

In the afternoon, they had sat in the little Creek Baptist Church, separated from the stomp ground by a row of cedars, an orchard, the cemetery, and the pastor's garden, and listened to Reverend Billy Harjo preach a memorial sermon over the box the Army said was his son. The sermon had disturbed Jake terribly. Reverend Billy came to a conclusion almost of ecstasy, an exuberant joy because Chitty no longer had to deal with the cruelties of the white world and had gone on to his reward, a better life. Jake's arm hurt so badly that the tears started streaming from his eyes. He begged Betty for a shot of morphine, which she refused; she did, however, allow him a codeine tablet. Betty was crying, too, but it was from grief for Chitty.

Jake had managed to walk to the cemetery where the squad from the National Guard fired a salute over the grave and the whole community participated in covering the box with dirt. Jake stood a short distance away from the grave, feeling awkward and inadequate. When there was a break in the stream of people, he moved up to the grave, lay his own pocketknife on the mound, and covered it with dirt. He knew that Chitty always carried a good pocketknife. In a daze, he turned away, not looking at anyone and blinking the tears out of his eyes.

Since the dancing had begun, Betty had alternated between crying for Chitty and translating for Jake what was happening. The *micco*, or stomp leader, was Alexander Harjo, Billy's brother. He had called for a number of Friendship and social dances, between the ceremonial dances for Chitty. He would announce to the gathering that the following dance was in memory of some aspect of Chitty's personality, or of some event in Chitty's life. And then most of the crowd would fall in behind the leaders and dance a shuffle-stomp for a half-hour, or more.

"The Dance of the Warriors, Going" had been full of courage and bravado, but it made Jake weep again, for he kept seeing Chitty's chest, shredded like sausage in a senseless war, a war everyone lied about, was still lying about. His own arm bent backward upon itself, drawn by a tension Jake had no control over. Betty had to give him morphine to get the arm to release.

Billy Harjo had taken off all signs of his ministry and dressed in a breech clout, leggings, and an Indian blanket. He sat, half-hidden by the women of his family. Alexander announced a Giveaway Dance. Betty explained to Jake that the introduction to the dance included references to Jake and Chitty's experiences at Okemah High and in Viet Nam. Jake was astonished when the first gift of the dance was an Indian blanket, which Chitty's youngest sister brought across the dance ground and lay in Jake's lap.

She stood in front of Jake a long moment, as if deciding if she would speak or not. Finally, she said, "Dad and Uncle Alexander forgive you and want you to have this blanket." Jake felt unworthy of the gift and tried to refuse it, but Betty whispered in his ear that it would be impossibly impolite to decline. Gifts went to dozens of the assembly, each gift diminishing in importance according to the recipient's degree of removal from Chitty's life.

The *micco* announced an Honor Dance to Jake. After two or three times around the dance ground, individuals began leaving the dance to come in front of Jake and drop some gift on his blanket—sometimes a dollar bill so tightly folded that he had no idea it was in their hand until they opened it above the blanket, sometimes a bit of beadwork or a piece of tooled leather. Some of Chitty's relatives gave Jake little mementos of Chitty's life—a pen he had used in high school, a feather that Chitty had wound with colored yarn in elementary school. He knew enough now not to try to reject the gifts, but he could not keep his eyes dry or his arm from hurting. He looked at Betty, pleading for relief.

"They are honoring you," she said, "because you were a warrior who fought at Chitty's side, and because you had the courage to come here and tell us that Chitty died with honor."

"It's a stupid, senseless war," said Jake. After a moment, he added, "We both knew they lied to us. The generals, the president, everybody lied to us; it wasn't a holy war."

"Yes, it was stupid and senseless," Betty admitted, "but Chitty did what he was called on to do. And he did it with courage and dedication. You did the same thing. You both earned the honor we give you."

Jake's arm bent backward, involuntarily, until he thought it would break.

No one announced the beginning of the *ohkalga*, or washing ceremony; the medicine man simply appeared on the dance ground, and Billy Harjo started a line in front of him. The medicine man poured a red root medicine over Billy's head four times. Then the next person in line stepped up to be washed.

"It gets all the gunk out of your eyes and throat from the grief," Betty explained. "It's really refreshing. C'mon, I think we both need some." She walked away, adjusting her shawl across her shoulders and not looking back.

Jake didn't know what to do amid so many strangers. Betty was his guide and his security, as well as his nurse. Before she disappeared from sight, he followed after her, like a child following his mother.

He stood to the side of the line, keeping Betty in sight. When she was washed, she circled around and took one of Jake's arms. Someone else tugged at his other arm, and, before he knew it, the medicine man was pouring red root medicine over his forehead. He sputtered with surprise and the sting in his eyes, but Betty was right: it was refreshing.

Dripping, he and Betty went back to their side of the stomp ground and sat on a wooden bench near his wheelchair.

At the "Dance for the Warrior Fallen in Battle," Jake struggled to his feet, took Betty by the hand, and said, "Come on. Show me what to do. I want— I *have* to dance this one."

Adjusting her shawl across her shoulders, she showed him the point-hold-stomp movement, and Jake began. After a couple of times around the dance ground, Jake stopped in front of Billy Harjo.

"I know it's too late to be sorry now," he said, "but I am. I didn't mean to be mean to him. But I was. From the time I was born, till we got to Viet Nam. Why, I never even sat down to a milkshake with him at Dairy Queen." He stopped and looked down. "But it wasn't the same in Viet Nam; I swear it wasn't." He scuffed his shoes twice across the stomp ground. "All those years, I didn't even know I was being mean, but I was." He stopped again, confused, at a loss for further words. He didn't know how to say what had to be said.

Billy Harjo stood up, put his hand on Jake's shoulder, and gazed at him for a long time. *"Mongas chay,"* he said at last and sort of pushed Jake and Betty back into the dance.

"What did he say?" Jake asked Betty.

"It was a kind of blessing," she said. "It means everything is right with the world. Everything is as it should be. He thinks you're a white man worth saving." She smiled and looked into his eyes, then added, "So do I."

Jake noticed for the first time ever that Betty had a great figure and was really kind of cute, with the red root medicine still dripping from her hair. He reached for her hand, but she withdrew it and hid it under her shawl.

After all the dances were done, except the final farewell, they were sitting again on the wooden bench near Jake's wheelchair. Betty shivered from the late night chill. Jake picked up his blanket, draped it across her shoulders, and pulled it across his own. She blushed, and then allowed him to fold the blanket around her as they sat, waiting for what was next. The dancers had gone twice around the stomp ground before Jake realized he was holding the blanket around Betty's shoulder with his right hand. And the wound in his arm didn't hurt.

Tour of Ácoma

We were a dappled mob that assembled on a Saturday dawn to tour the ancient pueblo at Ácoma. Grungy young people wearing backpacks and T-shirts with no bras. Painted social types in good quality pantyhose, short skirts, and four-inch spike heels. Old couples in Cadillacs who stayed in motels at Grants off the reservation, twenty miles away, and complained about quality, convenience, and service. Sinewy graybeards that made you hate them for their health and stamina; and round-bellied, round-bottomed, round-shouldered men who waddled on round feet. A few, like me and my wife, were mixed bloods.

We had bought our tickets, but there were plenty of signs saying "No Visitors Beyond this Point" and such; so the group had milled around like a trail herd, some studying items in the little museum, some gawking at the geegaws in the souvenir shop. The young grungies took the opportunity for a nap on the floor. One sinewy graybeard lectured whoever would listen on local geology, archeology, and Pueblo history. He quickly let it be known that he was a professor in some European university—English, I believe it was.

"What archeology?" I asked him. "They don't allow any diggers around here, do they?"

"No, perhaps not here. I was thinking of archeology in general."

"I thought Native Americans in general weren't very interested in artifacts," I countered. "I met a Navajo clerk twenty-five miles from Grand Chaco, who had lived there all her life, but had never been out to the ruins. I told her I thought it was a totally different culture from her own and something she might find interesting, might even learn from. She replied: 'We are taught to leave those Old Ones alone.' To her, Grand Chaco wasn't a pile of stones, but a collection of ghosts. And respect for the ghosts took precedence over interest in digging."

"There are a number of very interesting studies from the turn of the century, old chap," was all he said.

I recognized some of the photos from those studies, high up on the museum walls, behind the exhibits of old, exquisite pottery.

There were also some pottery and pictures of Casas Grandes, an ancient pueblo in Mexico some 200 miles south of El Paso. I wondered if they, too, were of the Grand Chaco stock.

At last, the busses arrived to transport us—powerful, shiny, glass and steel things, made with the latest technology in West Germany. The drivers and guides were young Ácoma people, the counterparts of college kids working at summer jobs in national parks, all carrying cell phones. We got on the bus, were cautioned not to take pictures of anything, and started winding our way up the asphalt road to the Sky City, sitting like a jewel on the top of its cliffs.

"For most of Ácoma history," the guide began his prepared talk, "there has been no road. In the old days, the only way to get up and down was by foot trails, which some of you may want to take on the way back to the visitor center. Every bit of adobe, every stone, every log you'll see in each building up there had to be carried up the cliff on the backs of workers. In the 1930s, some Hollywood people made a movie at the Sky City and cut a dirt road to get their cameras and electric generators and their stars up there. It was good for pack horses, and not much else. About ten years ago, the Ácoma council decided to widen and pave the road, to make it easier for the people to reach their homes. More recently, they purchased these modern, air-conditioned busses, to make your trip to Ácoma about as easy as it was difficult in the old days."

No one said anything, but I could tell that the professor wanted to know the name of that movie. He'd be sure to study the backgrounds of every shot. He had his notebook out and was making notes.

We came to a plaza at the top of the road and stopped. Before the guide opened the door, he cautioned us again to please respect Ácoma ways—not to stray from the group, not to take pictures of anything that was not approved, not to invade the privacy of the people who lived up here. There were plenty of late model cars parked in the plaza—Toyotas and Fords and Mercedes—it looked like a tourists' convention.

But there were no people, except the tour guides and drivers. "It looks like a ghost town," said the woman in four-inch spike heels. "Does anyone live here now?"

"Oh, yes," said the guide. "I believe there are about sixteen families currently in residence at Ácoma. Right this way," he said in a different voice to the crowd, "and please stay with the group." He led the way to the north rim of the mesa, where we could look at the foot trail and a view of the visitor center. This was one of the approved picture-taking spots, so several people took out their cameras and snapped the scene.

"As we go through the pueblo," the guide began another part of his spiel, "you see a mix of ancient and modern. All of the houses here are built of adobe or stones carried up here and plastered with a slurry made of adobe. Yet, in most of them, you will see casement windows and jam-hung doors with screens. What you won't see is electricity or plumbing. The Ácoma people believe in living simply. They still cook with wood and carry their water in jars called *ollas*."

"What kind of wood?" wanted to know the round man.

"Cedar and pine," said the guide, pointing to a stack of firewood. "The cedar burns more slowly, but the pine burns hotter; so a cook chooses the kind she wants for whatever she is cooking."

"And you get the wood here?" asked the middle-aged tourist, waving at the barren plain. There was not enough wood in sight to start many bonfires.

"We get it from the mountains you see directly north of you," said the guide. "All the timbers in the pueblo were cut over there and carried here. After they were cut, they were not allowed to touch the ground, until they were in place in the house here. That was one of our religious customs."

"Are you Ácoma?" asked the professor, eyeing the guide's wide-brimmed Stetson and new Nikes.

"I am a half-breed," said the guide simply. "I'm half Southern Ute and half Ácoma. My grandmother lives in the other street." He turned quickly and walked up the street, as if he had confessed more than he wanted to.

"Will we visit your grandmother?" asked one of the grungies.

"No, I'm afraid not," the guide said, letting it drift back over his shoulder. "She doesn't speak much English and doesn't like to be made fun of."

"No one is going to make fun of her, will they?"

The guide did not respond, except to walk a little faster. The women in spike heels were having a great deal of trouble on the cobblestoned streets.

Suddenly, the guide turned, a new smile on his face. We were beside an adobe house with several shelves and tables along its walls, facing the street. On them were displayed pottery, fetishes, and a few novelty items in clay. A woman came out of the house and stood on her porch, watching the tourists. She was the first Ácoma person, aside from our guide, that we had seen since we left the bus. "We will be stopping at the houses of a number of artisans on the tour," said the guide. "You are welcome to look over their creations, chat with them about their wares, and, if you like any of them, strike a bargain to buy your pleasure. Each potter has a specialty," he went on. "Some paint their pottery with only one yucca fiber in the brush, so that the lines on their creations are incredibly fine. Others specialize in the sheen of the pottery, or in fetishes, or other items. We will stop here for a few minutes, so you can look around. You can be assured that everything here is authentic; every artist here makes everything she sells."

The professor zeroed in on the display tables. He picked up pot after pot, examined the workmanship, asked the price, and put it down. He couldn't seem to find anything within his means, or to suit his taste.

The grungies went up close and asked questions about the fetishes.

Our guide withdrew to the shady side of the street—what scant shade there was—took off his hat and wiped his forehead with a red bandanna. He made a call on his cell phone. I sidled over to him and asked, "You been a guide very long?"

He looked at me, taken aback. He glanced at my shell-bead choker, which is really pretty hard to see under my shirt collar, and softened. "Not long," he said at last. "Does it show?"

"No, not at all," I said. "You're doing fine. It's just that you let some of the gringos get to you back there; a longtime guide probably wouldn't have allowed that."

"This is my seventh week," he said simply.

"And what do you do in the other seasons?" I asked. "Go to a community college?"

"How did you know?" he asked, and then didn't wait for a reply. "I'm studying business psychology," he added.

"Good for you," I said. "Guiding is good money for a few years when you're young, but it's hardly a career."

He glanced at his watch. "Time to head 'em up, move 'em on out," he said, then raised his voice so the whole tour could hear. "It's time to continue," he said loudly. "Note the number on the door post of this artist. If any of you want to come back later, we can arrange a private guide to bring you back." He started on up the street, toward the shallow pool in solid rock where people for generations have seen goats and their reflections kissing the surface of the still water. A number of the famous historical photos are just such a scene, some with children at the edge of the pool. No one was around it this morning.

"This is *not* the town's water supply," said the guide, heading off the obvious question. "This is water that collects from our frequent afternoon rains. But it is far too muddy to use. We get our drinking water from natural cisterns that are about fifteen to twenty feet below the level of the mesa, and which the water-maidens reach by special stairways and paths." He turned and walked rapidly toward the northeast rim of the mesa, overlooking a long expanse.

"The butte you see over there," he said pointing, "is called 'Enchanted Mesa.' Our traditions tell us that all the Ácoma people once lived on that butte, but one day while most of the people were down in the valley working the crops, a sudden thunderstorm washed away the only trail up to the mesa. A number of people were stranded. There was not enough food up there to survive, and no way to get more food. Several people starved in a few days. Rather than starve, an old woman and her granddaughter flung themselves from the mesa to their deaths. Since then, it has been called 'Enchanted Mesa.' No one goes there now," he added. "No one is permitted to go there. Several of our people died there and did not have benefit of burial; we do not go near their ghosts."

His cell phone beeped, so he brought it up to his ear. The conversation was very businesslike: Yes ... no ... twenty minutes ... okay ... bye.

"There is a funeral taking place in the mission church this morning," he announced to the crowd. "We usually try to include the church in our tour, but if the funeral is not finished by the time we get there, we'll have to skip it this time." He turned to go.

"Ah, young man ..." It was the professor. "Do your people have any knowledge of where they came from?"

"Oh, yes," said the guide, stopping and setting his feet for a mini-lecture. "Ácoma Pueblo has been continuously inhabited since about 1150. We are descendants of people who came here from Grand Chaco, just when it was breaking up. That's why our language is slightly different from the Keres people at the Laguna Pueblo or Isleta, and different still from those at Santo Domingo and up the Rio Grande valley as far as Taos. Those people are descendants from Tewas people who abandoned Mesa Verde and other cities on the Colorado plateau. We descend from the older, Keres people of Grand Chaco."

He was gesturing around, as if to point out a crowd, but there was not a single person in sight.

The woman in four-inch spikes had been stumbling around on the cobbles for some time. She finally broke a heel and fell, spraining her ankle. The guide was immediately at her side, examining the damage and comforting the victim. He was very professional. As soon as he had determined that no bones were broken, but that the woman probably would not be able to walk, he called someone on his cell phone. In just a few moments, a Chevy van containing a stretcher came along the vacant, dusty street, and two medics took over. In a few moments, the woman and her husband were transported away.

"Everything is okay," he announced to the crowd. "We have a small clinic and dispensary at the Visitor Center. She'll be given whatever care she needs."

"Actually," he added, "her misfortune may produce some benefit to the rest of you. With a little more delay, we may get to tour the mission church after all."

We stopped at another artisan's house (she specialized in what-nots and wall decorations), but no one was very interested in her wares. The crowd kept edging forward along the route they thought we were going to take, sometimes having to walk around the Fords and Nissans parked in the narrow street.

A bit further along, we came around a corner to a small plaza and saw a stand where fry-bread was sold. I bought a couple, along with a couple of soft drinks, and my wife and I gulped them down, for it was already very hot. The man selling the fry-bread also baked good looking squaw bread loaves. Almost everyone in the tour party bought soft drinks and many bought fry-bread. The grungies and the professor bought squaw bread and began tearing the loaves into pieces and eating them.

After another cell phone conversation, the guide announced: "The funeral is over, but they locked the church. I'll have to see if I can find the key. Stay here in this plaza until I come back." He left, to search for whoever kept the key.

We milled around in the plaza; there were a couple of pottery salespersons with their tables nearby, one with a variety of very large terra cotta objects. I heard someone ask when the lady found time to make pots. "In the winter," she said clearly. "There's not much up here to do in winter. So we work ahead."

"How do you get them so shiny," asked one of the grungies.

"We rub the clay surface with a smooth stone," said the woman. "The smooth stone burnishes the surface and makes it shiny and hard. I use the stones my grandmother gave me. Most of the artists here, and throughout Pueblo country, use polishing stones they have inherited. We're always on the lookout for new ones, because stones do sometimes get lost or broken, but the right kind of stone is hard to find. And it has to have the right shape, too."

The guide returned with news that he had found the key to the church. "Right this way, please." The first feature the guide pointed out was the shaded balcony tower, where, beginning in the early 1600s, Spanish priests taught Ácoma children Spanish language and their catechism. The wood holding up the roof was pretty weather-beaten, even though I knew they were replacements; I had seen pictures of the church with the tower in ruins. It had been restored as recently as the 1930s. "It was the coolest place in town," the guide added. "Up that high, you catch what little breeze there is."

In the cemetery directly in front of the church door, we saw the fresh grave. "Only people who live up here and elders are allowed to be buried here now," the guide went on. "The only exception is men who are killed in the military." He pointed to a row of military stones against one of the walls. "We're running out of space—again. There are three layers of graves here. Each time the cemetery has filled up, the people have brought up dirt from the valley, built the retaining wall higher, and covered the old graves."

The door to the church, being back in an alcove away from the weather, looked very old. The guide assured us it was the original door, first installed about 1610. Even the lintel looked original. Inside, the church was cool. The thick adobe walls kept the heat out, while the natural chill you find when you have dug a hole over three feet deep was allowed to express itself. Here, there were a few electric lights, no furniture of any kind, and several wall hangings—representations of the stations of the cross and a few very old paintings. The guide told a story of one painting, which, legend said, helped bring rain. In a terrible drought a few miles to the north, it had once been lent to the Laguna Pueblo to help them pray for rain. After the prayers were successful, the Laguna people refused to return the painting. This resulted in a small war, but finally the painting was returned to its place. "We don't lend anything out any more," the guide commented.

After we left the church, there was one more cluster of sidewalk sales places. Among the offerings were miniature pots, some with interiors no bigger than a finger. I recognized some of them as being in the style of Casas Grandes, the pueblo in old Mexico. I picked up one of the miniatures, turned it over, and was surprised to see it incised with the artist's mark and the words "Casas Grandes." So much for every artist here makes everything she sells.

Still it was a nice pot, beautifully finished, and would serve to hold toothpicks, so I bought it. I noticed the professor was buying a number of the miniatures, probably as Ácoma gifts for the folks back home. He was still eating a piece of his squaw bread. It looked so good, it made my mouth water a bit.

After several moments, perhaps after the purchases subsided, the guide announced that this was the end of the tour. We could see the open busses waiting. "Anyone who wants to walk down the footpath is welcome to. We'll escort you to the head of the trail and show you the way. And if anyone wants to return to any of the artists' houses, we can arrange an individual guide for you."

Several people elected to walk down the trail; some got on the bus. I said I wanted to go back and buy some of the squaw bread. In a few moments, the guide brought out a teenaged girl, who was dressed just like ninety percent of the teenaged girls in Albuquerque and Los Angeles. We chatted with her as we walked. She had finished high school in Grants and planned to go to college in Santa Fe in the fall.

The street and plaza were not exactly crowded, but there were plenty of people around: little old grandmothers in bright, colored rebozos; women in K-Mart housedresses; children holding dolls or toy cars; boys carrying sticks they might use in some game.

"Where did all the people come from?" I asked.

"Oh, they were here all along," said our guide. "They just don't like to come out when the tourists are in the street."

We had difficulty finding the man to buy a loaf of bread, because he was in the next plaza over, visiting with a cousin. But finally, I had a fat loaf of squaw bread under my arm, and our guide urged us gently toward the waiting bus and away from the life of Sky City.

Return to Zuni

In 1960, Raymond Zima finally left Zuni[*] to find work in Gallup. He felt he had failed for fifteen years to make a decent living for himself and his family in Zuni. Raymond had been a marine in the Pacific theater in World War II, where he distinguished himself with three Silver Stars and two Purple Hearts. The years right after the war were not bad; he was a triumphant warrior, returned with many honors from a victorious war, and he was accorded appropriate respect. He was the recipient of many an Honor Dance at local pow-wows and was praised with rich gifts at many Giveaways. With the occasional piece work and day labor he found, he was able to live fairly well. Before the war, he married Mary Dog-Trot, had one child in 1943—Marisa—and fathered three more children after the war.

But survival in the 1950s was nearly impossible in Zuni. He started a construction company, but found no one was constructing anything. He started a well-drilling company, but no one could afford to drill a well. He opened a gift shop for tourists, but soon found that the town of Zuni had successfully discouraged tourism. "I can't stand it any longer," he told his father, an elder named Zima, who sat on the tribal council. "I have to try my luck somewhere else."

"You talk like a Yankee," said Zima. "I feared this would happen when you joined their Marine Corps."

"I hear there are more opportunites for work in Gallup. I've got to try it for a while."

"Well, go then," said Zima sadly. "But remember always that you are a Zuñi. And true Zuñis always, sooner or later, return to Zuni."

Raymond understood and respected Zuñi ways; so before he left, he hosted a Giveaway. He gave his gift shop to the tribal council, so that they might do with it what they thought most proper. He gave his house and land to the poor, so that whoever would work the land and repair the roof would have basic subsistence. He gave his turquoise jewelry to his father and brothers. He gave his blankets to whatever friends came to the dance. He gave bystanders almost everything but the clothes that he and his family had on their backs.

---

[*] "Zuni" refers to the place, "Zuñi" to the people, the language, and the culture.

Raymond also understood how to use the American system, so as soon as he got to Gallup, he applied to the Social Security and the Veterans Administrations, who helped him with training, and he soon got a job on the railroad. He spoke good English, as well as Zuñi, and saw to it that his children spoke both languages with ease. He enrolled his children in the public schools of Gallup.

Marisa, the oldest child, was born while her father was island-hopping with the Marines in the Pacific. She loved Zuni, for she had known little else in her life, but she also loved her father. She was a diligent student for his sake, graduated two years later, and matriculated to the Nursing School at the University in Albuquerque.

Marisa adjusted to the city quite rapidly, became a top student, and graduated with honors. She was asked to stay on with the Nursing School as a demonstration nurse, who assisted the instructors with their teaching, by explaining the principles of nursing to the few Indian students the BIA insisted upon sending to the school. She worked with another honors student, a male nurse from Houston named George Anderson Jr., who was just two years older than Marisa. They soon fell in love and were married in 1965, with the blessings of both sets of parents. The elder Andersons in Houston, being Southern liberals, were elated to have Zuñi relatives, and Raymond Zima saw the match as a first step toward the assimilation, and thus well-being, of his whole family.

The Viet Nam war was heating up, and George was soon drafted into the Army, where his special talents as a nurse were ignored, since he was not a woman and could not be billeted with the other nurses. He was trained hastily as an infantryman and soon shoved into the front lines, where he was killed in 1967, shortly before his only son, George Zima Anderson, was born at Zuni, in the house of Marisa's grandfather, the old Zima. Marisa's grandmother, She-Bears-the-Water, brought the child into the world with proper Zuñi rituals, medicinal herbs, and incantations, along with Marisa's insistence upon antiseptic procedures. The only disappointment was that the baby was as pale-skinned as any white man.

Marisa, the young widow, found it convenient to stay in Zuni. The Indian Health Service there needed a good nurse, and her grandparents were more than happy to watch the baby while she was working. Thus it happened that the pale little half-breed acquired Zuñi as his first language, though Marisa saw to it that he also understood English. When Marisa's old grandfather Zima died, the much-loved child came to be called simply Zima, as if he had taken the place of the respected elder of the tribe.

In 1980, when Little Zima was thirteen, Marisa realized there was no future for her in Zuni; so she moved to San Franciso and landed a job at the UCSF Hospital. At the San Francisco Indian Center, she soon met a charming Southern Ute/Laguna half-breed, who proved responsible and ambitious. They were soon married, and, since neither spoke the other's language, English became the tongue of the household.

Little Zima, always called George Anderson in the Anglo world, did well in high school and was awarded a scholarship at UC Berkeley, where in 1990, he received a B.A. in hydraulic engineering. During a two-year stay with his Anderson grandparents in Houston, he earned an M.A. from Rice University and was invited into a job in his field with the Houston-Galveston Port Authority. He was paid handsomely and soon found himself able to afford imported clothes from England and France. He soon bought a red and white Miata convertible, so he could drive wherever he wanted in air-blown comfort.

In the summer of 1995, he, too, returned to Zuni.

He hardly knew where to begin, since none of his immediate family lived in Zuni. His Anglo grandparents were living in Houston and his Indian grandparents in Gallup, while his mother and her siblings were living Anglo lives in San Francisco, Seattle, and New York City. It was a Sunday afternoon, so almost no one was on the streets. He drove to the place where he remembered that his great-grandmother, She-Bears-the-Water, had lived. He approached several men sitting in cane chairs and asked, "Do you know where I can find She-Bears-the-Water?"

Although Little Zima spoke respectable Zuñi, admittedly rough from lack of use the last several years, he found no one who had heard of her. The Zuñi men he asked looked suspiciously at the little red and white Miata and were silent. Disappointed, he didn't know what to do with himself; he drove up and down the streets of Zuni—very little had changed—then stopped at some of the "Authentic Indian Jewelry" shops on the outskirts to ask questions. But he found they were all owned and operated by Pakistanis or Iranians or Lebanese, who knew nothing but how to add up dollar signs and haggle endlessly over prices. He bought an inlay "Sun-God" bolo tie for half the asking price and put it on over his plaid western shirt with mother-of-pearl snaps.

He was dressed in his usual Houston outfit: Texas cowboy boots, Levis, a plaid shirt, and a white, wide-brimmed, felt Stetson. He made another pass through town along the main highway, then parked in front of the Zuni Community Gift Shop, which his grandfather had once owned. He went in cautiously, hardly knowing what to expect. Two Zuñi men in plaid, Western shirts with mother-of-pearl snaps, hardly glanced at him, but they eyed his red and white Miata with distrust and envy.

In the shop, there was a plethora of things made in Taiwan: fiberglass bow and arrow sets with rubber tips and dyed ostrich feathers, and molded rubber six-shooters in plastic holsters—junk that would appeal to an Anglo child, but fall apart within a few days of their getting back to Kansas City or Louisville. The shelves were packed with things mass-produced by other tribes or Anglo companies: Minne Tonka mocassins, and such like.

Behind the tourist facade, he saw much nicer wares in glass cases, as well as items not for sale—saddles and old rifles hanging from the ceiling, and photo murals of the old Zuni pueblo, long since torn down and built over. He couldn't remember if he had actually seen the pueblo when he was a child, or if he had only seen hundreds of these photos and convinced himself that they were real experiences. He could practically feel the pressure of a ladder rung on his arches as he climbed toward an upper apartment.

"May I help you?" asked a clerk, a young woman about his own age, not immediately obviously an Indian. She wore Anglo clothes, with a few pieces of Zuñi jewelry to convince the tourists that she had a right to stand behind the counter.

"Uh—no, uh—" He was caught by surprise and stammered in English, "Uh, I was just looking around."

She smiled at his embarrassment, but said nothing.

George nervously brushed his nose with his forefinger. "Sure isn't much going on in town."

"It's Sunday," the clerk said, as if that explained everything.

"Everything's closed," said George.

She smiled again. "Everything but this place and all those junk shops run by 'East Indians.' They've got nothing better to do, so they hold their shops open sixteen to eighteen hours a day, seven days a week. This is the only Zuñi place the tribal council allows to be open."

"There's no one on the streets."

She knitted her fingers together and smiled again. He was aware that, if the shop had been busy, she would have excused herself and moved on to a customer more interested in buying something. But the shop was almost empty; she stood, waiting, maintaining eye contact with him.

"You're not from around here, are you?" said George.

"Oh, yes," she said. "I was born and raised here, but I went to high school in Gallup, and then I lived for a while in Los Angeles."

"My mother did the same. Except she went to San Francisco. Still lives there."

The clerk was not interested. She did not pursue that line of conversation.

"What were you doing in Los Angeles?" George asked, trying to pick up the dialogue again.

"Oh, you know. Just knocking about. Went to a community college for a while; clerked in a department store for a while...."

"That's where you learned to maintain eye contact with a customer, eh?"

She looked down and did not respond.

"Did you ever hear of Raymond Zima?" he asked.

"No, I don't believe I have," she said.

"He is my grandfather. He once owned this building, this shop."

She looked away, as if someone had just told an untruth.

"So you went to Los Angeles for some years? And then you came back here?" asked George.

"Yes," she said. "Sooner or later, every true Zuñi returns to Zuni."

"Well, I may not be a true Zuñi, but I was born here, and my mother is Zuñi; so I guess I've got a right to return if I want to."

"You were born here?" she asked in Zuñi.

"Yes," he responded in Zuñi. "In the house of old Zima and She-Bears-the-Water. Old Zima is dead, but I can't seem to find a trace of She-Bears-the-Water."

The clerk's manner changed. She let her arms drop to her sides, half came from behind the counter, and continued in Zuñi: "Maybe she'll be at some of the small dances that are usually held on Sunday evenings."

"Yeah, but how in the world would I find one of those?"

"Meet me at twilight, up at the grocery store, and I'll help you look." She smiled at him, maintained eye contact, and sort of rolled her shoulders.

Near nightfall, George parked his Miata beside the creek and walked to the area where the ancient Zuni Pueblo had stood. The area was filled with crooked, dirt streets, among mud houses with milled windows and doors, and ten-year-old cars parked helter-skelter among them. But it was as if the area was uninhabited. He could see, now and then, a curtain waver at a window, but no human being was on the street; they seemed to be forewarned of his arrival and vanished.

Baffled, he returned to his car and found a number of four- and five-year-olds gawking at it. "Pretty, isn't it?" he said in Zuñi. The children bolted as if he had said he was a devil or an Anglo policeman.

He drove south across the creek and stopped at the grocery store where just about everyone in Zuni came sooner or later. He looked around for the girl from the Zuni Community Gift Shop, but, stupidly, he had forgotten to ask her name; so he could not ask for her. He asked the clerk, in Zuñi, "Have you heard of a very old woman named 'She-Bears-the-Water'?"

The clerk looked at the mother-of-pearl snaps on his shirt, the Zuñi Sun-God bolo, and answered in English, "No. She live around here?"

"She did when I was a baby," said George in Zuñi. "I can't seem to find her or anyone who has ever heard of her."

"Well, people move. They come and they go," said the clerk in English. He turned to busy himself with some shelves.

Frustrated, George left his car at the grocery store and started walking the side streets, hoping he would see someone he recognized. Soon, away from the sounds of cars and the streets, he heard singing and drumming in the distance. He went toward it.

In a small plaza, a large number of Zuñis were assembled around a bonfire, with Kon-tiki kerosene flares around the sides. No wonder he hadn't been able to find anyone to talk to or ask directions; they were all here in this crowded little plaza. He recognized the dance and the ceremony, but could not remember the name of it. He moved closer, thinking he would identify the dance or some of the participants.

A polished cottonwood stick like a hiking staff or a lance was lowered across his chest. Four Zuñi men had come out to meet him, like sergeants-at-arms.

"Sorry," said the captain in English. "This is a private ceremony. Outsiders are not permitted here."

"No, it isn't," said George in Zuñi. "I recognize the dance, but I can't remember what it's called."

"Outsiders are not permitted here," repeated the captain. "You'll have to leave."

"I'm not an outsider," said George in Zuñi. "I remember this dance. Anyone who wanted could come to it. And dance if he wanted."

"Look, Bozo," said the corporal. "We said this is a private affair and you ain't welcome." He waved his staff threateningly.

The captain held up his hand to stop the corporal. "Look, Buddy. It's true that we don't object to tourists at some of our dances, as long as they stay off to the side and don't make themselve obnoxious. But this isn't one of them. This is a sacred dance and ceremony."

"This isn't sacred," said George in Zuñi. "I remember it as like a Friendship Dance. Everyone is invited in. Even the Anglos."

"Look, Bozo," said the corporal. "That's a nice shirt you got on, and a nice pair of boots. You wouldn't want to get them scuffed or dirtied up, would you? You better leave, like we said, before we have to...." He waved his staff across in front of George's face.

"I know my rights," said George in Zuñi. "You're just bluffing. Why, I don't know, since this isn't a holy dance. I know what's holy and what's not."

"Oh, do you?" said a third of the constables in English. "Well, if I poke a hole in that nice shirt, then it will be holy. Beat it, Buster." He feinted toward George's chest with his cottonwood staff.

George grabbed the staff and pulled the man off his feet, causing him to lose his grip on his staff. George grabbed it and brought it up in time to counter the downward stroke of the corporal's staff. The staffs popped like shots. George whirled and got behind the captain, pinning his elbows behind him with his own staff. "Is there no one here with any sense?" screamed George in Zuñi, using the captain as a shield against the attack of the other constables and dragging him toward the dance in the plaza.

"Here, here, stop that," said a Zuñi voice so soft and weak that everyone was forced to listen for it.

The constables immediately stopped and waited, while an old woman, hardly four feet tall, hobbled out of the plaza toward them, with the aid of the clerk from the Zuni Community Gift Shop. The old woman shook her walking stick at the constables, and they dodged, as if she had struck at them.

"You leave that boy alone," she said.

"But Grandmother," said the captain in defence. "He's an outsider. We're supposed to keep outsiders outside."

"Pshaw! He's no more an outsider than you are. This is Little Zima. See that mole on his forehead? I'd know it anywhere. He's my own granddaughter's baby."

Return to Zuni

George broke away from the constables and walked rapidly toward the old woman. "Grandmother? She-Bears-the-Water? Is that you?"

"Yes, Little Zima. This is what's left of She-Bears-the-Water. It lifts my heart to see you again, Little Zima. I had no idea of whether you were still alive, or had turned into a white man."

George dropped to his knees and touched his forehead to hers. "Oh, Grandmother. I was afraid I wouldn't find you. I went to where you lived when I was a baby, but the people there said they had never heard of you. I didn't know what to do."

"They were just trying to protect me. We Zuñis still know nothing when we think a white man is involved. They thought you were a paleface."

"I thought grandfather Raymond had returned to Zuni. Is he around?"

"No. He and Mary Dog-Trot came home when he was hurt on the railroad. But they went away again. Every one of the family is dead or has moved away, except me," she said. "I just seem to go on and on. That's the way Old Zima said it would be. But these young people nowadays, they haven't even heard of Old Zima." She waved her walking stick at the constables, and they retreated.

"They haven't heard of Little Zima either. They took me for an Anglo."

"Well, come on," she said. "You can sit with me, over by the drums. I can't stay on my feet for very long any more."

"Oh, I'll bet you could dance all night."

"Not all night, sonny. But maybe once around the plaza; then you can dance with Susan Red-Tail, this lovely girl that came and found me. Seeing you has put little wings on my feet. It's so nice to see you again, Little Zima." She took his arm in one hand and her walking stick in the other, and, slowly, she escorted him into the dance. Smiling, Susan hooked her arm in Little Zima's other arm, and they formed a trio.

"I had a feeling," said She-Bears-the-Water, taking up the step, "that some day, you'd return to Zuni. Every true Zuñi, sooner or later, returns to Zuni."

Cowboy

"Hey, Cowboy! Come and sit in on a few hands." Some of the truckers, Tilman Snyder from Memphis, Billy Billings from Los Angeles, and Frank Coppersmith from somewhere west of Denver that no one could locate on the map, were sitting around the poker table. There were two empty chairs. Tilman scooted one of them around a bit in a gesture of invitation.

Jolly Mankiller hesitated a moment, still tying the ribbon in one of his braids after his shower. He listened in his mind to the invitation again, trying to detect if there were sarcasm or hatred or aggression in the tone, but he didn't hear any. He strolled toward the game.

At least they didn't call him "Chief," as the whole company had in Viet Nam, even the lieutenant and captain. He made no secret of his Indianness: in addition to braids, he wore a turquoise watchband; a huge, silver, sand-cast belt buckle; cowboy boots; levis and a plaid western shirt with mother-of-pearl snaps. Even though he was from the Qualla Boundary and none of these badges had roots in Cherokee traditions, he still wore the uniform of a "breed" in Indian Country.

He sat down, rubbing the wound in his right bicep to ease the pain, and nodded to Frank Coppersmith. Frank was a half-breed like himself, and a Viet Nam veteran, but he tried to hide both. Jolly didn't hold that against him; every man had his own way of keeping the alligators off.

"What chu hauling this time?" asked Billy. "I heard your handle on the CB down in Texas. I tried to say howdy, but I guess you was out of my range."

"Yeah," admitted Jolly. "I was in Texas this morning. I'm on a cattle drive, just like the old days on the Goodnight-Loving Trail. Got a load of steers from San Antone. We're bound for Montan, to do the Hoolihan."

"I hate steers," said Tilman. "They shit all over a rig."

"Ain't that the truth!" said Frank.

Darlene Jones, Billy's driving partner and companion, came out of the shower room, still brushing her hair. "Hey, Cowboy! Good to see you! And congratulations! I heard you took 'All-around' at the truck rodeo in Albuquerque. You going to the Nationals?"

Jolly shrugged and mumbled, "I just got lucky."

"Lucky, hell!" said Darlene. "Don't give me that 'lucky' bullshit. Not many men, or women either, can handle eighteen wheels the way you do." She sat in the empty chair and tapped the table twice to indicate that Tilman should deal her into the next hand.

"How 'bout you, Cowboy? Are you in?" asked Tilman, lifting the deck slightly.

"I can't," said Jolly, caressing the scar on his bicep through his shirt. "Gotta head 'em up, move 'em on out."

"You work too much," said Billy. "It must have been six this morning when I heard you down in Texas. And now you talking about driving all night?"

"Well, I had a little rest down by Roswell. This company unloads the steers a couple of hours, so they can take on a little water and feed. And I took a shower just now. I can make it okay now. I'm supposed to be at the layover corrals north of Cheyenne by first light."

"Shit!" said Billy. "They ain't no beaver out, that time of day."

"You keep your nose to that doggone highway, like it was a grindstone," said Frank.

"Hey," said Jolly, getting up and heading for the door, "a man's got to do something to stay ahead of the twelve-steppers."

He took his hammer and went around to check all eighteen. The steers were restless tonight. Milling about in their cramped space, bawling, and Tilman was right, they were shitting all over everything. Every minute he could make up on the freeway gave them a few more minutes at the layover. He climbed in, cranked up, and pointed his Kenworth north on I-25.

"To stay ahead of the twelve-steppers," he had told the gang at the truck stop. Truth was, he was staying ahead of the bottle. He drove to keep from drinking. It was so easy, when the worms and alligators started crawling in a man's mind, to shoo them away with a shot of Wild Turkey. That first shot poured out so smoothly all over a person's insides and made him feel utterly safe, and that safety was plenty good reason to take a second shot. Then another, and pretty soon, the worms became friendly and the alligators started to smile. The only trouble was, you woke up with a brain full of alligator teeth. Then you started all over.

He got so bad at one time that the V.A. Hospital in Tampa put him in therapy. They said he was suffering from post-traumatic stress from his Viet Nam experiences. He hadn't noticed it. And the fact was, he didn't feel anything particular about Viet Nam. The memories were perfectly neutral. There had been hairy experiences, true, but he had worked it out so he could survive. He always asked the sergeant or lieutenant to let him walk swing, because he was the only cowboy in that outfit who was able to detect Charlie before he stuck his feathers up out of a gully or when he came over the ridge in a wave. He didn't like point, because too many point men caught a sniper's shot, like Jolly had with his right bicep, and he didn't like being in the herd because there was no protection when Charlie started throwing his shit. Two of the three times he had been wounded, all slightly, he had been forced to walk in the herd in the middle, while the sergeant or lieutenant walked drag.

He was good at swing. He had an instinct for it. He felt safe there, because he was responsible for himself and he trusted his own abilities, far more than he trusted any of his fellow soldiers. And, when he had saved the squad and the company a few times with warnings and carefully directed fire, he started hearing respect and love, mixed in with the sarcasm when the men called him "Chief." He was given a job to do, and he did it well. That required no particular praise and no blame. There was nothing there to cause post-traumatic stress.

But the group therapy sessions at Tampa were another matter. Now, there was a bunch of men with real nightmares. And Jolly soon found himself dreaming other men's traumas and feeling other men's pains. He couldn't help being infected. Their stories were so real, their agony so horrible, their need to be heard so intense and bloody, that the worms and alligators made Jolly sick with post-traumatic stress. He got so bad, he had to have individual analysis with a shrink, privately.

When he thought about it nowadays, he often saw a huge gray-green worm, the size of a Greyhound bus, slithering up to his truck, oozing over the cab, sliding down in front of the windshield, and eventually falling off the front of the truck, under the wheels, to be crushed into withering, stunted remnants of a bad dream. Driving kept him ahead of the bad dreams. Especially at a truck rodeo, the concentration kept his mind clean.

He sometimes thought he ought to have a co-driver, like Darlene. Someone who could drive part of the time, talk a lot of the time, and release his tensions when they got in the sack.

He pulled down his mike, broke into the airways, and asked, "Is there any coin-operated beaver within shouting distance?"

After a long moment, a female voice came on the CB, asking, "Who wants to know?"

"This is the Cowboy from Qualla, and I need to have my head rubbed."

"Tell me more, Cowboy."

Jolly understood that she wanted to check out that he wasn't the vice squad. After he had satisfied the woman he was okay and identified his mileage marker, she responded in an exaggerated southern plantation drawl, "We 're at that li'l ole rest stop about ten miles north of yawl, Cowboy. In a purple and pink Winnebago with red curtains. We-all call ourselves the 'Skirts of Cheyenne.' Come on in. We got jist what yawl need."

"Oh?" said Jolly, trying to sound surprised and skeptical. "What do I-all need?"

The woman began singing with a lilt: "We can sing, and we can dance. We've got purple, lacy _____." She left the rhyme blank.

"What do you do for a piano player?"

"Why, we-all have a eunuch, of co-urse, with garters on his shirt sleeves."

Jolly continued bantering with the woman: Truth was, he needed the banter more than he needed sex. Nevertheless, he pulled off when he saw the rest stop and let his truck glide. On smooth tarmac, a Kenworth would coast silently.

He spotted the "Skirts of Cheyenne" at once. He let his rig roll calmly up beside it. Inside, over the cafe curtains in the picture window, he could see two truck drivers and several busty women in dance-hall costumes, sitting at a red velvet booth and drinking. He let his Kenworth float past, then he eased his foot onto the accelerator again. He couldn't go in there. The bottle would be sure to swallow him again.

Jolly jerked awake and grabbed his right bicep where the sniper's bullet had gone through. The pain was back. He shook the images out of his mind and realized he was on I-25; he had been dozing in the saddle. The adrenaline of the startle reflex would keep him awake for a few minutes, but he would have to find some place to get out and do a few deep knee bends pretty soon.

The bicep still hurt. Funny, it was the most superficial of his wounds, yet it still hurt, after all these years. The bullet had gone through clean but hadn't stopped him. He had seen the sniper's gunsmoke and filled that tree with a fog of his own fire, which put an end to that one. He went to the aid station after the patrol; the doctor flushed out the entry and exit wounds, packed them with sulfa, and put on two big, oversized Band-Aids. He went back to duty the same day. But, damn! That thing still hurt. The shrink in Tampa thought that was because it had made him feel so vulnerable.

Walking point made you feel vulnerable. You were guide, trailblazer, scout, and first-contact, all at once. And the enemy always got first strike. Driving an eighteen-wheeler up I-25 was a little like walking point; only there wasn't any swing man and no one to bring up drag. Just a bunch of wild steers, milling around and rocking the rig like it was a small boat. Plus, the darkness and your own exhaustion always got first strike.

He shook his head and focused on the roadway. These were the kinds of thoughts that brought out the worms and alligators. He didn't need any of that. He was relieved to see a sign saying there was a rest stop in eight miles. Maybe he could keep his Gollybigs at bay for eight miles.

He eased into the rest stop, took his hammer as a matter of habit, and walked around to check all eighteen. The steers were lurching about violently, as if they expected a storm. Jolly scanned the horizon in the darkness. The stars were in their proper places; there was nothing else in sight.

He went to the john, relieved himself, and splashed cold water in his face. Though he hated coffee, he figured he'd better have a cup, so he went to the all-night vendor and got one. He stayed a good while, chatting with the clerk about how dark the night was, before going back to his rig. Grazing around like this wasn't making any miles.

As he got in the truck, he saw, far to the north, probably near Cheyenne, the first strikes of lightning. Ha, the steers are right, he thought. We're in for a storm. They were lurching around in the rig, making it rock more than before. He got out, walked all the way around the truck, checking the rails and slats. He didn't want to spill his steers, the way he had seen some men spill their guts.

Satisfied everything was secure, he headed up I-25 again. He couldn't get "Little Joe, The Wrangler" out of his mind. Little Joe had been riding point in a thunderstorm and got run over by the stampede. Not a good thought to have, as you were heading into a storm. The steers were thrashing about so much, they made the rig sway. He could feel the pressure in the steering wheel. He even thought he could feel it in his wound. The good thing about that was, it would keep him awake, paying attention to the driving.

He got to the layover corrals near Cheyenne before the storm hit. The crew there unloaded and turned the steers loose in the big lot. The cattle were much more comfortable with a little space, and there were several men on horses there to keep them in herd. Jolly's arm hurt fiercely, so he took a knock-out pill and slept for a couple of hours.

For the last thirty-five miles of his trip, the freeway paralleled the Little Big Horn River. He would soon be in the footsteps of Reno and Benteen. Biggest frigging irony in the universe, he thought, that the monument to the greatest of all Sioux military achievements, the Custer Battlefield National Monument, should be right in the middle of the Crow Reservation and glorify the losers. Such a gargantuan insult couldn't have happened just by accident; there had to be a malevolent, knowing intent in the white man that invented these markers and boundaries.

At Crow Agency, he weighed in just before dusk, unloaded the steers, weighed out, and parked the Kenworth in the truck-stop remuda. He had made a little under fourteen hundred miles in a little over thirty-six hours, including layovers for the steers. That would get him a small bonus from the company, but he was ready for some R & R.

Jolly walked along the street, gazing into shop windows and reading headlines at the newsstands. Some gringo mining company was trying to strip the coal out from under the reservation by claiming that the boundaries set in the Treaty of 1868 were invalid and that the land was rightfully theirs under the laws of mineral claims. Some federal Fish and Game official was being sacked-by-transfer, because he had successfully prosecuted some Anglos who had been poaching deer and eagles on the reservations. The news was more of the same old stuff. Just the thing to bring out the worms and alligators again, if you let it get to you.

As he was bent over to read the headlines and rubbing the pain in his arm, a Crow teenager approached him: "Hey, man! I can get you a cut rate for a three-hour tour to the Custer Bat—" Then the boy noticed Jolly's braids and decided he wasn't just a rednecked cowboy. "Jeez, I'm sorry, Mister. I just noticed your boots at first."

Jolly didn't hold it against the kid; he was only trying to hustle a buck, like all the rest of us. "That's okay. No offense. But tell me, where's there a good place to get a bite to eat?"

"Most people go out to the casino. They got a little restaurant in the bar, and they give you a good meal for a fair price."

"I don't want a bar. And I was thinking of something closer by."

"There's a powwow tonight, out at the stomp grounds. There'll be lots of Indian food out there. You into powwows and stomps?"

"Yeah. I've been to a few."

"You go west on Libby Avenue; it's about two miles out of town. You can't miss it."

"Sounds worth a try. See you there?"

"Naw. Not this one. Tonight's an Honor our Veterans and Warriors stomp. I'm not into that sort of thing. I like Grandfather stomps and Friendship stomps a lot better. You pick up a lot of chicks at a Friendship stomp." The kid waved a farewell and moved on.

A warriors' stomp. Jolly hadn't been to one of those since before the war. And as for Honoring our Veterans, the anti-war crowd had thrown plenty of tin cans, trash, and rotten food at their veterans as they got off the boat. It was enough to make a man hide his commendations and medals. It was worse even than walking point and getting shot in the arm. It drove a lot of good men, including Jolly, to drink. But he remembered the old men at a powwow putting on their American Legion caps, pinning on their medals, proudly, and carrying the American flag or the eagle staff in the entrance ceremony. And there were dances just for those old men. Yeah, he would go. It would be different from most of what he had to put up with.

There was some time to kill before the powwow, so he wandered on up the street. At a half-opened door, he heard the sounds of a juke box and the whir of a crowd. A bar, of sorts, though there wasn't any sign or lights. He thought of going in. There would be people to talk to, conversations to pass the time, and he might just have one drink for the pain in his arm. Just one, and then he'd move on. He looked both ways in the street. The teenager he had talked to was watching him from the corner opposite. Jolly waved and went in.

It was not what he had expected in the capital of a reservation; everyone in the bar was white—coal miners and oil field roughnecks, grubby ranchers with long-term leases on reservation grazing. Hank Williams was singing "Your Cheating Heart" on the juke box. Jolly stood for several minutes, just looking around. No one seemed to notice him. He knew he should just turn around and leave, but there were several empty stools at the near end of the bar. He inched his way toward them and sat down.

He kept his head down, avoiding eye contact with anyone. It was the early days in Viet Nam all over again. Everybody in the PX, drinking beer after a raid or a patrol, no one talking to him, him not wanting to talk to anyone. Tolerated only because he was a member of the squad. Getting drunk to ease the pain of loneliness. Getting drunk to pacify the alligators.

After several minutes, the bartender set a mug of beer and a shot of whiskey on the bar in front of him. "Compliments of a friend," he said, then turned away.

Jolly looked up and down the bar, trying to figure out who had set him up. Everyone was studiously avoiding looking his way. He didn't want the booze, because he knew it had more worms and alligators in it than a clear mind could invent in a week. But it was there, in front of him, shining at him with amber sparkles. One boilermaker wouldn't be the end of the world. He turned away, looked down again, averted his eyes. His wounded bicep was hurting. A huge gray-green worm was oozing up from the darkness below the bar.

A voice at his elbow interrupted Jolly's thoughts: "My grandson said you were looking for a ride out to the stomp grounds."

Jolly turned around. The man wore an old-fashioned business suit, a white shirt, and a thin necktie from the fifties, but there was no mistaking; Jolly was looking at a tribal elder.

"Yeah," he said after a startled moment, then he remembered his manners. "Yes, Grandfather. Yes, I would appreciate a ride."

"Then drink up, and we'll move along."

Jolly looked again at the mug of beer and shot of whiskey. "No," he said. "No, I don't need it now. You can have it."

"They won't let me drink in here," said the old man. "It's some sort of dirty trick or a joke, or they wouldn't have set you up. Let's go."

Outside, the old man indicated a four-year-old Chrysler Imperial, explaining, "Bingo profits," when Jolly raised his eye-brows. "Don't worry. It's mine, and it's paid for. Get in."

The old man turned onto a side street, then another, and another, and they were on Libby Avenue heading west. "I figure you're a veteran of Viet Nam," said the old man.

"Yes," said Jolly.

"You entitled to wear any medals?"

"Yes. Three Purple Hearts, a Bronze Star, and a Silver Star." Jolly was surprised that he was neither ashamed nor proud to say it matter-of-factly to this elder.

"I knew it," said the old man, slapping the steering wheel. "I knew you were a warrior, as soon as my grandson described you."

At the stomp grounds, the elder parked, saying, "We're a little bit early. But that's okay. Give us a chance to introduce you around. My wife runs one of the food booths. Makes an Indian taco you won't believe."

"I could use a bit of food," admitted Jolly.

There were already several men and women milling around the edge of the dance ground. Several of the men wore fancy-dance roaches and bustles, and mirrors and feathers sewn into their short sleeves. The women wore doeskin dresses, with long fringes at the hem and sleeves, and lots of necklaces and elaborately embroidered shawls about their necks. They were visiting in small, self-absorbed groups; none seemed the least anxious for the powwow to begin.

Jolly and the elder got Indian tacos and diet Pepsis, then sat at the nearby picnic table to eat them. Several of the older men paused briefly at the table, greeting the elder and waiting momentarily for Jolly to give them his name and origins. When the men had welcomed him and passed on, the elder often gave Jolly an account of how the men were related to others. Everyone seemed to be part of the same extended family.

When the line-up for the grand entry began forming, it was not the dancers in colorful bustles that stood in front, but old Indian cowboys in levis and plaid shirts, insurance salesmen in blazers and slacks, a few dancers in feathers and beads. Most of them wore American Legion caps and sashes draped from one shoulder to the opposite hip, on which were pinned their badges of honor, from boy scout merit badges, to community awards, to Purple Hearts, to U.S. Medals of Honor. The elder surprised Jolly once again by producing a sash for him, containing representations of his medals. "I added the Viet Nam Service and the Good Conduct Medals," said the elder, as he escorted Jolly to a place near the middle of the grand entry group. "We're proud to have you dance with us," he added. His own sash had a modest number of medals on it. Jolly could see pin holes where two medals, probably a Purple Heart and a Good Conduct Medal, had been removed. He wondered where the elder got the other medals.

The drum began. Women trilled a high-pitched *ulalah* to welcome the warriors home. Ankle bells started ringing with the drum.

The grand marshall, the flag and eagle-staff bearers, and the head dancers, both men and women, led the group forward, dancing

Cowboy 171

languidly from side to side, moving forward slowly to savor the moment of honor.

Jolly took out his keys, a large metal ring with several big keys on it, and used them as a dance rattle. It reminded him in a way of the jingling of spurs. As the group entered the dance area, he found himself dancing swing. It felt comfortable. He felt safe and secure, right where he ought to be. The worms and alligators and the pain in his arm were further away than the stars, which shone above in their proper places, telling everyone where he belongs.

Comeuppance
At Kicking Horse Casino

(Seven Conversations from a Play)

1

Billy Duc-Doc is working in his office at the Kicking Horse Casino, when an old high school classmate knocks at the door. He comes energetically from behind his large, walnut desk, and extends his hand to shake. "Gary! Gary Fitzgerald! I haven't seen you in eight or ten years. Come on in. Have a seat." Billy indicates one of the padded guest chairs, seats himself in the other. Billy is twenty-eight, rather Indian-looking with braids, which are bound at the ends with beaded clasps. He wears a modest amount of Indian jewelry, a turquoise inlay watchband; he looks like a young Russell Means.

Gary Fitzgerald is also twenty-eight, handsome, jock, liked by all, but has been in a series of go-nowhere jobs since high school; he looks like a young Paul Newman. "Jeez," he says, "who would've thought it? Billy Duc-Doc, manager of the Kicking Horse Casino!"

"Co-manager," says Billy, making a gesture of dismissal. "I've got a partner. Hokai Yellow-Stick. You remember him? The one that sang "Old Man River" at graduation? He's our accountant. Does most of the business and money side and working with the tribe, the government, administration, that sort of thing; I work on personnel, advertising, public relations, things like that."

"It's hard to grasp." Gary makes a sweeping gesture with both hands. "The Kicking Horse Casino and Turf Club. Where'd you guys get a name like that?"

"He was my great-grandfather. Quite a man in his time. He was never heard of, outside the reservation, but the tribal council thought everybody would recognize it instantly as a generic Indian name. Sort of a brand-name recognition." Billy gestures vaguely toward the front of the building. "Same thing for that windmill of neon feathers, rotating in the chief's bonnet on the tower out front."

Gary stands up, goes to Billy's mezzanine window, and surveys the casino floor. "Boy! Co-manager of a big concern like this! You sure lucked out!"

"Well, yeah, I guess luck has a lot to do with it," says Billy, looking at the floor and shuffling his feet slightly. "I didn't do too well at Central High, as you'll remember. All that razzing and torment. Especially about my name. And I was so dark, I didn't fit in. But, after we graduated, the tribe gave me some bingo money and I went to that community college that was just getting started across the valley to study journalism. Did real well, too." He straightens up and looks at Gary directly. "Got a straight-A A.A."

"Wish I could have gone on to school."

"So the circle of elders picked me to go to the university and business school, specifically casino and restaurant management." Billy stands, walks behind his desk, gives a little lecture. "The tribal council had it in mind for some time to do more than bingo on the reservation, but they didn't want to call in a bunch of professional gamblers from New Jersey. They think they're all crooks. Some gaming companies take seventy percent of the profits before giving the Indians anything. That's not skimming, that's scooping. The tribe didn't want that to happen. So they trained me and Hokey to run this show. Bit by bit, we've turned it into a pretty successful affair."

"I'll say! I bet Las Vegas couldn't even match it."

"Oh, no. We're way behind Las Vegas," he says, waving off the suggestion. "They've got generations of people whose only business has been schmaltz and glitz. We'll never match them. Just when you think you're getting close, they do something really off the scale, like they'll blow up a twenty-five-story casino-hotel and build something that looks like a mega-ton mushroom or an elephant in its place." He shakes his head, as if the image is hard to comprehend. "We don't even try to keep up with them. But what about you? What've you been up to all this time?"

"Oh, you know. Knocking about, taking whatever I could get." Gary returns to his chair. "I got married right after we graduated. Karen Johnson. You remember Karen Johnson?"

"The cheerleader that made us all drool! I'll say I remember Karen Johnson," Billy says, coming back out and sitting near Gary. "She always went for jocks like you. She was planning to go on to the university and study musical theater. God, she could sing! And dance!"

"Yeah, well. We had a little accident on prom night—and had to get hitched."

"That's too bad. She was—uh—sure intelligent. And God! she was a knock-out!"

"Still is."

Billy holds his hands up in an "it all comes out in the wash" gesture. "Hey, living with Karen Johnson can't be all bad."

"That's what they say. Uh—You guys advertised for blackjack dealers."

"Yes. We're putting on twenty-five new dealers, this round of expansion." Billy leans forward on one elbow. "You think you'd like to try your hand at dealing?"

"Yeah, I thought I'd like to give it a try."

"I heard you were driving truck for Simpson's Hauling?"

"Yeah, I worked for them a little over two years. Made pretty good money, too."

"Did you get fired or quit?"

"I quit."

"Why?"

"Oh, y'know. I was just driving around. Going nowhere."

"And you think dealing blackjack is a job that will go somewhere?"

"Hey, Chief, uh—Billy," says Gary, looking at his hands, flustered. "I gotta have a job. I got a wife and a kid to feed. The Kicking Horse Casino is the only place in the county that's hiring people." He faces Billy, appealing. "Come on, Billy, gimme a job. For old time's sake."

"Okay, I'll give you a job," says Billy, standing up. "But not for old time's sake. I'll give you a job because you're a handsome buzzard with a good line of b.s. You always were popular with the kind of people we expect to be coming in here and leaving seventy-two percent of their money. We can teach you to deal cards, but we can't teach you to be handsome and popular." Billy turns toward the door; Gary stands and does the same. "Report on Monday at eight o'clock. You'll get ten days of training—you have to learn all our games—and then we'll put you on the day shift. Commissions aren't as good on days, because the breakfast-to-lunch crowd is mainly Anglo senior citizens who want to play bingo, and the afternoon crowd tends to be people on fixed incomes, with a fixed amount they're willing to play. They aren't big tippers. They're just looking for a nice place to spend the day. But you got to have somewhere to develop and smooth out your technique."

"Smooth out my technique?"

"Yeah. Y'know. Your line of patter. The maneuvers. The come-on's. It's all pretty straightforward."

"Oh. Uh—you mentioned commissions—"

"Yes, we pay ten dollars an hour base, plus a fraction of a percentage of the take at your table, plus tips. Work it right, and you can make two-fifty, three hundred a day."

"Really? I've had jobs where I didn't make that much in a week."

"I know."

"And I heard you offer benefits...."

"Yes. We pay hospitalization insurance from the beginning. After six months, we add dental coverage and eye glasses. Also, you become eligible for our group insurance package: group life, reduced auto, coverage for dependents. After a year, we start contributing to a 401(k) retirement plan in your name, but we hook a string on that one: you can't touch it until you retire, or ten years after you quit."

"Well, gee, Bill. I sure appreciate this. I'll make a good one."

They shake hands. Billy puts his arm across Gary's shoulder. "I'll go out with you and tell the money people to put you on the payroll. I'll get you a copy of our promotional newspaper, too. It has come-on pictures of the big winners and a schedule of lure games and big prizes. It'll give you some idea of how we like to operate."

"You're a buddy."

Billy stops, tugs at the back of Gary's hair. "Remember how you used to come up behind me in the hall between classes, jerk my braid, and yell 'Duck-Duck-Goose'?"

"Yeah, I'm sorr—"

"And all those bad jokes in the locker room about my being a duck-doctor? And Chief Duck-fucker?"

"Kids are crazy. Cruel."

"Yeah? Well, I guess it couldn't be helped. Given the situation as it was then. Seeing you again just made me think of it. That's all. You just made me think of it again." Billy turns back toward his desk, leaving Gary, who stands a moment, baffled, then shrugs and goes out.

2

Karen Johnson timidly sticks her head in at the door of Billy's office, tapping on the door facing. "Hello. Billy?" She is also twenty-eight, blonde, blue-eyed, voluptuous, ex-cheerleader who still has "it," a talented Marilyn Monroe, married to Gary.

"Karen! Karen, doll!" says Billy, coming around to greet her with a warm handshake. "Come in, come in. God! You're looking as smart and beautiful now as you were then."

"You're just lying. I feel stupid and haggard. And I'm almost a grandmother."

"Every grandmother should have what you've got."

"What? A shitty life? Excuse my French."

"Hey, it can't be that bad?" Billy indicates a chair for her to sit in, sits in the other himself.

"Can't it? Gary never gets all the grease from under his fingernails. And his mother, Carla— Do you know Carla?"

Billy nods.

"She always just looks right through me. You'd think Gary and I committed the first and last sin that her lousy priests ever thought of. But she's nice to Jennifer. I will say that, she's a good grandmother. But she's the world's worst, most sanctimonious, self-righteous, evangelical mother-in-godforsaken-law. She just loves to make people feel guilty. Oh—" She catches herself, is suddenly very embarrassed. "Why am I telling you all this? I haven't even seen you in—what is it?—ten years, or more."

"It's okay. I'm safe. You've got it all corked up. If you need to blow the cork, blow away."

"She keeps asking why Gary and I haven't had any more kids. Ha! If she only knew. I take the pill. Every time I take one, I think of her and it's the sweetest pill in the universe. She's got a lot of gall, goading me, after her and Ed only having Gary, and him late enough to be a change of life accident. She was probably so repulsive that Ed never thought of getting close to her a second time. But he's got an eye that'll undress me every time I come into the room. His eyes— It's like he has fingers all over me. I don't even like to go over there. I've even thought of leaving Gary, but I don't know what I'd do with Jennifer. Oh, I don't know where it's all going. Did you ever get married? Do you have problems like this?"

"No. My problems—" Billy looks at the floor for a moment, clears his throat—"have always been of a different sort." He stands, goes to the mezzanine window. "And I've been so busy with school and making up for what the public school and mainstream America didn't do for me, that I still haven't married."

"I don't know why I let myself get into this mess," Karen goes on. "I was going to get an education and do big things. I was going to be a song and dance star."

Billy turns toward her again. "That has something to do with why I called you to come over. Have you ever thought of going back into singing and dancing?"

"What do you mean?"

"Well, you know we added a dinner theater to the casino last year. I know you've seen it when you and your in-laws have been here to eat."

"It's the nicest place in fifty miles to have dinner."

"Thanks. The way we have it calculated, it's about time to start adding a few dinner numbers on the stage and maybe something more riotous for the after-dinner show. Considering audience appeal, we're thinking of a crooner in a low-cut gown for the first, and, for the second, a hoofer who can show a lot of leg and a little bit of breast—nothing actually dangerous, you understand. It just has to look at every moment like the next move is going to be absolutely disastrous. I remember, in high school, you were good at both."

"You're offering me a job? I can't believe— I couldn't—" She fidgets a moment with her purse. "What would I do with Jennifer? Geez, Billy, I haven't danced since I was pregnant."

"Is it something you forget?"

"No. Yes." She pulls her skirt up a couple of inches and looks at her legs, as if they contain the answer. "I don't know."

"Do you want to try it for a while?"

"Yes. No. Wait a minute." She grabs her own forehead. "Stop the world. Job, that means independence; that means I can hire baby-sitters; that means I can leave the Fitzgerald clan; that means wheeeeee, I'm free. I could actually be my own person again?"

"Whoa. Hold on," says Billy, taking her hand in his. "You're swinging a little far and fast. Going for the grand slam in the first inning. We were thinking of trying it for a month or two." Billy stands while explaining. "We'll do some slick photos, take out big ads in all the papers and magazines, run a bunch of local-girl-does-good stories, hype you up on the radio and TV. In two months, we renegotiate. If the tribal elders and council like your act and you bring in the crowds, the tribe will send you to the theater program at Valley College for two terms to spiff up your professionalism. After another year on the job, everything is negotiable again. We haven't laid out any specific plans beyond that, but we're likely to need a choreographer and director of theater. And what I've outlined requires that you get over an "if" at every turn. So what do you say? Are you the casino's first song and dance girl?"

"God, Billy, I'd roll over and play dead for half of what— Why me? Why Karen Johnson? Why not a dozen girls that are in better training? And younger? Who don't have any stretch marks?"

"You're local. You're good. You're squeaky clean. You could play the Lawrence Welk show. We're thinking you'd bring in a kind of person that hasn't been in before."

"You've been watching me," she says, smiling knowingly. "Just like in high school. I used to see your eyes running all over my body." She squirms a little to show her figure. "You wanted me then, and I think you want me now."

"No, Karen. You've got it all wrong," he says, taking both of her hands and putting them in her lap. He looks her directly in the eye. "You're gorgeous, but this is strictly business. In high school, every time we made eye contact, I saw something, a steel curtain, something impenetrable, close in your eyes. You didn't look through me; you just never saw anything. If I'd seen anything else then, I might see something else now. But I don't need you now. I don't need the Fitzgerald clan now. If they'd done something then about the poverty and ringworm that were on the reservations, I might see things differently. But they didn't. You didn't. And now I don't." He stands, turns away. "This is a business proposition: we need a song and dance girl with a lot of cheesecake, who can also croon a romantic number in a soft spotlight. We think a local girl would pull in the local crowd. Down the line somewhere, we'll add a stand-up comedian, maybe add a chorus line. Maybe we'll do whole musicals. We'll have to see what brings in the customers."

"Gollee, things sure change fast nowadays. I'm changing too, you know," she says, standing up so she can look him eye-to-eye. "I don't see—people the same way I used to."

"So, are you our song and dance girl for sixty days? Or should I call in the next girl?"

"God, Billy, let me think a moment. If I leave the Fitzgeralds, I'll never be able to go back. That'd be crossing the river of no return. At least, that's a plus. But then it's me and Jennifer, sink or swim. That's scary. Am I good enough to make it? I don't see any safety net. Oh, I don't know, Billy. Yes, I'll take it. Oh, yes, yes, I'll take it."

"Good for you! I'll walk out with you and tell the money people to put you on the payroll. Show up Monday and start your practicing and getting your costumes together. Let me know what kind of supplies you need."

"Sometimes, when Jennifer and Gary are gone, I still pull on that frontier dance-hall costume I used to dance in. I ooze out like toothpaste at both ends, but the men used to love it."

"You've got the idea. You still got that black-velvet sheath you wore to the prom? That would be good for the torch song."

"The one I have to wear without underwear? Yeah. I always felt sexy and—and—beautiful, in that dress. I just couldn't throw it away."

"Good. I'm sure Carla will be happy to keep Jennifer for the first week or so. After that, you'll be able to manage on your own." Billy puts his arm across her shoulder to escort her out.

"You're a prince, Billy, you know that? Why wasn't I born a princess?"

"Ask your grandmother. It wasn't the Indians that laid down the terms of the relationships between your people and mine." They meet Billy's grandfather, who is entering.

3

"**I** come to talk," the grandfather says, an elder of the tribe who wears conventional working man's clothing and uses a walking cane.

"Grandfather! How nice to see you! You honor me with your visit. Karen, this is my grandfather, Woodrow Wilson Kicking Duc. Grandfather, this is Karen Johnson, uh, Karen Fitzgerald. She's going to do a song and dance for us evenings."

"Then I'll have to go against my principles, even if I am eighty-three, and come to the casino in the evenings."

"You're too kind, grandfather, but I'll do my best, just for you."

"You hear that, Billy?" He waves his cane toward Billy. "She's a real Indian princess. Why don't you find a princess like this and settle down?"

"You're sweet, grandfather." She tiptoes and kisses him on the cheek. "But I'll leave you two to your business, now. We can take care of the payroll stuff later, Billy."

"Leave your Social Security number with Diane," Billy yells after her. "I'll do the rest later today, Karen-doll."

"She sure turned into a beautiful young woman," says grandfather, looking after her. "I was in love with her grandmother in grammar school."

"I didn't know that."

"Her grandmother didn't either." He waddles toward the guest chair, tapping his cane on the floor, and sits. "She only had eyes for Kyle Johnson. No way was she going to notice a murky, scruffy kid like me. No way she was ever going to kiss me on the cheek. Times sure change."

"Why, I'll bet you were a handsome kid." Billy sits in the other chair.

"Nope. I was bright—bright enough to catch a half-breed wife." He rests both hands atop his cane, standing between his feet. "Bright enough to have become a mechanical engineer, if I'd had the opportunity. But not handsome. Your grandmother always said I was the ugliest man on the reservation. Still does, and we've been together a little over sixty years. You'd think she'd be used to it by now."

"How is grandmother?"

"Same. Grouchy as ever, God love her. I don't know what I'd do if she ever quit grumping. Probably start digging her grave."

"Let me burn some tobacco in your honor." Billy goes behind his desk, slits a cigarette, dumps the tobacco into an ashtray, and puts a lighted match to it.

"Thank you, *Illio cha-la*. We never know whether our tribal gods or the Christian gods are listening, so it's always best to hedge our bets."

"You know I don't believe in any god, grandfather. I burn the tobacco for you."

"I know. Can you also stop someone from gambling for me?"

"I didn't know anyone in our family gambles, except of course for the Indian guessing games we've always had."

"It's not one of ours. It's some Mexican workers. Since we've been getting the per-capita distribution from the gambling profits, things are sure looking up. Your grandmother and I decided we'd like to have our little house plastered, both inside and out. Buy some new furniture. You know, sort of raise our standard of living."

"Last time I was by the house, it looked real good to me." Billy comes back and sits in the other guest chair.

"Yes, they're doing a fine job. We hired that Whiteside Plastering Company that Ed Fitzgerald owns. He and I were kids in school together, you know."

"Yes. But I'll bet he doesn't remember it."

"You're right about that. Anyway. He hires illegal immigrants to do his work. They do good work, but he gets to pay 'em less."

"Always pays cash, so there's no way to trace him, and doesn't withhold any income tax or social security, or offer any benefits. Greed and capitalism, those two go together. It's the American Way. I don't see what the problem is."

"It's Jorge and Jaime. They no sooner get their money in hand than they head straight to the casino. Think they're going to multiply their money in a few flips of the cards or a flicker of the electronic slot machine. But they always lose everything they've got. And if they do take a pot, they shove it right back in the slots. Don't even stop to send part of it home to their kinfolks in Mexico. Then someone like me has to lend them money to eat on the rest of the week. Next pay day, it's the same little game."

"Haven't you told them that the game is always rigged, so that the house wins in the long run?"

"Oh, sure. But they always know someone, who knows someone, who knows someone, who struck it rich. It's never any of them, or anyone they know personally. Their dreams are built on hearsay."

"Hearsay by relay. Long distance. That's the way it works for everyone. At least, they don't bet on horses."

"We want to know, your grandmother and I, is there anything you young people can do about it?"

"Young people?"

"Yeah. Used to, when I was a kid, most of the young people died, or moved to town to starve, and that left the old folks on the reservation to run things and make decisions and all that. And we managed to lumber along with the old traditions. But nowadays, it's not the same. Somebody besides a white man finally discovered a profitable way to use Indian land, and it was our own young people. You young fellows are running the show now, but some of us old-timers don't much like this 'economic' development."

"Believe me, grandfather, if there were any other way to get rid of ringworm and bubonic plague, I'd take it. Plague can be cured with a thirty-five cent shot of penicillin, if you can only get the shot to the right place at the right time. It takes a bunch of money to deliver that thirty-five cent shot where it's needed."

"Anyway, we were wondering, your grandmother and I, if there's any way you can keep Jorge and Jaime from coming in here?"

"I don't see how, grandfather. I'll be glad to talk to them personally. But we can't close the door selectively to anyone, not even the Devil himself."

"He gets in without doors. Piggybacks on anyone that'll carry him." Woodrow stands up to go. "Thank you, Billy, I'll appreciate it if you can nudge their personal liberties a little bit in the direction of good sense. I'll be going now. I know you got a lot of business to attend to. No, don't get up. I can find the door on my own."

"Seeing you to the door is the least I can do, grandfather. I wish I could guarantee you more." He gets up and follows the old man toward the door.

"I'll tell you, Billy, this casino business is going to be the death of the Indian. I don't think the Indian will come out of this one."

"Sure he will. But he'll be changed. That's what always happens. We were changed by defeat in the frontier wars. We were changed by the reservation system. We were changed by the denial of social and economic opportunity. But the people always survived. We'll come out of this thing, too, and we'll be different. Some on the tribal council call that progress."

"I know they do. Time marches on, and all that. Like they used to tell us on Guadalcanal and Borneo. But I don't think I'm going to like the Indian that survives the casino gambling wars." He goes out.

4

Hokai Yellow-Stick, twenty-eight, very Indian, co-manager of the Kicking Horse Casino and Turf Club, a modern, young Red Cloud, comes into Billy's office with a sheaf of papers in his hands.

"Hi, Hokey," says Billy. "What's up?"

"Quite a bit, Goose. I thought we'd better go over what my half of the partnership has been doing lately."

"Okay. Shall I close the door?"

"Yeah. You'd better." Hokai half sits on the edge of Billy's desk and shuffles through his papers.

"Did we get the Fitzgerald land?"

"Yeah. That's the biggest item. We closed with Ed Fitzgerald yesterday. We probably paid twenty percent over market, but the tribe is now owner of the 300, 400, and 500 blocks between State Street and Reservation Road. Our architect thinks the 400 block is the best site for the Regional Inter-Tribal Health Center and Hospital, and the council has budgeted two million to get things started. We'll demolish that junky honky-tonk and the three souvenir shops right outside our gate, and break ground for the hospital within the week."

"What's taking us so long?" asks Billy, with a melodramatic gesture. "I'd better put that scholarship plan into action. If we don't start training some Indian doctors and nurses right now, we won't have anything but palefaces in the building, not counting janitors and accountants, of course."

"You're a wise-cracking duck-fucker, you know that?"

Billy ignores his comment. "I'll send the carrot to all the reservations, all the medical schools, and all the universities where Indians are even maybe thinking about going into pre-med."

"Don't forget the urban Indian centers."

"Right. I'd better make a note of that."

"We're going to leave the 300 and 500 blocks the way they are for the present. Eventually, the council is thinking about a factory-outlet shopping mall. They gave Steve Ochoa ten thousand to start a feasibility study. But, for now, those are fairly decent buildings, and we have good tenants. Those rents will make the payments on all three of the blocks and leave about thirty grand a year left over."

"Oh, my, my," says Billy, putting on an imaginary shawl and holding it at his throat. Whatever will yawl redskins ever do with that much money? Drink it all up?"

"We got plenty of rat holes, Ma'am," Hokai responds, but immediately drops the game. "Actually, the council also started the planning stages on another tract of low-mortgage, three-bedroom houses on the res. Now, that things are looking up, Indians are actually moving back home. Bungalows, lawns, the whole nine yards of picket fence. Tribal enrollment is up over fifty percent."

"Geez! And to think that when you and I were kids, the people lived in unpainted ramshackle huts and decomposing masonite trailer houses."

"Ah, yes," says Hokai, with fake nostalgia. "The life of a happy boy on the res: throwin' rocks, hittin' dirt."

Billy matches his nostalgia: "And it looked like it would last forever."

"Well, things change. Thank goodness for bingo!"

"The way the casino is taking off, bingo is going to look piddling in no time."

"Yeah. The council talked about that. The consensus was that we ought to start some public service grants."

"Like?"

"You know how all the media have been bitching and moaning about the city's symphony going broke? They say it's all but bankrupt."

"What?" says Billy, putting the back of his hand to his forehead. "Don't the Fitzgeralds have culture enough to support the arts?"

"Not this week," says Hokai, matching Billy's gesture. "The tribal council voted to make them a gift of two hundred thousand dollars. We haven't let it out yet. You're to plan the media campaign that announces it."

"There goes my golf on Thursday! And my trip to the races."

"Be serious for a minute, Goose. They also voted a hundred thousand to the city library system, to make some of those repairs that the city can't, or at least won't, fund. You're to coordinate the releases on that project, too."

"Do you ever think of singing again, Hokai?"

Hokai is nonplussed, caught off guard. "What?"

"Singing. You've got a good voice. Do you ever feel the urge to sing, like you used to?"

"Sure. I sing to my bathroom walls all the time. (*Sings*) "When I'm calling you, oo-oo-ooo, oo-oo-ooo...."

"You know, Hokie, it's a great day to be alive!"

"I thought that was supposed to be 'It's a great day to die!'"

"Five hundred years, and we never had it a thousandth-part this good. I'll bet it won't last. Some politician or preacher will find a way to pop our bubble. Indins weren't meant to own land that produces income."

"You're hopeless, Chief. You know that?" says Hokai, exasperated. "But you're right. We need to broaden our economic base so that we don't depend entirely on one thing that can evaporate at any time. The council is inquiring into the possibility of buying the Municipal Bank."

"He-ya, Hey-yahh," says Billy, starting to dance. Hokai lays the papers on the floor, and they do a little dance around them.

5

Norman Bird-Feather, thirty-five, a mixed-blood Wintu, casual business dress, no Indian symbols or badges of identification, appears at Billy's open door. "Mr. Duc-Doc? Bill Duc-Doc?"

"Yes?"

"I'm Norman Bird-Feather, from the Wintu tribe of Northern California. I believe I have an appointment with you."

"Yes, of course, Norman," says Billy, coming around his desk to greet him. "Come right in. I've been expecting you. Your council wrote us a letter, asking us to teach you all the ropes. Our activities here are so frazzled that we may not look like we've got our hands on any ropes. But you're welcome. We'll do what we can. Would you like a cigarette?"

"No, thanks. I don't smoke." He takes the seat that Billy indicates.

"I don't either. But a lot of Indians, even modern Indians, like to do the tobacco ritual before talking. I see being bound to that kind of tradition as another sort of rope."

"The story on the moccasin telegraph is that you've managed to keep the ropes out of the hands of outsiders, Bill. Especially the professional gamblers on the one hand, and the church people on the other."

"Well, we've tried hard to tie our own knots. Had a lot of good luck, too. A lot depends on having good luck."

"You sound like a gambler."

"Hey, from one point of view, everything's a gamble," say Billy looking out his mezzanine window. "Hunting. Farming. Investing in the stock market."

"Most people wouldn't think of those as gambling."

"The difference is that they require some input from the gambler, and society condones them because of that. The hunter has to have skill and patience. The farmer has to have knowledge and be willing to work long hours. The investor in the stock market has to understand money and stocks, and he usually has the sense that he's producing not only a profit for himself, but a needed service to the larger community. In a sense, those gamblers earn their winnings." Billy turns back to Norman. "But this isn't what you're here to hear. What can I do for you?"

"Well, I thought it might be a good idea if you gave me a rundown of your projects. And tell me at each juncture how your tribe managed to keep control. We've had plenty of offers from outside concerns wanting to set up operations on our land, and they all promise us a big pie."

"Don't they all!"

"But some of our council, especially a couple of mixed-bloods, have been assimilated, or partly assimilated, for some years, and they say those promises are just sucker bait. Like our California Lottery. It was supposed to produce millions every year for support of our schools. There was money in the fund the first year, I have to admit that. And money for elementary schools for two years. After that, it just doesn't seem there's ever any left over."

Billy continues for him. "So the people lose their money at the lottery, hoping their school taxes will be lowered, but then find they pay both ways."

Norman nods his agreement. "At best, the scheme was a way of shifting the burden of supporting the schools and running the state to the lower and middle class. In practice, it's a way of shifting money from the pockets of the poor to the pockets of the big-time gamblers. And now the state and the school districts find they're saddled and bridled by a bunch of skunks that nobody has a way of deodorizing."

"Sounds pretty bad."

"It's enough to sour you on lotteries, that's for sure." Norman takes out a small notebook and prepares to take notes. "We're afraid that bad experiences with the state failing to finance projects with gambling money will sour people on gambling in general, and the door will be shut before our tribe gets in at the window of opportunity."

"I sort of know what you mean," says Billy. "I was reading an article in the newsletter of the Anti-Gambling League. This one preacher figures that the current gambling craze will only last twenty, maybe twenty-five years, because by that time, one of two things will happen: either the churches will regain enough power to make it illegal, or gambling will collapse on its own when the players finally discover—no, realize—that the house always wins."

"Exactly. I must have read the same article."

"We try to counteract the possibility of player burnout by constantly inventing new games to bring in a new generation of gamblers. In fact, we're working on one now. Walk with me over to our math classroom. I've got to give them a task. We can talk along the way, and it's a way to see our layout." Billy leads Norman outside.

"You have a classroom on the res?" Norman makes a note of it.

"Actually, we have several. They're in those trailers up on the hill over there," says Billy, gesturing as they walk. "The Anglos call them portable classrooms, but they're really trailers. We have eight, I believe it is, right now, and some of them have two or three classrooms in them. Air conditioning and everything."

"I'll bet you hire only Indian teachers."

"When we can. Otherwise, we try to find Anglos who have a bit of empathy for our kind of students. Half-bloods and mixed-bloods make good teachers. We started as an extension of Valley College, just offering a few classes over here, like our vocational nursing program. Then we became a satellite campus of Valley when we brought in the trailers. In the fall, we're expecting that we'll get accredited as an independent branch of Valley College and be authorized by the state to offer a regular two-year curriculum, with all the arts, sciences, and humanities."

"Well, it's great to offer so much to Indian students. A real comeuppance." Norman makes some more notes.

"Actually, we're open to anyone, now. We get some financial support from the state. It's a sort of partnership."

"So does that mean you had to give up control? We want to maintain control in Wintu country."

"It means we had to share control with the state. It works out best that way, I think. We're a part of the general public, and they're a part of us. It's a sort of marriage of the two cultures."

"I'd expect the Indian to lose in that kind of marriage," says Norman, a wry smile on his face. "I'll guess: your dean, or whatever your chief administrative officer is, is a white man?"

"Yes," admits Billy. "It's pretty hard to find an Indian with enough Anglo education to run a campus—those that exist can command much better salaries than we have to offer—so we're forced to settle for an Anglo who has some knowledge of Indian culture. But, as I say, it's not all bad. Our dean has brought in a professional linguist from the university, teamed her up with four of our elders, and they teach our native language. The elders know things about the language that linguist has never dreamed of, but she knows things about language structure and patterns and methods that those elders would never have dreamed of on their own. The product of the cooperation is a good thing that neither side could have created by itself."

"Sounds great. I hope all of your Indian students take that course! It sounds like the opportunity of a lifetime."

"I took it when it was first offered. My trouble is, I'm so busy with the casino and our projects that I didn't have time to do the homework. About half of our student body at the moment is non-Indian, and eighty-two percent of our staff is non-Indian. Our vocational nursing program and our firefighter school are the only ones that are heavily Indian; they're over three-quarters."

"And the curriculum for those is controlled by outsiders, right?"

"Right. We want our students to get standard certificates, so they can move anywhere in the dominant culture they want. Or they can stay on their reservations if they like."

"Are there jobs on the reservation for so many?"

"Hardly. Most of these people will work in the Anglo community. But we'll make a space on the reservation for those who want to work here. Anyone from any tribe who wants to work at the casino or anything connected with that gets a job."

Norman makes a note. "But some don't want to be involved with gambling or any of the people who are."

"Of course, but they don't object to the per-capita distribution of casino profits or the scholarship money." Billy and Norman enter the schoolyard, where a number of students are lounging around, waiting for the next class to begin. "All these boys and girls you see get a scholarship here. Including the whites and blacks. They're mostly from the socially and economically disadvantaged segment of American culture. We give them a chance to find themselves."

"And do they? Do they find themselves? In an Indian environment?"

"Some do, some don't. Most just need a real start. Somehow, they got out of step before beginning and just never caught up. We try to help them find their path."

"And it's working out?" asks Norman, writing in his notebook. "No strife? No friction? I've heard it said that blacks and chicanos can be among the most bigoted, because they see the Indian as competing with them for their piece of the pie. The stairway to the stars is built on the backs of your inferiors. And everyone tries to put Indians at the bottom of the heap."

"Yes, that's a problem we haven't solved yet," admits Billy. "We wish we had more middle-class Anglo students. We think our Indian students could learn things just by being around them. You know: assumptions about following schedules, and managing money, and paying bills, and even duty and public service. Of course, the whites could learn a lot of things, too, by associating with Indians: respect for the world we walk on, old people, tolerance for cultural differences, that sort of thing."

"I suppose most of your vocational nurses will want to work at the Indian Health Service when they get their licenses."

"A few will. And we'll hire them first when our hospital is completed and encourage the best ones to become registered nurses. Some of our nurses are taking our course in our native language, so they can work with elders of the tribe. Of course, we don't have hardly any elders now who don't speak English, but we do have a fair number who feel more at home with our native language. Elders will accept modern medicine and hygiene more readily in their own language than they will in English."

"Well, we're having a slightly different experience with our native language," says Norman, closing his notebook. "We have five elders who can still speak Wintu, so we started a program in the community hall: five nights a week, an elder holds conversations with anyone who wants to learn. A lot of the assimilated and mixed-blood crowd can't see any reason to learn Wintu now. It's not like studying French, they say, which is a usable language in the world. It's not even like learning a dead language like Latin, where you, at least, have a literature to read and a body of politics and philosophy to study. To them, it's not even setting up a living museum, where descendants can learn the conditions their ancestors lived under. If they're going to have to study, they say they want something that will act like a wedge to get them into Anglo society. As if that were the aim of all Indians!"

"Not all our people want to join the Anglo culture, either. Our fire-fighting school, for example, has been popular with young Indian men from a lot of tribes, partly because it isn't an admission ticket to the dominant society. They seem to like it because it has something of the old warrior society in it. You know: a hard fight against a difficult enemy, which requires a heroic, dedicated, and well-trained warrior."

"Plus it deals with the protection and preservation of the environment," adds Norman.

"Right. That appeals to their feelings for Mother Earth. All our graduates go into State or National Forest Service fire crews, where they've already begun to change them with their values. I wish we could infiltrate more Anglo institutions like that. It would be a step toward making our two cultures understand and respect one another."

"You say you teach math here at Kicking Horse College? How far up do you go?"

"We have an advanced calculus class going right now. They're the ones I want to give a problem. Our Games Committee wants them to figure out the chances of two red jacks coming up together in one deck, two decks, and six decks. We're thinking of inventing a new game that we think will keep the gamblers' interest up. We'll multiply the odds by six—professional gaming companies usually multiply by seven-point-five or eight—but we stick with six and still come out all right. We think we can charge people five bucks for ten chances to play, and offer a prize of five thousand."

Norman stops for a moment, dumbfounded. "Calculating gambling risks is a proper task for an advanced math class?"

"They have to know all the right stuff, too. They get tested on it by the accreditation agency. They do this sort of thing on their own time. The teacher has been real good about staying late or coming extra when he's needed. Sort of gives our young people a chance to feel like they're participating in the tribe's activities."

"At least, it's a form of control. And you think five thousand bucks will pull in the crowds?"

"Sure, it will. You can practically see the greed dripping from their eyes when they see the announcement. But I wish we had some other way to do it."

"Some other way?" says Norman, again stopped by surprise. "What do you mean, some other way? You've got them by the nose. What more do you want?"

"What we're teaching the gambling public is not good for them, or good for us. We're destroying the work ethic. We're undermining the idea that one earns what he gets and that there is honor in the earning. We're substituting an ethic of luck, the big win, the free lunch. And that's not good for the culture the tribe is striving to join. We're messing in our own nest, even before we've had a chance to call it home." They enter the math room together.

6

Billy picks up his ringing phone: "Hello. Kicking Horse Casino and Turf Club."

Carla Fitzgerald, fifty-five-ish, stylish, Gary's mother, a bland Angela Lansbury, is on the phone in the den of the Fitzgerald home: "Mr. William Duck Doc, please."

"This is he."

"What? Oh. Ah. Excuse me. I just didn't expect you to answer your own phone. This is Carla Fitzgerald."

"Hello, Mrs. Fitzgerald. Long time, no see."

"Actually, I've seen you. Off in the distance. When we've been out to the casino and restaurant. You always seem so busy."

"Well, we busy bees think we have to make honey while the grasshoppers fiddle."

"Speaking of money and fiddles, I understand you've made a gift to the symphony."

"Not me, Ma'am. The tribal council."

"And that's gambling money?"

"Oh, no, Ma'am. We saved that out of our annuities and reparations."

"Annuities?"

"Yes, Ma'am. Didn't you know the government supports the Indian tribes with annuities? It's to pay for the land they took away from us ages ago. We each get forty cents a month. It's all in the treaty."

"Treaty?"

"Yes. Didn't you know we have a treaty with the U.S. government? It recognizes us as a sovereign nation, with all the rights of self-determination. That's how we can sponsor gambling on the reservation, when you can't in town."

"Money taken from gambling is tainted money. Ill-gotten money."

"What do you mean, 'ill-gotten'? Is it any more ill-gotten than church bingo money, or money from lotteries, which you call raffles, or the Las Vegas Nights your church sponsors to raise money for its activities, including a parochial school? So what do you mean, 'ill-gotten'?"

"Why, uh—you know. The scriptures say money got from gambling is ill-gotten money."

"I never heard of that in scripture. In fact, my understanding of the Bible, which may be faulty because I'm not a Christian, in fact, I'm anti-Christian, is that scripture is quite ambiguous on the issue of casting lots and all forms of gambling. My understanding is that your church does not condemn gambling per se, but only the abuse of gambling. But I couldn't agree with you more, Ma'am. And I—"

"That's what I mean: the abuse of gambling. All that money taken from all those Indian mothers who abandon their children in the parking lot for the day."

"Excuse me, Ma'am?" gasps Billy. "Indian mothers?"

"Everyone knows about it. How you take advantage of the Indian's weakness for booze and love of gambling."

"Everyone knows?"

"Taking advantage of people who spend their whole paycheck in your casino and then can't feed their families. And we, who don't gamble, we have to come to their aid with food packages and pay their utilities bills. And now you're digging up our land on State Street. Ed just told me he sold that land to the Indians. I suppose you're going to put up a casino there, too."

"I don't quite understand, Mrs. Fitzgerald. Are you against gambling out of moral indignation or because it's happening in your neighborhood?"

"Well, uh—People are going to gamble whether we want them to or not. I just say, let them go somewhere else to do it."

"Like Las Vegas?"

"Yes. I certainly don't want a casino right across the street from me."

"I see. You'll be relieved to know that's a hospital we're building on State Street."

"Oh. Do we need another hospital?"

"Maybe you don't, Ma'am. But we do. That's to be an Indian hospital, for the benefit of Indians of all tribes."

"Oh. Whites won't be able to use it?"

"Not in the beginning. Maybe later, if our two cultures ever come to understand each other."

"And it's being built with gambling money?"

"That's right, Ma'am. Every ten million that goes into it came right out of the casino's ill-gotten gains."

"You ought to be ashamed. Gambling is evil. You ought to be ashamed, all of you."

"Oh, I am ashamed, Ma'am. I think gambling is grossly immoral. You look at the people in the casinos and you'll see that they are the segment of the population that is least able to lose money. They tend to be white working-class poor, middle-class at best. They're there to win a fortune, strike it rich, make a killing, get a free ride. Such hopes are very unrealistic and psychologically damaging. A study done by the Illinois tax commission regarding river boat gambling on the Mississippi shore of Illinois showed that, of all the money that went onto those boats in the pockets of tourists, only eighteen percent came off the boats in the pockets of tourists."

"Wow! Someone sure is making a killing, all right!"

"That's for sure; they're killing human spirit right and left. The immorality to me comes in what this process is doing to the psyche of the white man. Forget about the damage to their pocketbooks; the damage to their psyches is apparently irreparable. Gambling is a sickness that grows out of false hopes. Each time a person places a bet or rolls those dice, he's staking himself, his soul, on a false dream of salvation: if he wins, he's somehow saved; he's a hero and worth something. If he loses, his self-esteem goes down. He's damned and worthless. In extreme cases, it can even lead to suicide."

"I don't think it's that bad. Bingo, raffles, a hand of blackjack now and then seem pretty harmless. I think you're overstating the issue."

"It's worse. People get addicted to the gamble, in spite of the knowledge that they're going to lose eighty-two percent, because most casinos keep eighty-two percent; we only keep seventy-two percent and still make out. What the gamblers get is despair, depression, a loss of esteem. With each bet, they are worse people, more base, more sick, more demeaned for having taken part in this monstrous robbing of themselves. Less able to see right, and wrong, and compassion, and love."

"Honestly! This has got to be another of your practical jokes. You're putting me on."

"Oh, no, Ma'am. I'm deadly serious. Gamblers are almost entirely focused on their psyche's greed and grabbing and what's petty in their own souls, not in giving of themselves for what they receive. You don't *do* anything to win at gambling, so it's a hollow, undeserved gain. To win without earning or deserving diminishes your spiritual worth in your own eyes; it is precisely an ill-gotten gain. Win or lose at gambling, your spirit loses. Listen to gamblers' conversations in greasy-spoon restaurants in Cimarron, New Mexico, and you'll hear it in the quality of their voices."

"I've never been in Cimarron, New Mexico."

"And you know something else, Ma'am? It's ruining the Indians, too. Because when we manipulate the gambler's greed, we dirty our own hands and souls by contributing to the degeneration of others. Of course, I'm glad to see improvements in the standard of living on the reservations and the per-capita distribution, but this improvement comes at a terrible price to the Indians. We Indians are participating in our own corruption by feeding the gamblers' illness, by helping them in their self-destruction. And that diminishes our spirit, because we do it knowingly. We make ourselves mean when we encourage meanness in others. We ought to be working to make our fellow man better, more healthy, instead of feeding his addiction and illness. I'm not sure that the gambling business is good for the Indians. On the other hand, hunger, illness, poverty, unemployment, segregation are not good for the Indian soul either: they tend to encourage alcoholism, irresponsibility, indigence, even mental illnesses like de-personalization and anomie. I don't have any very good answers, given that my neighbors are as strong as ever in their bigotry and small-mindedness. I seem to be limited to drawing small pictures of what I see as small truths, on soggy napkins in cocktail lounges."

"I didn't know you drank in cocktail lounges."

"I don't, Ma'am."

"If gambling is so bad, why don't you quit it?"

"I'm ready, Ma'am. I'll quit in a wink of a gnat's eye, as soon as your church or your nation offers Indians a tenth of the opportunities for economic development that gambling does. Because with economic development comes all the rest: education, housing, health care, wholesome food, pride, the will to live with the dignity that Americans think is their birthright. We are Americans, you know. We're Native Americans."

"Oh. Well, I'm a native, too." She looks at the phone a moment, like it was an alien from outer space, then hangs up.

7

In the gaming room of the Kicking Horse Casino, Gary Fitzgerald is shuffling cards at a blackjack table and trying to keep up a line of patter. "Step right up, gentlemen. Place your bets. Two red jacks get you five thousand."

Ed Fitzgerald, seventy or so, successful, prominent businessman, Gary's father, an Ed McMahon type, comes up to Gary's table. "Hello, Gary."

"Oh. Hello, Dad. Hello, Uncle Tom." Tom Fitzgerald, sixty-five-ish, bigoted, Ed's brother, is a Walter Mathau look-alike. "You two gonna try your luck? Special this week is Indian Red-jack. The prize is five thou."

"Maybe later, son. Have you seen Karen's act?"

"Yeah. She's good. I never realized she had so much in her. I sure wish she'd come home. She don't act mad, or anything like that. She's just— She's like a person I never met."

"When's she come on?"

"Her torch song has already passed, but her duet with Hokai comes in about a half hour. You could catch it from the bar."

"Good idea. We're supposed to meet your mother there anyway. See ya later, son."

Tom tugs at Ed's sleeve. "Don't we have time for at least one slap at Indin Red-jack, Ed?"

"Not now, Tom. Maybe later."

"I'd sure like to win that. It'd put me on top of the world. This is my lucky day. I'm gonna solve all my money problems at once."

"Not now. It's a pretty long shot. Odds must be out of this world."

"I could win, Ed," says Tom, looking back. "I know I could. I feel real hot, tonight."

"C'mon, I'll buy you a drink. Cool you off."

"I hear them damned Indins are buying up all the land around the reservation, Ed."

"They made me too good an offer, Tom. Way above market. I couldn't afford not to sell."

"Do they have the right to do that? To own land off the reservation?"

"Why, I don't know. I guess they do. I hope they do. I made a killing."

"I mean, do they have the right to buy our land? Our land that we've got clear title to, fair and square? Can they just take our land like that?"

"I reckon so."

"And do they have the right to hire a white man? I mean, a man like Gary, and pay him good wages, too? Do they have the right to hire a man to wear a tux and deal blackjack on green velvet in as ritzy a casino as you'll find anywhere?"

"He's doing better than he's ever done in his life. Taking some responsibility. Beginning to settle down. This job's been good for him. There's Carla at that back table." They thread their way through the tables and chairs. "Hello, dear."

"Hello, Ed. Hello, Tom. What are you up to these days?"

Tom takes her hand, saying, "Just complaining about everything, as usual, Carla. Have to keep my curmudgeon's license active."

"Well, sit down and teach me how to gripe."

He sits beside Carla and stretches his neck to look around. "D'you think we'll be able to see the stage from way back here? They sure have a lot of cocktail waitresses, don't they? Almost one for every table."

Ed beckons to a waitress. "Two Scotch and sodas, honey. Do you need a refresh, Carla?"

"No. I can nurse this one for a while yet."

Tom looks around. "This damned casino sure hired a bunch of people. Getting so a honest man couldn't find an able-bodied man to work for him, even if he had a job to offer."

Ed draws lines in the tablecloth with the back of a knife. "They've certainly been a shot in the arm to the local economy. They've put on more than eleven hundred people in all their activities here, including construction. Biggest employer in the county."

"And I hear from Oliver Perry's boy that the Indins take income tax out of the employees' checks, but that they don't have to pay any themselves. And no property tax either."

"That's because we're on an Indian res—"

"That ain't right, Ed. Them damned Indins ought to have to pay taxes, just like the rest of us. They're getting filthy rich. They ought to have to pay taxes, just like the river boats in Illinois, or the casinos in Las Vegas and Atlantic City."

"I don't think those places pay taxes, Tom."

Billy Duc-Doc comes up to their table: "Hello, Mr. Fitzgerald, Mrs. Fitzgerald. Mr. Fitzgerald. I hope you folks are enjoying your evening."

"Oh, Hello, Bill— uh, Mr. Duck— uh—Just what are we supposed to call you now, now that you're a big success?"

"Call me whatever you want. Call me Billy, like you never

bothered to. Call me Chief Duck, if you like. Names don't matter any more."

"How come you Indins don't have to pay taxes?" asks Tom.

"Some we pay, some we don't. As citizens, we all pay individual income tax. The treaty says we're a sovereign nation, with the right of self-determination."

"What's that mean?"

Billy puts on his patient lecturer tone and voice. "It means we're a little country in the middle of your country. It's like the Mexican or Russian embassies. You can't tax them, because those embassies are considered a part of Mexico and Russia, and those countries' laws apply within their boundaries. We wouldn't want the Russians to tax the American Embassy in Moscow, would we?"

"They wouldn't dare! Them damned Russians better not try to tax the American Embassy in Moscow. That'd be war!"

"Well, the whole mess is like a Ninja star," says Billy, "no matter how you approach it or which angle you try to pick it up, you're sure to get lacerated."

"I guess so. What's a Ninja star?"

"Well, you've certainly made this into a ritzy place, Bill," says Ed, taking over the conversation. "A real credit to the county. Nothing like it within a hundred miles."

"Except those other Indian casinos, eh?" says Billy, smiling wryly.

"Looks like we're goin' to have wall-to-wall Indin casinos before long," says Tom, complaining.

Billy holds up his palms in a what-can-I-do gesture. "Well, whoever has the most toys at the end, wins. Right?"

"There is such a thing as too many lights," says Ed.

"We didn't learn that by ourselves, now, did we?"

"Gaudy," says Carla.

"Yes, Ma'am. But that's the idiom of the white world we're imitating. When in Rome, speak Roman. Would you folks like to join me and my grandparents at my table up front? Karen and Hokai are about to sing a suite from *Rose Marie*. Karen's a nightingale on 'Indian Love Call.' You know: 'When I'm calling you-ou-ou-ou...'"

"We'd be honored, Bill," says Ed. "Can I buy you a drink?"

"No, thanks. I don't drink. Or gamble."

"Don't drink or gamble?" says Tom, amazed. "Whatta ya Indins do for fun?"

"Play with rubber bands," says Billy, smiling wryly again.

"Play with rubber bands?"

Comeuppance at Kicking Horse Casino

"It's just a little joke, Tom. Remember in one of the Peanuts comic strips, years ago. Linus is sitting among a pile of toys, playing delightedly. Lucy comes through; swish, there are no more toys, and she says 'You can't play with those.' Then she tosses him a rubber band, saying, 'Here. Have fun with this.' In the last frame, Linus is having a ball, jerking that rubber band up, down, back, every way you can imagine. Indians have been calling out for love and 'toys' for over a hundred years, but no one has answered that call. Now that we've found a lever to lift ourselves up with, everyone wants to take it away from us. We're not supposed to have that much fun with our rubber bands."

"Well, uh—" Tom is caught without words.

"And the next day, she came back and took away the rubber band, saying 'You weren't supposed to have that much fun.' That's the history of Indian/White relations in America in two comic strips."

"I'm sorr—"

"We won't settle the question today, will we? Let's sit up close and see if that Mountie and that Indian princess ever get up courage enough to marry and start respecting each other's culture. That's what has to happen in the long run. White Americans have to become more aware of Indian values, maybe even adopt some of them into their lives. And Indians have to merge their values with the ton of trash they have to accept from the white culture. Some of it: iron pots, flushing toilets, and so forth, isn't hard to live with. To me, it's not really a question whether or not this is a happy or unhappy marriage. It's the only alternative we have, and we have to make it work. We *have* to make it work."

(*Closing tableau on casino's stage*). A very Indian Mountie with braids is singing with a very blonde, blue-eyed, very voluptuous Indian princess.

Rose Marie:	*When I'm calling you,*
	oo-oo-oooo ooo-oo-oooo,
Mountie:	*I will answer you,*
	oo-oo-oooo ooo-oo-oooo,
	That means I offer my love to you,
	To be your own,
	If you refuse me, what shall I do?
	Just waiting all alone?
Rose Marie:	*But when I hear your love call ringing clear,*
Mountie:	*And I hear your answering echo so dear,*
Duet:	*Then we will know our love will come through;*
Mountie:	*You'll belong to me.*
Rose Marie:	*I'll belong to you.*
Duet:	*That means I offer my love to you,*
	To be your own,
	If you refuse me, what shall I do?
	Just waiting all alone?
Mountie:	*But when you hear my love call ringing clear,*
Rose Marie:	*And you hear my answering echo so dear,*
Duet:	*Then we will know our love will be true:*
	You belong to me. I belong to you.

[Situation and Lyrics modified very slightly from Rudolf Friml, *Rose Marie*, 1923.]

Other Books by the Same Author

Works of Fiction:

Killing Cynthia Ann, a novel (Fort Worth, TX: Texas Christian University Press, 1999), =vi + 209 pp.

Contemporary Insanities, Short Fictions (Arroyo Grande, CA: The Press of MacDonald & Reinecke, 1990), 160 pp.

A Snug Little Purchase, How Richard Henderson Bought Kaintuckee from the Cherokees in 1775 [Documentary novel] (La Mesa, CA: Associated Creative Writers, 1979), 152 pp.

The Other Side of Love, Two Novellas (Denver: Alan Swallow, 1963), 88 pp.

Whatta Ya Mean, "Get out o' that Dirty Hole"? I LIVE here! [Poems and Cartoons] (Spring Valley: Helix House, 1974), 36 pp.

Works on Creative Writing:

Creative Writing: Fiction, Drama, Poetry, The Essay (New York: American Book Co., 1968), 476 pp. Reprinted by D. Van Nostrand Co.

Developing Creativity (Spring Valley: Helix House, 1974), 72 pp. Reprinted 1975, 1978

Creative Writing for High School Students (Ann Arbor: University of Michigan Bureau of School Services, 1968), 224 pp.

Creative Writing Handbook (La Mesa, CA: Associated Creative Writers, 1990), 280 pp.

The Structure of Essays (Englewood Cliffs: Prentice Hall, 1972), 326 pp.

A Writers' Toolkit, How to Write Poems, Essays, Stories (San Diego: Associated Creative Writers, 1999), 288 pp.